Woody Starkweather

MOLP

MOLP | 2nd edition

Text © Woody Starkweather, 2013, 2016

Cover by BEAUTeBOOK, 2016

Published by Birch Tree Books, 2016

ISBN 978-0-9981822-0-9

Also available in eBook and audio

Table of Contents

MAP OF FRANCE AND KAZAKHSTAN

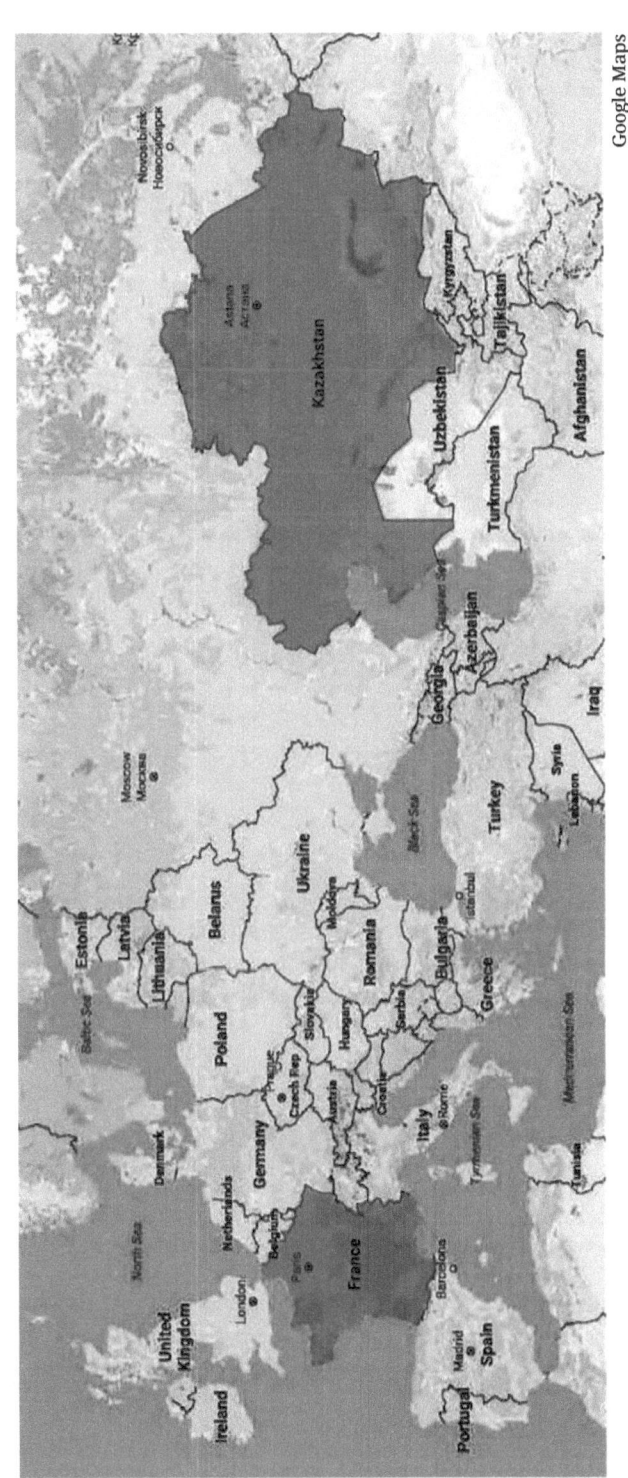

Chapter 1
The Grab

Stepping outside the café, Charles and Louise were still shading their eyes from the blinding sunlight of the Central Asian summer when two men grabbed them from behind. Louise yelped like a puppy and tried to twist away, but her attacker's grip was too strong. Charles protested loudly but kept his cool and stayed in his role.

As she was pushed roughly into the back seat of a waiting Russian Lada, Louise looked back, hoping someone had seen the abduction, but the street was empty. Her satellite phone was hidden deep in her bra, but she knew the battery was low and decided to wait.

Next to them in the back seat, a young man held a machine pistol but said nothing. Charles recognized the converted Intratec TEC-DC9. The man was lank and snake-like, grinning smugly. The driver looked ahead silently. A third man, in the front passenger seat, turned around and looked at them with a satisfied grin. The car sped off, lurching through the streets. Pedestrians scurried out of the way. The man in the passenger seat was massive, with a blond crew cut, beefy-faced and stupid-looking. He pulled out a gun–the same type as the one held by their back-seat companion, and held it loosely at shoulder level, just so they could see it.

Earlier, walking in the streets of Zhezkazgan, a former gulag town deep in the Kazakh steppe, they'd been parched by the 110° heat. The café had been an oasis.

Now this.

"Blindfold them," the grinning man in the front seat said in Russian. Charles, fluent in Russian and many other languages, noted the Moscow accent that seemed to have too many "o" sounds. He also heard coarse street lingo. Louise checked her watch just before the blindfold was tied tightly over her eyes.

She felt her purse snatched from her lap, heard it snap open and someone rummaging in it. Heard it snap shut. Hands patted her down, fondling her breasts briefly but missing the miniature cell phone tucked low between them. Satisfied that she had no weapons, the man shoved her roughly into his seat as he stepped over her to pat down Charles. Finding nothing, he shifted back to his original seat, pushing Louise to the center again so he could keep his gun pointed at both of them.

Louise sat upright, facing straight ahead, concentrating on the car's turns and speed to keep track of their location. She cursed silently at her cell phone's low battery. Ironically, she'd been talking on the phone moments before to Henderson, their State Department contact, suggesting that a solar-powered cell phone would be useful. Too late for that.

The blindfold didn't handicap Charles. He'd have been lost anyway. But he had an uncanny ability that no one could detect. A genetic mutation had made him hyperosmic; his sense of smell was as acute as a bloodhound's. He'd taken advantage of the genetic gift and trained himself to recognize the odors of chemicals and products associated with criminal activities–bomb-making materials, handguns, and the residue of fired ammunition. He also knew the smells that distinguished individuals–soaps, shampoos, perfumes, and the natural oils of the body.

He smelled re-aspirated alcohol from the man sitting next to him, mixed with the bitter scent of unwashed hair and, from the floor, recently applied shoe polish. He quickly noticed that the driver had bathed not long ago using strong Kazakhstan soap. But the blond crew cut in the front seat was unwashed, and–Charles wrinkled his nose in distaste–had an advanced case of gingivitis. Charles then turned his attention to less obvious odors and filed them in his memory until he knew he could identify any of the three men. Each had a characteristic odor, underneath the other recently acquired smells, that was his and his alone. He also memorized the smell of the car.

Charles and Louise had never even discussed what they might do in such a situation. They didn't need to. They'd been kidnapped once before on another mission, and these same skills–Charles' amazing nose and Louise's ability to orient herself–had saved them. They were confident that could manage this situation, too. The guns pointing at them were a problem, however. They didn't carry weapons.

The car turned and turned again as they sped through the town, pulling their bodies unexpectedly from one side to the other. Louise noted each turn carefully. Finally the car settled into a long run in one direction, the speed increased, and she confirmed their direction of travel by the warmth of the sun on her left leg. They were heading a little east of due south, toward Kyzel-Orda hundreds of miles away. But why? She knew there was nothing out there but empty steppe. She estimated their speed from the sound of other cars going by in the opposite direction between 60 and 70 mph. Charles too listened carefully. He hoped later they could compare notes.

They both heard the sound of cloth rubbing against cloth as the blond crew cut turned in his seat to look at them, and Charles got a blast of gingivitis breath. Louise stayed focused on their speed and direction. Without turning his head Charles focused his attention on the man he knew was looking at him. He didn't want the kidnappers to know how well he perceived the situation.

Gingivitis Breath spoke.

"Who you guys anyway? Couple of old farts messing around, I think. Stumbled on something way out of your league."

"It's beginning to look that way," Charles said, then asked, "Where are you taking us?" Charles spoke in Russian, but used an American accent and forced his voice to shake. He knew there'd be no answer, but the question–and the fake fear–went with the innocent, naïve role. He was on high alert, but not scared–that might come later.

"We'll see, won't we?" The smugness in the man's voice was expected. Louise was concentrating so carefully that she might've been in a trance. Their captors ignored her.

"Who are you?" Again Charles knew he wouldn't get a straight answer.

"OK," said the bad breath. "Let's talk. You messed up, that's what. You made a bad mistake. Your big pal pretended to be a friend of Nikita. That was bad. The Koreans got pissed at Nikita, and Nikita didn't know what was goin' on so he was pissed. Jesus, he got pissed. He don't like not knowin'."

Charles began to understand. They'd been kidnapped as payback. They'd recruited a bilingual American marine, who pretended to be a Russian gangster in order to scare the drug ring in Almaty. It had worked, the guys running the drug ring had fled from the Russian mafia's well known ruthlessness. But now the tables were turned. Their kidnappers really were the Russian mafia.

"I don't understand. Who's Nikita?" Charles kept up the *naïveté*.

"OK," Gingivitis said dismissively. "You gonna play innocent. What else is new."

There was a period of silence. Charles broke it.

"We're journalists from America. We work for a magazine you wouldn't know about."

"Yeah, yeah," said Gingivitis. "I heard all that. I don't buy it. But you don't look like any kind of cops I ever seen neither."

"We're not cops. I have ID I can show you if I can take off the blindfold."

"Don't bother. It don't matter. You won't fuck over Nikita again. For sure."

"Where are you taking us?"

"If I told you, you still wouldn't know."

Then there was a long silence. The odor of gum disease faded as he turned to face front.

So, Charles got the picture. They'd offended the Russian mafia and were being taken somewhere by three men, at least two armed. He was glad the ride was long. It meant they weren't going to be quickly shot and dumped in the street.

They left the highway and turned due south. Louise felt their speed decrease, and the bumps told her they were on a dirt road. It went on for a long time. Charles tried to get them talking again, but no one answered.

They left the dirt road and traveled over what seemed like loose sand for another half hour. Then the car stopped. Charles and Louise were both suddenly nervous. They were far outside the city; if they were shot here no one would ever know. The doors opened and they were pushed out, stumbling blindly in the soft sand. Would they hear shots or just suddenly be dead?

There was a malevolent chuckle before the last door slammed and the car sped away. When the sounds of the car had faded, they took off their blindfolds and peered after it. But there was only ruffled dust, and that soon settled. And then there was nothing. Only silence, relieved by the soft whistling of the wind against the scrubby brush and sharp stones.

"Why didn't they just shoot us?" Charles wondered.

"Leaving people on the steppe to die is used here to scare others. Dying alone is a terrible fate to the family-oriented Kazakhs." Louise's research wasn't comforting.

A faint screech sounded high above, and they looked up. A tiny dot moved across the sky–a steppe eagle hunting, seeing the movement below of the two Americans, assessing their potential as food. They stared until with a shudder they realized they were prey, but they said nothing.

They looked around, alone on the immensely vast steppe. Louise thought carefully, calculating time and distance, direction, and speed.

"I think we're about 90 miles southwest, maybe southwest by south, of Zhezkazgan. The nearest village is over 40 miles away."

"Too far to walk."

"Yes." She was quiet for a moment. "But I think we're close to a direct line between Kyzel-Orda and Zhezkazgan."

"But they're what, a thousand miles apart?" Charles looked around impatiently trying to figure out how to cope with the situation.

"Well, maybe 300, but a long way," she conceded.

"How does that help?" he asked.

"There should be a power line along that straight line, and a telephone line," she answered easily.

"Can you tap into it?" he asked, a little hopeful.

"Do you have your jackknife?"

"No. What good would that do?"

"If we had some wire or a piece of metal..."

The skepticism in her voice confirmed his suspicion. They couldn't tap into the line, even if they could find it.

His hopes fell. Nothing in the desert could conduct electricity.

"They didn't get my satphone," Louise said.

"Why didn't you say so?" Charles sighed with relief. "Call the Marines."

The Marines guarding the embassies had been prepped as to their general whereabouts and could mount a search and rescue operation. The satphone had a GPS, and Charles and Louise had a well-memorized number to call.

"Well, the battery's low, and I don't know how long it'll take them to get here. I can give them the coordinates from the GPS system, but we might need the phone to guide them in. We have to conserve the battery. Let's make sure we know what we're doing before we place the call."

Charles looked around, and sniffed the air. "It's cooling off a little."

Louise added, "It'll be really cold later, and that'll be uncomfortable, but we'll survive that. It's tomorrow's heat I'm worried about."

Charles became decisive. "First, let's try to contact the Marines and tell them what's going on."

"OK, but we'll have to make it short." Louise punched up the numbers. Almost instantly a voice said:

"This is Lieutenant Gemelli, U.S. Marine Corps Central Communications Command. How may I help you?"

"This is Iguana, Code 666."

"One moment ma'am." Then another voice came on the line.

"This is Special Operator Delta. Describe your situation."

"We've been kidnapped. We're at 47.36 North by 68.29 East, about 90 miles by dead reckoning, bearing 170 degrees, from Zhezkazgan, Kazakhstan. There are two of us. No supplies. No shelter. We could use a ride."

"Yes ma'am. You have top security clearance. Can you talk freely?"

"Oh yes. There's nobody around for about a hundred miles."

"Can you describe anything in the terrain that'll help the pilot find you?"

"We see nothing but empty steppe in 360 degrees, but we should be near a power line running from Kyzel-Orda to Zhezkazgan."

"Roger that. What's your power situation? I see you're calling on a satellite phone."

"Probably an hour on standby, much less when in use."

"OK. In a second I'm going to have you shut down. You have our number and now I have yours. If you see any aircraft, call us. Use the code Red Dog. Good luck, and shut down. We're on our way."

"OK." She switched the phone off completely.

Silence. Only the faint rustle of wind. They had no food or water and no way of getting any. It'd take some time for the rescue craft to reach them from the nearest base, in Tajikistan far to the south. The coordinates would get them close, but at the end the pilot would have to start a search pattern. They were dressed in light, summer clothing, and it'd be uncomfortably cold during the night. If they weren't found by the next day, however, they faced life-threatening heat from a blazing sun and no water.

And there was that steppe eagle.

"These guys know what they're doing," Charles commented as much to reassure himself as Louise, "We should be grateful we're not in a hostile war zone."

"Let's do what we can to get ready for tomorrow," Louise suggested.

"I guess we shouldn't try to find the power line," Charles said.

Louise thought about it. "No, probably not. If I could be sure which side of it we were on, then it'd be worth the walk, but without that information, it's a fifty-fifty chance that walking would make our situation worse. It's better to let the helicopter do the searching."

They looked around carefully and as far into the distance as they could see, but saw only a flat terrain of sand, small rocks, and little tufts of dried, brown grass. Charles reached down and pulled up a clump of it. It came up as if there were no roots at all.

Louise, an avid gardener, explained. "When it does rain, it's only briefly, at least in this season. They need to get what water they can before it evaporates or drains away, so the root systems are shallow."

Charles noticed something. "There's a flat rock over there. I can dig us a little hole with it, while it's cool. Why don't you get as many of these clumps as you can and make a pile of them?

It'll make a little warmth tonight and maybe some shade tomorrow."

They both set to work. The sandy soil was soft and peppered with small stones, hard to dig in. After an hour of digging and assembling clumps of dried grass, they were both sweating and exhausted. Charles had managed to dig an impression in the ground that was about eight inches deep and long and wide enough for them both to lie in. Louise had assembled a pile of dry grass, enough for one layer over the two of them. They stopped to rest.

After regaining her breath, Louise asked, "You don't have any matches I guess, do you?"

"No."

"This brush would make a great signal fire."

"Yes it would."

"Maybe with our glasses tomorrow, when the sun is bright."

"Yeah maybe."

Neither was too hopeful about that possibility. They knew that eyeglasses weren't strong enough to focus the sun into a fire-starting temperature. The sun was setting and already there was a slight chill. A steady breeze from the west made them colder.

"Let's work a little more while we have light." Louise had regained her energy. Charles, whose hands were roughened and arms tired, was slower, but he pushed himself, recognizing the gravity of the situation. They worked for two more hours until the hole was two feet deep, enough so Charles could hollow the sides out laterally about four inches on either side. They would have some shade except when the sun was directly overhead. Then they would have to rely on the grass and roots Louise had been able to gather. Finally they could rest. Charles tried lining the bottom of their grave-like hole with grass, but it was too coarse and pricked them unmercifully. They were more comfortable lying directly on the sandy dirt, after picking out the stones. They laid down next to each other and covered themselves as best they could with the wiry grass. The wind wasn't very strong, but it chilled them anyway, ignoring their bristly covers.

They tried to sleep, but it was no use.

"Warm enough?" Charles knew she wasn't, but asked anyway.

"No. Not really."

He reached his arm farther around her waist to increase contact. They were nestled spoon fashion, half buried by spiky clumps of brush. It was hard not to dwell on the grave-like shape of their sleeping place. The cold didn't help.

"Are there any nocturnal animals we need to think about?" she asked.

"I don't think so. There used to be onagers, wild asses, that were supposed to be quite vicious, but they disappeared long ago."

"Good. I'd hate to have to tell my friends that an ass got a piece of me."

Charles chuckled. Her good humor was helpful. He remembered that there was some unpleasant insect life–scorpions, huge spiders–but he hoped they weren't active at night. Getting up in the morning might be dicey. Warmth-seeking critters might come into their little nest. He wondered about snakes but couldn't remember if there were any.

Boredom and fear were an odd combination he recognized from earlier missions. And feeling unprepared. Of course, they couldn't carry special equipment. It might compromise their role as elderly journalists.

Expectations preyed on Charles' mind, lying huddled in what seemed like a shallow grave. He didn't really expect to die, but it was a distinct possibility. In fact, he expected to be rescued. But when? Louise, on the other hand, knew they'd be rescued, but it had to be soon.

They slept for a few hours, off and on, listening for the sound of helicopter blades, waking often, hugging each other for warmth and, finally, long before dawn, they gave up on sleep. They talked about their home in Virginia, about their grandchildren, and wondered aloud when they might be rescued. It would take a couple of hours to get the crew together to check out and fuel up a helicopter. It was unlikely that one would be kept on standby. Rescue was a part of the Marine mission, but they weren't in an active war zone, so there was no call for it. It would then take a couple of additional hours to reach them. Figuring all this out, they decided that the chopper should be searching already, but they'd heard nothing.

"Maybe my dead reckoning was off." Louise reviewed the blindfolded trip for the third time. The many turns they took while the car was in the city could easily have thrown her sense of direction off, but she remembered that after they'd left the city and were traveling in a straight line, she'd felt the sun on her left leg, and consequently knew they were south and west of Zhezkazgan. Her estimate of distance was the one most likely to be wrong, since the speed of their car changed from time to time. But she knew almost exactly how long they'd been driving after they left Zhezkazgan, and it had been in one direction. They'd been going 55–60 mph, at the most 70, which meant that her distance estimate couldn't be off by more than 15–20 miles. Of course they weren't visible at night, and couldn't light a fire, but they didn't hear anything either, and this worried them. They dozed off again.

Louise woke up around 4 a.m.. It was cold, but she had to pee. She sat up slowly, trying not to disturb Charles, and the prickly, tumbleweed-like plants cascaded down her chest and piled up on her outstretched legs. She brushed most of them aside, carefully making a small pile to the left of their grave-like bed.

"You OK?" Charles was awake. She wasn't surprised.

"I'm fine. I just have to pee."

"I might as well, too, or I won't be able to get back to sleep."

Charles also brushed off the little shrubs that passed for their blanket. A soft breeze brought the desert smells to his nose, and he sampled each separately in his mind. None was familiar— a good thing. There was a faint odor of gasoline-engine exhaust, the lingering remnants of their captors' car engine probably. It seemed odd to him that the smell was still in the air, given the wind, and he tried to account for it as he got himself up. Maybe the air had become still during the night and was only just beginning to stir. The exhaust fumes could have remained stationary until this very moment. He walked off a few paces and urinated. To his left he heard the sound of Louise doing the same, and the strong smell of urine, both his and hers, each slightly different, mingled. He found this faintly romantic but kept the thought to himself.

For her part, Louise, squatting in the night air, felt the cold on her bare bottom and looked up at the stars for distraction. She oriented herself to the sky in this latitude. Then, from the position of the constellations, she calculated the time. Daylight would come in a few hours and rescue shortly thereafter, she hoped. She pulled her pants back up and shuffled back to their makeshift bed.

She got there before Charles and stepped down into the depression. Finding a few pieces of the dry, prickly shrubbery they'd covered themselves with, she set them on the piles they'd both made. Charles, guided by the sounds of Louise's housekeeping, and her scent, picked his way slowly back to their "bed."

"We've got a couple of hours before daylight," Louise said. "Are you holding up?"

"Sure. It's actually not as cold as I thought it would be."

"Nevertheless..." Her voice trailed off, leaving the sentence unfinished.

Charles tried for a moment to figure out what thought she'd abandoned.

"Right. A good soft bed and a shower will be welcome."

"Hmmp." Her grunted response meant she hoped Charles would try to get back to sleep and not go off on some rambling scientific discourse. And Charles, knowing the meaning of her grunt, clapped his mouth shut before saying anything about the psychology of human temperature perception. He decided also not to mention the automotive smell he'd noticed before.

Chapter 2
The Assignment

It had begun, as their missions always did, in the President's office.

When the call came, Louise was working in her small garden at the log house in Virginia. The smell of salt air and marsh grass mingled with the strong rose scent, caressing her nostrils as she reached deep into the rosebush toward the lush peach-colored blossom. Her eyes were fixed on the flower's deep orange interior, her hands steady despite her years, as she held the stem for snipping. At that exact moment, the cell phone in her back pocket rang, and the vibrations on her butt made her jerk. A rose thorn stabbed deep into her thumb.

"Shit! That hurts!"

She whipped off her garden glove and stuck her thumb in her mouth. The phone buzzed a second time, and she opened it with her other hand.

"Hello?" She snapped, her voice muffled by her thumb.

"This is Mrs. Skolnick at the White House. He wants to see you."

Her heart thumped. "Do you know where we're going?"

"You sound as though you have something in your mouth."

Louise jerked her thumb out. "It's just my thumb. I..."

"You're way too old for that, dear."

"I pricked it." Louise rolled her eyes.

"I see."

Damn the woman, she thought. She always makes me feel small.

"Do you know where we're going?"

"Sorry, I don't. Better pack twice."

"Thanks." Louise hoped the President's secretary hadn't heard the sarcasm in her voice. "Bye."

The rototiller was too loud to outshout, so Louise walked over and tapped Charles on the shoulder. He leaned down and pressed the "off" button.

"The President wants to see us."

"OK." He looked at Louise, hoping she might say more, then pushed the little machine to the shed. His step was measured and resigned and his shoulders drooped. Here we go again, he thought.

It was the first time they'd worked for this particular President, and Charles was curious to get to know him. His predecessor had died suddenly in office, and the Vice President had taken over immediately, keeping the staff and cabinet of the former White House.

They'd been doing their unique brand of assignment for several years, since Charles had retired as a Linguistics Professor at a northeastern university. He'd honed his keen sense of smell over the years with studies in biochemistry and by carefully categorizing in his mind various substances by their smell. Bloodhounds couldn't do that. His linguistic skills were another asset, helping him learn languages quickly and pronounce them flawlessly.

Louise had special skills, too–the first was an ability to orient herself virtually anywhere in the world. She'd studied, and taught, astronomy and had excellent protensity, the ability to estimate the passage of time. She'd taught celestial navigation at the U.S. Naval Academy until her early retirement five years ago at age 55.

"She said pack twice," Louise reported when he got back from stowing the rototiller.

"OK," Charles said, "so they want us to drive straight to the airport after we get the assignment. Thank God they're not sending the damned helicopter." Neither of them liked the lurching motion.

They packed two suitcases apiece, one for a tropical climate, the other for a colder place. Louise called their next-door neighbor.

"We're off again on another business trip. Can you keep an eye on the house?"

"Sure thing. Where're you going this time?"

"Europe first, after that it depends." She used to find it hard to lie to the neighbors. Now it was easy, even to her grandchildren.

Charles appeared, carrying suitcases.

"Europe, maybe," Louise mused, thinking that the cover story might come true.

"We'll find out soon enough," Charles said.

Charles packed his guitar and Louise's harmonica case in the car. Music was an old friend, relieving tension and helping them celebrate successes.

As he nestled Louise's harmonica set in the trunk, Charles remembered meeting her at a party given by a mutual friend in Manhattan. She was playing folk tunes and old-timey blues, his kind of music. So he'd unpacked his guitar and waited for a pause. When it came, he started up a Leadbelly song. Her improvised riffs told him they belonged together.

Their laptop, with its secured, encrypted satellite linkup and various hacking programs, also went into the car. Then they drove the little hybrid across the Chesapeake Bay Bridge, and south into the District. A few minutes later they showed passes to the guard, who waved them toward the parking lot. If he recognized them, his face gave nothing away.

"It won't be more than an hour," Charles told the attendant. The young man nodded and handed them a chit. They entered through pure white French doors, where a waiting aide introduced herself.

"Follow me, please." Through the stately hallways, into an elevator, down another hallway, and they were standing in front of Mrs. Skolnick's tiny alcove outside the Oval Office.

"Good morning," she said as if regretting even those two words. No trace of a smile. No small talk. Just a brief wait. A small light blinked on her desk.

"You may go in now." She leaned toward the little intercom, which looked hopelessly out of date. "Louise Danvers and Charles Dereva," she announced as the older couple walked in. The President was sitting at his desk but rose to greet them. Henderson, who was their State Department contact and well known to them, stood next to the desk. Louise's heart raced as she sat on the small sofa President Borden gestured to with a warm smile. He was boyishly handsome and had the graceful manners of the Old South. For a moment she felt like a teenager meeting a rock star.

"I'm glad to meet y'all. I've heard so much. You're gonna help us hassle some of our so-called friends." The southern accent seemed to fade in and out.

"We're glad to meet you too, Mr. President," Louise said, "and glad to do what we can for our country."

"I'm curious about something. What you do is similar to espionage, but..." he chuckled, "kinder and gentler. You're certainly not spies. How do you describe what you do?"

Charles sat up a little straighter. "We've tossed that one around a bit and never come up with a satisfying description. We're tricksters, dirty tricksters, really. We annoy, embarrass, hobble the targets, always in secret–but no violence."

"Dirty tricksters eh? That's pretty good. As you surely know by now, there are times when a dirty trick in secret is just what we need."

"Thank you, Mr. President."

"I won't go into the details of this assignment. Henderson'll brief you. If you're exposed, we'll just have to say we don't know who y'all are, but of course you've worked under this kind of pressure before." He pushed his famous shock of chestnut hair back from his forehead and glanced at Henderson, the only other person who knew what Charles and Louise did. Henderson nodded briefly.

"OK then." The President stood up, looked at Henderson, and the interview was over.

"Thank you, Mr. President," Louise said. "We'll get right on it."

Charles and Louise shook his hand and the three went quickly out the door. Henderson raised his eyebrows at them and shook the folder in the air, indicating its importance. In it was their assignment. They all smiled at Mrs. Skolnick, who just barely smiled back as they filed silently past her desk. Then, escorted by the same aide who'd brought them to the Oval Office, they left the building.

Henderson's car was waiting by the entry.

"Step in the car for a minute," he said, gesturing for them to get in.

Charles shook his head. He'd known the interview would be short, but its consequences were huge. Their lives would change drastically, probably for several months. They'd be in different countries, speaking different languages, engaged in activities that were often dangerous and usually illegal, all as a result of a five-minute talk. It still made his head spin.

Henderson handed them the folder with broad gestures, almost ceremoniously, and Charles accepted it gingerly, as if it were a little hot.

"There's a full description in there. Some new software, too. The French counterintelligence boys have gotten creative, but we've developed some countermeasures. Where should I drop you?" Henderson said, eager to leave them, as if they were contagious. Well, they were, thought Charles. And the disease had a number of different names–plausible deniability, secrecy, espionage, or simply danger. People exposed to it could get hurt.

"You don't have to drive us. We have our car," Charles said.

They got out and said goodbye, and were left standing at the entrance to the White House garage, Henderson's "Good luck" ringing ominously in their ears. They were on their own. Sure, they could call him on a secure line, and he could consult with experts from any department of government. More than once his support had meant the difference in the success of a mission. But Charles still felt abandoned. He and Louise would have to study the mission, research the "target," decide on strategies, and implement the scheme.

They retrieved their car and drove off the White House grounds.

No one ever mentioned money, and they had learned not to ask. They were paid very generously, the cash deposited electronically in an anonymous Costa Rican account. The amounts varied somewhat, and they had no idea why; maybe Henderson himself placed a value on each mission. The payments came at odd times, and never on completion of their work. If they had to spend money, they weren't directly reimbursed. All this to maintain distance from the President. From time to time they withdrew most of the money and moved it to another account.

"Henderson mentioned French counterintelligence," Charles said.

"Yes, I heard. Paris is lovely this time of year."

"Let's hope it's Paris and not some grimy industrial city."

Louise opened the folder and read the opening paragraphs. "France certainly," she said, and then "Yes! Paris it is."

"We have to talk. Let's go to that little cafeteria on M Street, between 10th and 11th," Charles suggested.

They often discussed important missions over food in public places. There was no reason for it, just a custom, although the background noise and the last-minute locations were helpful in making sure they weren't being bugged.

Louise made a turn and sped down an avenue, then into a cross street. After a few minutes they found a parking place. Before they left the car, Louise read the mission statement aloud.

"Embarrass the new French President," she repeated. "Those are the important words. I wonder why."

"He's done a lot of damage to U.S. policy, playing to French anti-American sentiment," Charles said. "And I believe he's coming up for election next year. But, ours is not to wonder..." He didn't need to finish the aphorism.

Louise nodded. It wasn't the first time the rationale for their mission had been kept from them. Nevertheless they wondered what could be important enough to send them on a mission of embarrassment requiring secrecy. Why embarrassment anyway?

Inside the cafeteria, they considered what they could do to embarrass the French Head of State. His name was Rene Michaud-Benoit, followed by a host of academic letters. Trained in the law, intensely French, a lover of good food, good wine, and beautiful women, not all of them his wife.

"It has to be a money scandal," Louise said definitively.

"Why?"

"Because sex scandals don't really work in France. The guy may be embarrassed, even have to divorce, but in the average Frenchman's mind, his reputation is enhanced."

"And the average Frenchwoman?"

"Even more so. After a sex scandal involving 'other women,' the French female vote is almost guaranteed." Louise had read some recent polls. Although the recent scandal involving the Foreign Minister had put a damper on the typical French attitude toward sex, the change was small, and probably temporary.

"I'm glad our target isn't a female politician. That would be harder to figure out."

"What about a homosexual scandal?" asked Charles.

"Wouldn't be enough. It's just not that big a deal in Europe, certainly not in France."

"OK. So money then."

"Yes, the French can't stand greed; it seems so"–she rolled her eyes–"so American, the worst sin for a French politician."

Their conversation sketched the outline of a plan to embarrass the new French President–catch him taking a bribe, perhaps, or rigging an important local election, or spending state money on private affairs. Any of these would do, and if they couldn't find a real scandal, they knew how to make it look like one. But they left the details until later. They usually worked that way. Now they had research to do, research that would provide the necessary details, and that meant flying to Paris.

While Charles was driving to the Baltimore-Washington airport, Louise called an airline and ordered electronic tickets. By the time they drove into the long-term parking area, they knew their flight number and departure time. They retrieved a few items from the warm-weather set and repacked them in the cold-weather set. Then they locked the unneeded luggage in the trunk and headed to the check-in desk.

Chapter 3
Paris

Landing at Orly, they were tired and grouchy. Neither spoke as they waited impatiently for their luggage to appear on the belt. When it did, they loaded it onto a cart and headed for the taxi stand.

"Place de L'Odéon," said Charles gruffly.

The cabbie was surprised at the excellent French, but heard the gruffness even more clearly and sensed correctly that his tip would be more generous if he didn't talk. So, they all rode in silence to the hotel, where they found that the room they'd reserved wasn't ready. The desk man apologized with French effusiveness. It would be several hours. The small lobby was already occupied by other listless, or sleeping, patrons, so they stored their bags and headed out into fresher air and some place, any place, where they could sit and wait.

The sun was still weak, and they kept their coats on, sleepily watching the few briskly walking passersby, all better rested than they. A breeze off the Seine lifted a handful of last year's leaves and sent them chasing the pedestrians. Charles could see the river off to his right, grey in the morning, and calm. Gulls wheeled and dipped, searching for yesterday's edible leavings. A mist rose and drifted ashore, brushing a row of old boatmen who sat in folding chairs on the quay, nursing their cafés au lait and smoking silently between sips.

Charles wrapped his coat a little more tightly around him, thinking about the miles of flowing water and the slow, inevitable mingling of it with the sea, somewhere–he couldn't remember exactly where–with the Channel far to the north. His mind drifted to their mission. He felt a little nervous about it although never doubted they were doing the right thing. It was not for them to stay home like other retirees and grandparents. He looked at Louise, who was excited to be in Paris and absorbed with sketching the scene in the notepad she always carried. She actually enjoyed danger, and she'd know without the slightest hesitation just where the Seine emptied into the sea.

She put her pen in her bag, thoughtfully closed the notepad, and looked at Charles, knowing he was going to say something.

"The President would want us to get started as soon as possible."

"Yes, I know." Louise couldn't hide her sleepy irritability. We'll begin tomorrow."

"Of course. We want to be in top form." He agreed, and she could tell that he was trying not to be impatient.

"But," he went on, "what's the plan?"

"We need information on our target," she said. "I'll go to the Sorbonne library and get his history for background. You find a city library for more current information on the President, then hit the streets, talk to people, read the newspapers, get a sense of how he's perceived."

"It's a plan," he said, satisfied.

They sat in silence for some time, waiting for the sun's warmth. An ounce or two of grouchiness sloughed off. A waiter came and tried to solicit more business, but they were both still sipping mineral water.

"*Monsieur, voudriez-vous de...* Would you like...?"

Charles interrupted. "*Pas maintenant. En effet rien.* Not now. In fact, nothing." The waiter looked startled. Louise almost laughed. People were always surprised by Charles' good pronunciation.

"*Je m'excuse.* I'm sorry." The waiter mumbled something additional and backed away.

Louise reopened her notepad and was sketching again. Ten or fifteen minutes crawled by. The waiter reappeared, and there were more curt exchanges in French. Charles stood.

"Let's go for a little walk–stir ourselves up."

"Just a second."

Charles sat back down heavily, hunched a little against the chill. He felt his fatigue, which reminded him of his age. A cute Parisian thing in high heels and a tiny little skirt walked by, distracting him momentarily. Louise took note and smiled. She was glad to see that Charles, tired as he was, still had the fatigue-shredded remnants of a libido. She closed her notepad, and they both rose–Charles left some money for the bill and a very small tip because he didn't like being pestered–and walked to the crosswalk. The street was almost empty. They walked parallel to the river, which was far down and to their right. At the piers the sightseeing boats rocked gently, waiting for moneyed tourists. The row of boatmen in folding chairs watched the boats and said nothing.

The day warmed, and they opened their coats. Cars whizzed by. As the couple crossed a bridge, a group of school children, dressed in black and white, hurried by. At the end of the line, a small boy pulled his green book bag by its strap, dragging it across the pavement.

Louise nudged Charles to look.

"It's gonna wear through eventually." She imagined books spilling out in a long line behind the child like the wake of a small boat. She didn't think he would stop.

Charles smiled.

They turned down a little side street and ambled along. Charles hadn't the faintest idea how, but Louise knew exactly where they were and guided them through a series of small back streets until they arrived at their hotel from the opposite side.

"How'd you do that?"

"I just looked at the map before we left. You could've done it."

"I doubt it."

They paused outside the hotel, and Charles turned to face the light breeze from the river.

"The tourists are beginning to arrive at the sightseeing boats," he said, although the river was now out of sight behind two blocks of buildings.

"You must smell something."

"Yes. The boatmen are putting out their cigarettes and finishing their coffee. Some of them haven't bathed in quite a while."

"Your wonderful nose doesn't always smell pleasant things."

"Unfortunately not."

They turned and went into the hotel, where they found their room ready. They dropped their luggage on the floor and fell simultaneously on the bed, which fortunately didn't collapse. Soon the sounds of American snoring drifted out the window, mingling with the horns of Parisian taxis.

* * *

They slept through the afternoon and into the night, waking at dawn, refreshed and eager to get going. The desk clerk told them where they could find an open restaurant, and they set off, hungry from having missed dinner. They found it, an unpretentious restaurant serving breakfast at an early hour. The waiter was half asleep. After two apiece of what the French typically eat for breakfast–a piece of bread or a brioche and café au lait–they went their separate ways to gather information on MOLP.

The Secret Service always referred to the U.S. President as POTUS, an acronym for "President of the U.S." So, Charles and Louise, in a spirit of gentle mockery, referred to their target as "MOLP," short for Monsieur Le President. They liked the sound of it, as though they had stepped in something.

Before setting out, Louise painted a clear coat of flexible skin bond on her fingertips so that she could touch computer keys, telephone buttons, or anything else, without leaving prints behind. Her plan was to hack into MOLP's financial records and get them downloaded before the new hacker-detection programs Henderson had told them about sent gendarmes to find her.

She taxied to the main "campus" of the Sorbonne–a set of buildings in the middle of the city. The air was thick with tradition. Over 500 years old, the Sorbonne was one of the first universities in Europe, a Parisian showplace. The city took good care of it, kept it true to its ancient history, and restored parts only when necessary.

Inside the main library, vaulted ceilings echoed footsteps on marble from the high heels of those few women, who, like herself were long past university age; the students wore plastic sandals. In the main room an officious looking woman at a desk examined books being taken out or returned. It could've been a university library anywhere. To one side, Louise found a set of public access computers. Several students walked in and sat down at empty workstations, so she did the same. She inserted her flash drive.

To get at bank records and other very private information, Louise used a program devised by the CIA that generated all possible combinations of letters and numbers to find passwords. The program went through with four-character, then five-character combinations, until the account opened.

Using the hacking programs she knew so well, she soon brought up MOLP's bank records, then other troves of information–records of his elementary school grades, his prep school record, and his university friends. Before he became a public figure, he'd had several mistresses, and Louise marked their financial and educational records for copying, too.

The French Sureté's new countermeasures against hacking were simple and effective. Each password used by a government official contained a character, visible only to the official, that triggered an automatic trace on the location of the computer user typing or copying the password. A hacker could get into the account, but his location was quickly known. To counter the

French program, the CIA had developed Bird Dog. It detected the trace and flashed on her screen that Louise's location was known. She'd have to move fast before she felt a heavy Gallic hand on her shoulder. But she didn't know how long the gendarmes would take to reach her.

She cut it a little close.

She also received an email from Charles.

He'd found another library, a small branch of the city's public library system. He'd read recent issues of *Le Monde* and identified employees who came in regular contact with MOLP–bodyguards, housemaids, chauffeurs, his barber–and his closest political and governmental advisors. When he found an associate who looked promising, he emailed the name to Louise for further investigation.

Two Sureté officers, one fat and red-faced, the other tall, thin, and slack-jawed, had been assigned to Internet security, but they were away from their computers smoking American cigarettes with French intensity when they heard the beeping sound that meant someone was hacking into the President's private accounts. They'd put their computers on speakerphone and turned the volume up, so they could sit outside on the library steps and "enjoy the fresh air" while they smoked. So, the "beep" was extremely loud, like a 700-pound chickadee, and they jumped up.

"*Zut! L'alarme sonne!* Jesus, it's the alarm!"

Only two months old, the new system sounded often, but they still hadn't learned to maintain their composure. Turning together, they bumped in the doorway like Keystone Kops, then, swearing, raced back to their monitors. The thin one arrived first, punched in some keystrokes and saw that the hacker was in one of the Sorbonne University's libraries at a public access computer. The officer turned his head to the phone on his shoulder and spoke rapidly to headquarters, giving the address and room number and the computer's identification number.

"*C'est les étudiants émmerdants de l'université!* It is those damned university students!" said the fatter of the two. He'd lost the race to the computer and tried to redeem his failure with an extra helping of indignant anger at the students.

"*Encore?* Again?"

"*Oui. Cette fois peut-etre...* This time maybe..."

"*Nous lui attrappons.* We can catch them."

"*Je l'espère.* I hope so."

"*Moi aussi.* Me, too."

A cruising police car took the call, sounded its siren, and rushed to the scene. The officer ran up the library steps, flashed his badge at the front lobby guard, and headed for the computer room.

Louise, keeping her eye on her watch, saw that almost ten minutes had elapsed. Probably not much time left. Quickly, she saved the information to her flash drive, closed the site, and ejected the drive. She heard the door behind her burst open, and she stood up with the drive in her hand. An intense, whispered French conversation behind her made her heart beat faster. Without looking back, she walked slowly away from the computers and into the nearby Reference section. Her steps echoed in the cavernous space, and she regretted her hard-soled shoes. She felt incredibly conspicuous but hoped that the officer would be searching for the computer. She sat down and opened a large dictionary. While she ran her finger down the column of one page, she slipped the flash drive under the spine of the huge book. If someone remembered that she'd been at the computer, at least the incriminating evidence wouldn't be on her person. Frowning as though deep in thought, she moved to the adjoining table to consult another reference book. She heard the officer walk over to the line of computers. Glancing up, she saw him consult a note in his hand, verifying that the computer in front of him was the hacker's.

Again she studied the reference books. Now, she thought, he'd be looking around the room trying to identify the hacker, who must be near by. The room was full of students, not all of them young, she noted with some relief. She hoped he wouldn't suspect the elderly lady at the encyclopedia. He moved away and spoke to some students, gesturing back at the computer. She couldn't understand, but surely he'd asked them if they'd seen who'd been using it. They shook their heads; they'd been too busy, and besides, rough police tactics at recent street demonstrations had made most students unwilling to cooperate with the law.

Louise, however, thought it might not be long before someone remembered her. She walked slowly into the stacks out of sight. She removed the gray wig she'd been wearing and put it in her large purse, pushed her short blond hair back to make it a little spiky, and took off the black vest she'd been wearing and stuffed it into her handbag. Her bright yellow silk blouse with the low vee neckline was now more prominent. She took off her glasses. Then she slid a book from the shelf, pulled in her stomach a little, and went over to an empty carrel. She sat down to read, glancing at the dictionary once to make sure her flash drive was still safe.

The Sureté officer was still looking around the room. Maybe someone had told him that there'd been an old lady sitting at that computer. She hoped her altered appearance would evade suspicion. The officer turned 360 degrees twice but could find nothing. Finally, he slapped stiff arms against his sides in a classic gesture of frustration, inadvertently banging his hat on his knee. He looked around one more time before clapping his hat back on and stomping toward the exit. Louise listened to his footsteps, still pretending to read. When the sound stopped, she knew he'd turned back to take one last look. She heard another click of the boot's heel on the marble floor and looked up to see the back of his uniform disappearing through the doorway.

She was interested to note that, even in this age of terrorism, he hadn't confiscated the computer, or dusted for fingerprints. Louise made a note to tell Charles that the Sureté's operations in the field were not as advanced as their computer software. Well, people don't like change, she thought.

She retrieved the drive from under the dictionary, sliding it into her handbag, then headed for another exit. She came out on a side street, walked two blocks south, and hailed a taxi. With a sigh of relief, Louise gave the cabbie the name of their hotel. He scowled at her American accent, but didn't pretend, as some did, that he couldn't understand her.

Chapter 4
The Chauffeur

That same morning, Charles found several interesting items in last week's papers. MOLP had a chauffeur, René Delacroix, who was, according to the stories, a bit of a celebrity himself, mostly because of his good looks. There was a picture of him holding the door for the President and smiling at the cameras that were pointed not at his passenger but at him.

Charles walked to the Ministry and was lucky enough to see the President arrive. Sure enough, the paparazzi were more interested in the chauffeur than the President. After the President entered the building, Delacroix parked the car in a reserved place alongside the imposing building and walked away. Charles followed.

He stopped at a little café less than a block away, took out a cell phone, and placed it on the table, probably Charles thought, to receive his boss's call. Then, he opened a paper and ordered a drink, tall, iced, and clear, more like an Englishman, Charles thought, except that it was morning. That part of the scene seemed more French.

Charles took a table downwind, not too far away, and pretended to read his paper. In a few moments, he could discern the chauffeur's scent against the background of ink and newsprint from his paper. He also filtered out the powerful odor of gin. Slowly, item by item, he noted the soap the chauffeur had used for his morning bath: the cleaning fluid from his fresh uniform, stale tobacco, and one other smell, quite faint. It took him a while to remember what it was–a certain perfume, quite elegant and fashionable, certainly expensive. He knew from the gossip columnists that Delacroix wasn't married and had a substantial reputation as a ladies' man. According to the columnists, Delacroix enjoyed the excitement he created in women and the power he had over them. And it's not simply his good looks; he was supposed to have unusually imaginative ways in the bedroom.

While he was wondering how a truly enterprising gossip columnist could lay her hands on such information, and chuckling to himself at the obvious answer, he smelled a powerful wave of the same perfume he had detected faintly from Delacroix. At the same moment, an elegant woman breezed by, a woman the French describe as "of a certain age." She stopped at Delacroix's table, but for only a few seconds, then walked on.

He knew immediately that an assignation had been arranged. Nothing else could explain the brief stop and the same perfume. After a few minutes, as Charles predicted, Delacroix carefully folded his newspaper, paid his bill, and left.

Charles put on a faded little beret taken from his ever-present shopping bag, changed his glasses, and took his coat off and draped it over his arm, just in case he'd been noticed. Two blocks away, Delacroix turned into an entrance, and Charles could see that he pressed the second button from the top. As soon as he was inside, Charles went up to the door and looked at the list of tenants. There was the name of the Minister of Agriculture–G. (for Georges) Mijoux.

It had to be the Minister's wife, judging from the way she was turned out.

Mmmm. An interesting development, thought Charles.

* * *

As she met with Charles over *croques monsieurs* and excellent coffee in a small restaurant, Louise told him about her brush with the Sureté.

"How long did it take them to get there?" Charles asked.

"Not more than ten minutes from when Bird Dog beeped."

"Not much time."

"But enough. If I hadn't had a change of clothes with me…"
Her voice trailed off.

"Right. A good lesson, I guess."

Sitting back in her chair, Louise changed the subject.

"Who do you think we should work on first?" She'd been busy with the minutiae of accounts and email correspondence, and wanted now to focus on the larger picture.

Charles nodded decisively. "I think Delacroix the chauffeur should be first. He'll know everything about MOLP's movements inside and outside the Residence."

"How can we influence him?"

Chewing a mouthful of brioche rapidly and swallowing, he revealed his morning's discovery.

"He has two small vices, although few Frenchmen would consider them that–he likes to drink at a small café not far from here, and he has a mistress. The mistress is also married–and this is interesting–her husband is a high cabinet member, a confidant of MOLP. Here's a picture of Delacroix."

Charles unfolded the morning's paper and presented it. Louise looked and smiled.

"He's gorgeous!"

"So they say." Charles shrugged. "Even has his own groupies."

Louise stared at the picture of the chauffeur–a man in his mid-thirties, athletically built, strikingly handsome.

"His current love interest is Anne Mijoux, wife of the Agricultural Minister," said Charles taking the picture back. "She's older than Delacroix by ten or more years, but very attractive. I don't have a picture, but from what I saw, I'd describe her as blonde, artificial of course, but the color of excellent quality and the styling perfect. She was impeccably dressed."

"They must make a handsome couple."

"Sure, but I'll bet no one's ever seen them together."

Louise paused and put her cup down, puzzled. "But with the clothes she must have to buy to keep up her appearance, the hair and nail salon visits, and the many social functions she has to attend with her husband, how does she have time to see Delacroix?"

"I don't know, but love often finds a way."

"How did you find out about the mistress?"

"I saw them arrange for a meeting, and I followed. When he went into the building, there was the Minister's name, plain to see. The maid was probably sent out on an errand, or paid off with a gift so she'd keep quiet. The same with any other house servants. It's a way of life for the upper-class Parisian."

Louise leaned forward. "This is really not enough to embarrass MOLP. A public cuckolding of one of his closest associates is too light."

"You're right, of course. I'm thinking it'd be better to threaten the wife and her lover with the embarrassment and get something else, something more powerful that we can use to help create a financial scandal for MOLP."

They both sat quietly then, pondering the possibilities as they finished their *croques* and a small salad and watching the fashionably dressed Parisian women on their way to expensive shopping sprees. But some of them, the two Americans imagined, were probably on their way to a more exciting day.

Chapter 5
The Plan

Charles and Louise dined that night at "Ventre" on the Rue Gascogne—a small restaurant, seating only forty, with a reputation for unusual dishes combining "nouvelle cuisine" with French and Italian styles. Charles had discovered the place when he read a review, adjacent to a story on MOLP's aides. The chef and owner was a young man who hadn't studied cuisine in any formal way, and the Parisian restaurateurs were scandalized that such an upstart was winning prizes and public attention. His success came from his imaginative cooking and a practice not common among Paris' elitist chefs–he came out of the kitchen and chatted with the diners from time to time.

Charles closed his menu. Louise was still studying hers.

"I'm thinking of having the veal cheeks," she said. "I've never had cheeks of anything." She closed her menu. But Charles knew she'd open it again.

Charles ordered in flawless French.

Louise asked many questions, which Charles painstakingly translated, being very careful not to roll his eyes. At last, knowing she'd covered all possibilities, she ordered what she'd originally chosen. Charles grumbled inwardly but admired her patience and self-care.

The sommelier came and made his recommendations.

"Shall we make an exception?" Charles asked. "It seems wrong to have dinner without wine in Paris."

They followed the sommelier's recommendations and, after a sip, balancing a wineglass stem in his fingertips, his palate awash with floral and acidic combinations, Charles started the conversation that would create their strategy for embarrassing MOLP.

"How would you summarize your findings about MOLP's financial holdings?"

"Summarize? That's easy. He's squeaky clean. Before the election, he put all his holdings in a trust. On paper, at the moment, he's quite poor. Of course, with one word he can be one of the richest men in Europe."

"What do you suggest, then?"

"We could create some conflict of interest. Dozens of possibilities for that, but my guess is we'll have to go beyond conflict of interest to embarrass him."

"Yes, I imagine so." Charles smiled. "Do you have anything specific in mind?"

"No, not really–only vague ideas at this point–a more serious financial scandal, perhaps a tie to criminality, something like that. How about you? What ideas do you have?"

"Well, there's the chauffeur, Delacroix, and his highly placed plaything. She'd be mortified if her affair were made public. Her lover is, after all, only a chauffeur, and her husband is a Minister. Discovery could mean divorce, and that would ruin her financially. She has no money of her own. Delacroix also wouldn't want to be discovered. He'd lose his job, which he values. They're both vulnerable. But I worry that the danger of discovery will throw ice water on their ardor before we can use it. Right now, they're hot, and if we apply some pressure, we might get something of value against MOLP. But I'm not sure about the particulars."

Louise pursed her lips. "We can always use pictures."

"In flagrante?" He said with mock horror.

She laughed. "No, no. Nothing like that. Nothing so obvious."

"What then?"

"I'm thinking."

"We have no real plan yet, do we?"

"No, but pictures can be used later for a financial scandal. Perhaps a photo of money being passed."

Charles sat forward and nodded. "Sure, we can do that. Suppose the Minister's wife is found out, but by someone she trusts not to reveal her indiscretion. That person could ask for some innocuous favor, swearing it's unconnected to her discovery, but scaring Mme Mijoux enough to agree, but not enough to make her discontinue the affair. Something, anything really, could be passed. We can doctor the picture to make it look like sensitive data or money."

Louise was nodding vigorously. "I may have to buy some equipment. I don't have a press camera or a telephoto lens with me."

He sighed. "We have so much of that stuff at home."

"I know, but remember we didn't want to bring anything so–specialized–through Customs."

"Oh, right. I remember now." Charles sniffed at his wine and sipped to hide the fact that he was being sarcastic.

She tapped his hand. "You aren't getting dotty, are you?"

"No, I don't think so. But then, if I were, I probably wouldn't think so, would I? So perhaps I am."

"Wonderful!" Louise's sarcasm was evident. Just then their first course arrived, and this time she said "wonderful" without the sarcasm.

Charles was served the onion soufflé, which he sniffed with considerable appreciation. Across the table, he saw Louise eyeing with faint misgivings a small molded shape of jellied wild boar, which quivered on her plate. The sommelier came again and recommended a new wine for the new course. They didn't order it. Charles had purposely avoided learning about wine. He'd have outsmelled the best connoisseurs, and they couldn't afford the publicity that would surely follow.

They ate without talking, only making quiet little "mmms" and "ahs" at the exquisite flavors. Between courses, a few more details of their plot developed.

"We'll need to hire an actor or two," Charles said.

"Right. I'll buy the photographic equipment. I confess to having done a little window-shopping at a camera store yesterday. They're hard for me to resist."

Charles sat back. "So we'll stage a brief encounter and photograph it. The pictures can show a close associate of MOLP giving an envelope to someone."

"One of the actors, I imagine."

"Yes. We'll want to establish a false identity for him or her, in case there's an investigation later."

Before they could plan much more, the main course arrived, and they stopped talking again.

Chewing, Charles looked up. "How are the cheeks of veal?"

"Wonderful, but there's a flavor in it I don't recognize."

"It's chervil. I noticed it when they brought your course."

"You and your nose. I think I preferred not knowing."

"You asked. Anyway, there's nothing wrong with chervil."

"I didn't actually ask. I just commented that I couldn't identify it."

"Yes, you're right. I assumed you wanted to know. Why wouldn't you?"

She shook her head. "Sometimes you're annoyingly like a man."

"Hmmm, probably am."

They called the waiter and ordered dessert, and while they waited for it, they filled in more details of their plan to obtain incriminating pictures.

"We'll need the two actors to alter their appearance," Charles said.

"Will they agree? An actor's face is his trade mark."

"I'll pay them well and give some phony artistic reason."

But like the main course, the desserts arrived quickly before they could think more about a plan.

The desserts were playfully presented and delicately flavored, and they finished them, paid the bill, and left, satisfied with dinner, but not with their attempts at planning.

Walking back to their hotel, Charles hardly noticed the charm of the Parisian spring evening. He was deep in thought, and Louise was equally silent. He thought about the possible dangers, and the twists and turns their assignment might take. To both of them the little plan to take a picture of the Minister passing an envelope to someone seemed like a huge effort with a small payoff, but it would be fun to carry off, and of course the pictures they got would be useful in many ways.

When they reached their room, Charles took out his guitar and strummed a bluesy beat. He smiled when Louise fished a harmonica for the same key out of her collection. Soon they were playing an old Leadbelly tune, "DeKalb Blues," with Louise filling in the long rests between phrases with harmonica licks. During the music, Charles had no thoughts of MOLP or his family and friends. After "DeKalb Blues," they took up another Leadbelly song. The blues rhythms and the wailing harmonica took Charles away from thoughts of their job as he watched Louise, sitting on the edge of the bed, her head moving, her eyes closed, and her feet tapping.

But when they stopped, they couldn't help wonder what tomorrow would bring. Louise's close call with the police was unsettling. They'd have to be more careful.

And they had no idea that their efforts would end up taking them to Central Asia and the vast steppes of Kazakhstan.

Chapter 6
The Italian Producer

The next day they went their separate ways again. Louise found the equipment she needed in a shop on the Champs Elysées and was back in the hotel room by lunchtime loading fresh batteries and checking it out.

Charles' task was more complicated. He rented a room in a glitzy hotel. The lobby displayed elaborate art deco figures and prints from the '20s. The doormen wore uniforms designed to resemble zoot suits. The idea was to attract wealthy tourists, but it also suited Charles' purpose.

He'd grown up the son of middle-class parents living the year round in a resort town on the Connecticut shore. He'd learned at an early age to match his outlook and his personality to two different sets of friends–summer and winter. He also had some theater in his blood. His insurance executive father was a frustrated actor and singer who seized every opportunity to perform in public. Charles had inherited the theatrical bent and used it in his current work, adopting disguises and playing different roles with pleasure.

In the hotel room, he changed into a brightly colored sport coat and an ascot, then taxied to a prominent theatrical agency in the Latin Quarter, where he introduced himself as an Italian producer and director of films. He was quickly introduced to an agent, Mme DeVore, a tall, slender, faded beauty who exuded excessive emotion like cheap perfume. Decades earlier, her emotionality would've passed for theatrical sensitivity. Charles suspected she was one of the agency's less important representatives, but that was just as well.

Charles wasted no time on chit-chat. Using Italian-accented French, he explained that he didn't make films of the "old" sort.

"Our films are based on a new concept of cinematic reality, an extension of the Danish protocol. We go beyond that concept. We want the world to know that the Americans don't even begin to understand film."

"Of course." The former actress behind the desk seemed charmed by the Italian accent, particularly the "Americaines," with an audible vowel at the end. Charles hoped that to her French ears, it would make the Americans sound like a group of schoolgirls. Whether it was the accent, the clothing, or the exuberant charm of the "Italian," Mme DeVore became decidedly sympathique, if not lustful, and her face, faintly grotesque with rouge and lip gloss, became animated. She waved her hands as she spoke, and many heavy rings flashed in the light. "They do not understand, the Americans. They have no real culture of their own, and they think every idea they have is a new invention." She banged some papers on the table to emphasize her point, and the loose flesh under her arms trembled and swayed like bags of suspended pudding.

Charles, containing his amusement, tried to look sage. "So, I'm looking for two young actors. One male, one female. I'll need to meet them, of course, but not for a regular audition."

"Ah but we have many actors, Monsieur, or should I say Signor," she said looking quite directly at Charles and holding the eye contact a bit longer than necessary.

He turned one hand up and tilted his head slightly in an Italian gesture of appreciation. "It doesn't matter. I'd like the woman to be young, but able to pass for thirty-five, attractive, well dressed, wealthy. The man should be younger, mid-twenties, somewhat countrified."

"I see." Mme DeVore smiled knowingly. "Oui. Some stories are ageless." She paused, as if remembering something from her own past, and a smile spread over her face. Her yellowed teeth reminded Charles of automobile fog lights appearing in the dark. "You will show such an affair," she concluded. "No?"

He let her think so. She turned to an array of open files behind her chair and located a half dozen, three for each of Charles' requests, with 8 × 10 glossy photos, brief bios, and the accompanying addresses and telephone numbers. She fanned them out on the desk, pressing Charles' arm flirtatiously as she did so. He looked them over gladly and smiled, staring at the photos, pretending not to have noticed her hand on his arm. After ensuring that their physical characteristics matched his needs, he eliminated those who were experienced or successful, and chose two.

"I must have actors who are not known to the public," he explained to Mme DeVore.

"I see. Yes, of course." Her tone was suddenly business-like, Charles noted with relief, as she sat back in her chair.

"*Merci, Madame, très bien, merci.*" His thank-yous were perfunctory, and he *au revoired* quickly and left, shuddering slightly, but satisfied with the outcome.

Returning to his hotel, he called two actors. He introduced his Italian identity to Henri Clous, the young actor. "I'm staying at the Hotel des Trois Arbres, room 463. Can you see me here later today? Say three o'clock?"

"Yes, of course. I'll be there."

Actors were much the same the world over, eager when young, desperate when old. Unless they had become successful, in which case they were insufferable.

Charles then called the actress and arranged for a second appointment a few hours later.

Then, he called Louise. "Are you done with your camera shopping?"

"Yes. I found it all easily. Can we meet for lunch?"

"I don't think so. It's a little after twelve now, and I've made two appointments. The first is at three."

"Where are you?"

"A hotel near Montparnasse."

She sighed. "Too far I suppose."

"I'm afraid so. I'll just have the hotel bring something up, then take a short nap."

"Good idea. I'll join you." She paused. "Well, in spirit anyway."

"Spirit'll have to do, I think."

He hung up, aware suddenly of his hunger, and dialed for room service. Keeping his Italian persona, he ordered a small lunch, another *croque monsieur* and a salad, and fell back on the bed to wait, thinking how he'd deal with the actors who were coming. The simple meal arrived, and he ate it quickly, then stretched out on the bed for a short sleep.

The phone rang at 2:55–the front desk announcing that Henri had arrived. Charles had him sent up, then hastily straightened his hair and clothing. He set out a notepad the hotel supplied, pulled a chair up on the other side for the interview, and turned on the desk light. He was ready by the time Henri knocked.

Henri was in his early twenties, built like a wrestler, which would help him look like a farmer. The young man was also good looking, with a shock of black hair that kept falling across his forehead. He was, in fact, a little too good looking, but that could easily be altered. Charles described the task for him, which was easy and would pay very well, with a generous bonus in three years if the arrangement had been kept secret.

"I know these arrangements are a little unusual," Charles said. "I'm sure you're familiar with the Danish ideas about film-making, the restrictions on technology, and so on."

"Yes, of course."

"In Italy we're also extending this idea to the cult of personality. Trying to make movies without famous actors. Of course, others have done this, but we want the actors to remain unknown. It's our credo that by doing this we'll obtain more authentic films. No playing to the camera with an eye toward future fame. So, we'll change your appearance quite a bit, and your real name won't appear in the credits. And as you'll see, your contract specifies also that you won't use this same look or name in any of your future work."

Henri sighed and brushed his unruly hair back off his forehead. Charles could see that he was disappointed. The job couldn't possibly further his career. Charles hoped, however, that the generous salary and the small amount of time required would balance out the shortcomings.

Henri signed the contract, and Charles did too, with a dramatic flourish.

"I'll call you when the time comes," said Charles, handing him a copy of the contract.

The woman came a few hours later. She looked perfect for the part. Just a little overweight, she could, with a touch of grey, pass for ten years older yet still be attractive. She wore a suit tailored to fit her generous figure, linen, softly yellow, fresh as spring but muted. Discreet jewelry: small amber earrings and a matching necklace. The plain band on her left hand said she was married. Her elegance was classically Parisian. She might have been a descendant of some long-forgotten royal family of old Europe. But would she accept the role and its conditions? The approach he'd taken with Henri would probably not work with her; she seemed a little too bright to fall for phony artistic blather.

She introduced herself as Sara Chalice, surely a stage name, but that was no matter. Charles concluded that the Italian director ploy was out the window. She'd see through it. But he had no plan B. He wasn't at all sure what to do. He dropped his Italian accent and plunged into unknown territory. "Mlle Chalice, I'm not a film director at all. I work for the government of France. I can't tell you which department. In fact, I can't tell you very much of what you'll want to know. Furthermore, no one must know that you're here talking to me. Any breach in this secrecy will nullify our agreement."

Charles felt his heart beating.

Mlle Chalice looked a little alarmed. "But what must I do?"

The plan came to Charles out of nowhere, but he found it nerve-wracking to be winging it.

"In the beginning, it's very simple. You'll become a certain person, a person we will invent–a little older than you. As this person, you'll strike up an acquaintance with the wife of a Minister of the government. She's a pleasant lady. I think you'll like her. She's done nothing treasonous, but she's having an unwise affair. We believe it's a weakness in our security, and we believe the Americans are trying to exploit it."

She looked shocked. "Are they spying on us, then?"

"*Bien sur*. Of course. They've been doing it for many years, but they've learned nothing of importance. They don't realize that we're many steps ahead of them."

Mlle Chalice smiled with patriotic satisfaction. Charles also smiled. *It's going to work*, he thought.

"In the beginning, you must simply become her friend, and after a while–we'll tell you when–you'll reveal something about yourself that shows you trust her very much. We hope, then, that she'll share her secret with you. If not, we'll arrange for you to discover it. By then she should trust you enough to be only a little disturbed that you know about her affair. You will then continue to meet with her, and from time to time remind her that you know her secret. You will assure her that you'll tell no one. Then one day you'll ask her for a favor, a very small, insignificant one. She'll certainly comply, and then your job will probably be finished. We expect she'll then bring to an end the situation that might compromise our national security."

"It seems very simple. Is there any danger in it for me?" A wrinkle appeared in her elegant brow.

"I don't think so. Of course it would be a problem if the American spies discover that you're working for the French government. But even if they do find out, you won't be a threat to them. It is possible, however, they might try to 'turn' you. That is, employ you to work for them. They would almost certainly pretend to be French counterespionage agents. If this happens, all you need to do is tell us."

"Of course, of course. I'm a loyal Frenchwoman." She straightened her back and took a deep breath.

"Yes, we know that. We've investigated thoroughly," Charles lied. "You'll be paid very well, as this agreement shows. There will be other benefits as we go along–some very nice clothes for you to keep, manicures, coiffures. Possibly some enjoyable time at a spa. And when you're finished, and some time has passed–three years should be enough–with no publicity, we'll provide a substantial bonus. You may sign here."

And she did, smiling and waving her copy of the contract.

Charles too smiled a little as she left, and felt some relief that his impulsive gamble hadn't gone awry.

Chapter 7
The Actress

The trap was set–baited with the gullibility, passion, and vanity of its unwitting participants. Louise liked the plan because no one but MOLP and his colleague the Minister of Agriculture would be hurt by it. The end result, however, would be trivial–something that could probably be used later in a bigger scheme. They sat in a small bistro looking out on the Boulevard Michelin, both wondering if the small result was worth all the effort. But in the end, they clinked their glasses of mineral water. It might even be fun.

From a tabloid that Charles translated for her, Louise learned that Mme Mijoux bought her gowns at a well-known couturier on the Rue Mignet, a fashionable area not known to be commercial. One gossip columnist had written that Mme Mijoux didn't like publicity, particularly when it focused on her appearance, and quoted her as saying, "There's so much of that in Paris–which wife of which Minister wore what couturier's gown." So she preferred not to be seen buying anything, but then, the columnist noted with catty undertones, she'd be stunning at some public event, and the journalists would ask her where she got her gown. She never revealed the little couturier on Rue Mignet, where Louise followed her. As soon as she realized it was a dress shop, she called Charles, who called Sara and asked her to meet him nearby.

On the street, Charles gave Sara enough money to buy a new gown, shoes, and accessories. He told her that for the first meeting it was important only for Mme Mijoux to see her there in the little home-like shop. Charles, posing as a man looking for his niece's birthday present, saw a smile pass between the two women. It is only a beginning, he thought, but just the right kind of beginning, a mutual smile that meant they both knew they were there for the same purpose–to look good and please men. From that smile, a little ingenuity and planning and subterfuge could produce a friendship between Sara and Mme Mijoux.

* * *

Two days later, Charles stood near a newsstand reading a paper. He saw Mme Mijoux leave her apartment building, looking elegant in a beige skirt and an ivory top with a scoop neck showing a bit of cleavage. Her face was delicately framed by medium-length gold earrings that made her hazel eyes look darker and more mysterious. Charles saw that she was carrying a box, but he was too far away to read the exquisitely modest label. He followed her, and as soon as he realized she was headed for the couturier, he called Sara and told her to come right away; but by the time Sara was made up, dressed, and taxied to the location, Mme Mijoux was ready to leave the store. In fact, as Sara hurried in, she bumped into Mme Mijoux in the doorway.

Sara, startled by the bump, was also taken aback by Mme's elegance, unimaginable in Sara's middle-class origins. She swallowed the impulse to curtsey and tried to play her role, but knew she was blushing.

"I beg your pardon," Sara said.

"Oh, you were here just two days ago, weren't you?" Mme Mijoux' beautiful face lit up in recognition.

"Yes, and I remember you, too." Sara struggled to regain her composure, praying that some minor slip of the tongue or reversion to the Lyonnaise accent she grew up with wouldn't reveal her humbler background. "Um, oh yes. Emerald green taffeta, off the shoulder. You looked beautiful in it." Sara was a pro and overcame her class-consciousness. She recalled a role as a countess she'd performed not long ago and found an authentically aristocratic voice and manner. She thought, however, that she shouldn't overdo it, or Mme Mijoux might wonder who this aristocrat was that she'd never seen before.

"Thank you." Mme Mijoux was already charmed. "It was very nice, wasn't it?"

"Was? You're not keeping it then?"

"*Hélas* no. My husband's attendance at the affair was cancelled, and there'll be no state dinners until we're well into summer, and then the taffeta wouldn't be suitable."

"Too bad." Sara's adorable nose wrinkled up a little in sympathy. "Your husband must be high in the government."

"He is Minister of Agriculture. But puh," Mme made that very French sound, a little like spitting out a small seed, "it is very boring."

"My gown too was very nice." Sara accented the "was" to indicate that they were in the same boat. "Do you remember cream-colored silk, rather tight but not too tight? Nevertheless I must lose a few pounds," she added breathlessly, rolling her eyes in resignation at the never-ending battle. "But the shoes don't fit. They seemed to fit in the store, but when I got home and tried them on again I knew my feet would be unhappy before the evening was out. And without the shoes, the gown would never work, so I'm going to look for another pair. Perhaps…" Her voice trailed off.

Mme's head tipped to one side as she smiled sympathetically. "I know, for me too it is always like that with shoes."

A warm look passed between them.

"Perhaps we'll meet here again," said Mme Mijoux.

"I'd like that," said Sara, as she stepped into the store with her shoebox.

Mme Mijoux hailed a taxi and disappeared with a friendly wave.

* * *

Later, after Sara had returned the shoes for a size larger, Charles met her in the hotel, and they went over the encounter in detail. He could've kissed her for doing such an excellent job, but remembering his own role as a professional French agent, he congratulated her with Gallic reserve. "A fine beginning. The next time you'll ask her to join you for coffee or tea and perhaps then or perhaps on a subsequent occasion, it'll be a glass of wine." He paused and appraised Sara, nodding his approval of her appearance. She was wearing two shades of green, a pale top with a vee neck that revealed just a hint of her generous breasts, and a darker skirt that was tight enough to show off her figure, which was somewhat full but still quite attractive.

He added, "She is very nice, isn't she?"

"Yes, indeed. I hope in the end, our subterfuge doesn't cause her any embarrassment." A furrow had appeared on Sara's forehead, and Charles noted it.

"On the contrary, you'll be saving her from considerable difficulty, even ruin. As I said before, she is having an affair, and not at all a wise one. Both she and her husband would be seriously embarrassed if she were found out, and it would probably be disastrous for her financially. Eventually you'll tell her that you know about it, she'll trust you to tell no one, and you'll convince her that you can indeed be trusted. But after a while she'll come to think that if you can discover her secret then someone else might also, and she'll break off the affair, we hope, which will seal up the little hole in our security."

"I see. I had no idea the French government could be so understanding."

"No, no. We are not understanding." Charles had the air of one tutoring an adolescent. "We simply don't want our Ministers to be publicly embarrassed."

"Of course." The furrow disappeared from Sara's pretty forehead.

Chapter 8

The Minister's Wife

The next week, Sara encountered Mme Mijoux in the street near the same shop where they had originally met and suggested an afternoon cup of tea. They were both dressed very well, and many heads turned as they entered the small café. The shop owner fawned over them, knowing the value of such beautiful customers. They too knew how gorgeous they were and doubly enjoyed their time together.

As they sat down, Mme Mijoux began, "I haven't formally introduced myself." She reached her hand across the small table. "Anne Mijoux."

"Clothilde DuVal," Sara replied. She and Charles had spent some time preparing a more detailed background for Sara to use, in response to the discomfort she'd felt in the previous encounter.

"DuVal, DuVal," mused Mme Mijoux. "I can't think of..." Her voice trailed off, but Sara got the message.

"My father made a lot of money in shipping, and I grew up in Lyons," she said. She was grateful to Charles for having picked the childhood in Lyons. It provided a cover for any traces of accent. Mme Mijoux' curiosity seemed satisfied. Her own background wasn't particularly aristocratic; her current status was a direct result of her husband's political success. In fact, she was only a little less socially edgy than Sara.

They sat outside in the warming spring sunshine and fell easily into a commentary on the fashions of the women passing by. They were both aware of fashion in a way that is uniquely French, and they made intelligent and forthright assessments of the women in view. As they talked, their comments grew more intimate.

"I don't understand how they can wear such short skirts, even though they do have beautiful legs," Mme Mijoux complained.

"I'd wear them if I could get away with it," said "Clothilde." She tossed her beautifully coiffed hair.

"Yes, I suppose I would too. Fashion is a hard mistress, but I don't think I'd like men looking at my underwear." Mme Mijoux shook her head slowly and laughed quietly at the idea.

"And Anne, these thongs! How do they stand them?" Clothilde acted horrified at the very thought.

"I can't imagine. Anyway they're going out of fashion. " Both women smiled at each other, appalled at the idea, one genuinely so. "But, you know, if I were ten years younger..." Mme Mijoux' voice faded and there was a brief silence.

"Anne, listen, I have to tell you something." She and Charles had planned this move for today, and she leaned forward and spoke in a quiet voice.

"Yes, Clothilde." Anne leaned forward too, apparently ready for a confidence that would increase their intimacy.

"I'm having an affair."

Anne's eyes rolled and she moved her head from side to side in an obvious show of disappointment. Apparently, she had hoped for something juicier. "Yes, so am I. Every woman in Paris is probably doing the same."

"But Anne, listen, I'm having an affair with a Member of the Chambre des Députés, and he is very highly placed. I don't dare say his name, but you'll know him, oh, I must tell someone," she said, pretending to give in to a need for confession, "it is M. Hervé, who leads the Green Party."

"Mon Dieu!" exclaimed Anne Mijoux, "But it is so dangerous for him. He has been married for a long time, and if you were discovered it would be a big scandal." Sara saw that she paled a little and was sure from the reaction that Mme Mijoux had thought of her own situation. This conclusion was confirmed when Mme Mijoux admonished her, "You shouldn't have told me."

"Oh, I know, I know," whimpered Clothilde, "but I couldn't keep it inside any longer. You won't betray me, will you?"

"Of course not. Your secret is safe with me." It was exactly the reaction that Charles had hoped for. Sara even imagined Mme Mijoux feeling as though she had acquired considerable power over Clothilde although with no interest in using it

"I'm so relieved." Sara's feelings of social inadequacy had drained away, and she was now playing with skill the role of a courtesan who can't keep her affairs to herself.

"How is he in bed?" Mme Mijoux asked, suddenly leaning forward and smiling in anticipation.

"Not bad, not bad at all," said Clothilde, recovering quickly from the shock of hearing the question. "He is considerate. But he has so little time."

"I know the problem," said Anne sardonically.

"Ah, no. I don't mean that. He is a grown man," Clothilde stifled her laughter and hurried to reply. "I mean it literally. He is very busy and we don't get to see each other very often."

"Mmmm. Well, it is perhaps better." Mme Mijoux touched Clothilde's hand in a gesture of reassurance. "There's less risk of discovery and, of course, absence makes the heart grow fonder." Sara laughed inwardly at the cliché. In a play it would've ruined the script.

"I love him to distraction already," Clothilde offered.

"Still," said Anne, "you must be very careful."

Sara realized that Anne had mentioned the danger of "Clothilde's" liaison several times and decided that she'd gotten the message. She was feeling quite proud of having accomplished her patriotic duty and changed the subject by commenting again on the passing scene. They talked in this way for another fifteen minutes until Anne glanced at her watch quickly and said "Mon Dieu, I'm late. Excuse me, please." She fumbled in her purse for money to pay her share of the bill, but Sara waved her off.

"Please, let me pay."

"*Merci, merci.*" She closed her purse and hurried away, looking at her watch and shaking her head.

* * *

Sara and Charles went over the conversation later.

"It sounds excellent," he said, "And you were quite right to reveal your supposed liaison, as I instructed. I'm nevertheless surprised that she took the bait so readily. But that may be a good thing. We need now to test her loyalty to you in some small way that will mean nothing. Perhaps you could ask her for some small favor." He pretended to think for some few seconds. "Would you ask her to ask her husband if he'd give an autograph to a friend of yours, or to your brother, yes that would be better, your younger brother, who admires his work on behalf of farmers. He is a farmer himself and believes the French farmer is the backbone of the economy... you know the usual political phrases."

Sara nodded. "The Minister does champion their cause."

Charles elaborated, "Your brother should be portrayed as having political ambitions of his own, a large following in the country, and great chances of success. This will make it more likely that the Minister will respond favorably, thinking he may gain a political ally in the future."

Charles watched Sara nod slowly. She did indeed understand what was expected of her. Soon he'd be able to spring the trap and complete the first step of embarrassing MOLP.

Chapter 9
The Reaction

Charles and Louise were having dinner in an excellent but not distinguished restaurant on the Place de l'Odéon, across from their hotel. Charles briefed her on the latest developments.

"It seems likely that Mme Mijoux would do a small favor for her new friend, if she has an incentive."

"And what might that be?" Louise's sarcasm was evident.

Charles smiled. "Of course her friend 'Clothilde' has to find out about Delacroix. But how?"

Louise was silent. Charles waited, hoping for a brilliant idea.

Their main course arrived, and they ate in silence. Louise had ordered only a salad, and the waiters protested but were quieted by a withering look. Charles was less restrained, ordering a lamb chop, a potato, and *haricots verts*.

When her salad was gone, Louise took up the conversation. "I hope you don't mean that you want Clothilde to find her and Delacroix in bed together. We've already discussed this idea and dismissed it; it would be altogether too dramatic."

"Louise, believe me I have no such thought. It is enough for Mme Mijoux to know that her friend knows who her lover is." Charles paused. "What makes you think I'd pursue such a plan?"

Louise hesitated, her lips pursed. "I think you like these over-the-top scenarios."

Charles twiddled his fork. He wasn't sure how to respond to Louise's accusation. "Well, perhaps I do lean toward the dramatic. But I don't let it get in the way of our general purpose."

"OK. I'll accept that. But I'm still going to, to, keep my eye on you."

"Fair enough."

A long and decidedly uncomfortable silence followed, which Louise broke.

"I have an idea," Louise said.

"Yes?" Charles punctuated the relief he felt by spearing one of his remaining *haricots verts*.

"Well, Delacroix is nearly a public figure. We see him on television whenever MOLP is coming or going. And he has a kind of fan club, you know."

"I don't see where you're going with this."

"Well, it wouldn't be out of place for 'Clothilde' to comment on Delacroix's looks. Mme Mijoux would surely react, perhaps visibly, and Sara could pretend to discover from her reaction that Delacroix is her lover. Mme Mijoux is so afraid of being caught, she'll be ready to believe that her new friend has figured her out–that it's Delacroix who makes her toes curl in the afternoon."

"But what if Mme Mijoux shows no reaction?"

"Charles, sometimes you're dense."

Charles eyebrows went up. He treasured his intelligence, but if pressed, he would admit to some difficulty understanding the emotional side of life. "OK. I'm dense. Please explain to me how Sara will see a reaction when there is none."

"Don't be smug. It's simple. There doesn't have to be any reaction at all. Mme Mijoux will assume, because of her own fear, that she has blushed, or paled, or blinked. It doesn't matter what she actually does."

"I see, I see. And you're right. It should work." He thought for a moment. "I'll explain it to Sara. She's been excellent so far."

* * *

The next day, Charles briefed Sara.

"The President of Italy is visiting in two days, and I'm told that during his visit the Opéra de Paris will give its last performance of the season. It'll be Verdi's *Il Trovatore*, and the Italian and French Presidents will both attend. Delacroix will surely drive them, and the television coverage at the arrival will be intense. We can only hope that it will be aired. Other news of the world could interfere."

"And what should I do?"

"If the chauffeur is shown on TV, I want you to meet with Anne soon after."

"That will be easy."

Noting that Sara seemed fully on board, Charles continued. "During the conversation, comment on how good-looking the President's chauffeur is. She may react or she may not, but in either case, you should comment on her reaction."

"Do you mean you want me to act as if she has reacted, even though she has not?"

"Exactly. That'll give you an opportunity to let her know that you know who her lover is. She'll be very upset, I'm sure, and you'll reassure her that her secret is safe with you. It would be helpful to remind her that she keeps a similar secret about you."

The next meeting between Clothilde/Sara and Anne Mijoux took place in the late afternoon at a café on Rue Griot, where they sipped an apéritif.

The arrival of the two Presidents at l'Opéra had been aired, and most of the channels included a brief clip of Delacroix opening the door for MOLP. The press knew the value of his photogenic face.

The two women were again watching the passing fashion scene, but quietly. Sara was feeling, as she had before, that she was out of her social league. She hesitated to initiate Charles' plan, which seemed presumptuous. She stole a glance at Mme Mijoux and thought about her foolishness in taking up with a chauffeur when her husband was so prominent in the government. The idea that Mme Mijoux was acting irresponsibly helped reduce Sara's sense of social inferiority.

She began to implement Charles' request. "Did you see that chauffeur Delacroix on TV last night? He is gorgeous!"

Sara thought that Mme Mijoux reacted. But was she jealous of Clothilde's attention to her lover or nervous at hearing his name mentioned so publicly? Sara let a moment pass to make her next utterance seem more real.

"Why Anne, whatever is the matter? You look as though you might've seen a ghost." Clothilde allowed some sarcasm to show in her voice.

"Not at all. It is nothing."

Madame doth protest too much, thought Sara. She let a smile, sly and knowing, spread slowly across her face.

"It's him, isn't it? It's Delacroix you see."

"No, no, not at all." Mme Mijoux hesitated at first, and then denied the accusation so vehemently that Clothilde chuckled.

"And is he good in bed?" she asked, laughing out loud.

"Mon Dieu," gasped Mme Mijoux. "You can't possibly believe that I..."

And then she too began to laugh.

"Glorious, just glorious." But her laughter died quickly, and Sara noticed that her voice quivered slightly. "But you must swear to me on your most sacred belief that you will tell no one."

"Absolutely," said Clothilde, growing serious. "I know how bad for you it would be if the truth came out. I'd never hurt you like that. Or in any way."

The reassurances seemed to help, for Mme Mijoux straightened her back.

"Besides," said Clothilde, "you hold the same weapon over me. We're even."

Both women laughed, softly at first, then loudly.

Mme Mijoux called the waiter over and ordered another round, which she drank quickly.

* * *

Charles was at first elated when Sara gave him the full report over this last meeting, but then he wondered again if events hadn't moved too quickly. It wouldn't help their plot if Mme Mijoux became fearful of discovery and ended her friendship with "Clothilde." Maybe her fear would make her want to keep Clothilde close by. Nevertheless, he worried over those risks and shared his fears with Louise.

"There's no way to avoid all risk," she reminded him as they dressed in their hotel room the next morning. "It's a part of what we do."

"I know that," Charles replied, pulling on a sock, "but it doesn't make me feel any better."

Louise didn't answer him right away. She bent over to pull up her panty hose, first one leg, then the other, then straightening and wiggling her hips in the last part of the maneuver, while she thought of an answer.

Finally, she said "It's like an investment–you can take a lot of risk and maybe make a lot of money, or you can take many small risks, each with a chance of modest gain. We've usually followed the second philosophy, although there have been some exceptions. I'm thinking of that time in Lisbon when we slowly built up the kidnapper's fear, piece by piece, until he got rattled and revealed his location."

"Yes, I get your point." Charles' voice moderated somewhat. "And it does calm my nerves a little to see it from that more philosophical perspective." He straightened his flamboyant tie and assessed his appearance in the mirror. Satisfied that he looked like a French agent trying to look like a French-Italian film director, he turned to Louise, who wouldn't be dressed for another twenty minutes.

"All right, it'll work or not. In either case, we'll move forward."

Louise smiled at him. "That's more like it." She enjoyed this aspect of their relationship. She thought of her role as a combination of mother and therapist. She'd done both jobs in her former lives and done them well. Now she applied her skills and wisdom to helping them–the team of Danvers and Dereva–function smoothly and efficiently.

* * *

Charles met with Sara later that morning and gave her the next set of instructions.

"Perhaps at this next meeting, perhaps the one after, depending on how she still feels about your discovery of her secret, you'll ask her to ask her husband for a brief meeting and an autograph for your brother, who so admires his work for the farmers. Some flattery of her husband will also help her see him in a better light, so that she'll be more likely to break off the affair that is such a danger to France," Charles explained. He didn't add that it would also help persuade Minister Mijoux to consent to the meeting. "Please use your judgment about whether the timing is right to ask her for this favor."

"I'm not sure I understand," Sara said. "Why does he ask for the autograph? It seems to me that if she is sufficiently frightened by my discovery of her lover to break off the affair that we've accomplished our purpose."

"I understand your question." Charles noted with satisfaction her use of the pronoun our. "It is a common practice in our line of work to ask for some tangible evidence of a 'fish's' loyalty. You will appreciate the metaphor behind our jargon. A 'fish' is someone who has taken the bait." Sara's brow wrinkled a little, and Charles quickly added, "Of course, usually we're carrying out a plan that isn't in the fish's own interest. So the metaphor isn't really appropriate in this case."

Charles watched with some relief as the wrinkle disappeared from Sara's brow. He began to think of her brow as a gauge of how well he was running her.

"We call this tangible evidence of loyalty a 'token.' But in this case it isn't exactly loyalty. Getting the autograph is a token of her friendship for you. But believe me, it works. She'll be even closer and more committed to her friendship with you after she's done you a favor."

"Yes, I see. It makes sense in an emotional way." As an actress, Sara was interested in the motivation behind her actions.

"Unfortunately, as soon as we know she has this level of commitment we must begin to unravel it. We don't want the Americans to know what we're doing."

"Certainly not."

"Perhaps we could arrange for you to have a little vacation, away from Paris for a while."

"That sounds very pleasant."

Chapter 10
The Photograph

Anne and "Clothilde" met later that day but hadn't decided how to spend their time together. Anne wanted Sara to try a new hair stylist, but Sara demurred, knowing that her artificial graying would be discovered and with it her false role. She claimed to be satisfied with her stylist, and they settled on a joint shopping venture in a boutique on Rue Delattre.

An outlet for the creations of a famous couturier, but known in French as *"deuxieme étage,"* or "third storey" and a complicated tale explained the term.The boutique held creations not good enough for the shows but ones that could still be sold without embarrassing any reputations. The two women enjoyed looking at these designs but didn't buy any. Some were only half finished, others too bizarre to consider. They often laughed as if to say, "What was he thinking?"

Afterwards, they sat together over coffee in a small nearby café.

"May I ask you for a small favor?" Clothilde asked.

"Of course," Anne offered quickly.

"I've told you before about my brother, who's very talented and politically active up north."

"Yes, I remember."

"He'd enjoy meeting your husband, if only briefly–I know how busy he is–and perhaps also an autograph? It may sound silly to you, but it would mean a lot to him."

"I'll certainly ask my husband," Mme Mijoux said, "but I can't promise he'll do it. He is far too *sérieux*, and he could refuse. He doesn't want to be a celebrity. But perhaps if I emphasize your brother's political connections, he'll think of him as a future ally. I believe that he doesn't have many allies in the north."

When the Minister, M. Mijoux, heard his wife's request for an autograph and a meeting with his wife's friend's brother, he was at first a little angry that Anne would ask for something so trivial, even though it wouldn't take much of his time. He hesitated, too, because only a few weeks ago, the agency that handled the President's safety and security had lectured all the Ministers on the importance of avoiding contacts with people they didn't know. But when he heard that the brother had a following among farmers and had also political ambitions himself, his uncertainties about the appointment vanished in a cloud of political ambition. He consented to meet the young man briefly on the following Monday.

After news of the agreement passed from Anne to Clothilde to Charles and finally to Louise, there were only two days in which to prepare. The photographic equipment was ready, so Louise spent a good part of Saturday examining the corner where the brief meeting was to take place.

At the same time, Charles explained to Henri the importance of talking to the Minister as long as possible. Henri had been told that a cinematographer would be filming, but he didn't know, of course, that Louise would take only still pictures. Nevertheless he seemed eager to do his job as requested, and that meant keeping the Minister engaged in conversation for as long as possible before giving Henri the picture. During the conversation Louise would have time to set up the shot. Charles also helped Henri choose a look that would be appropriate but also alter his appearance as much as possible, so as not to interfere with any later roles in movies or theater that Henri might have. These changes also helped Charles achieve the secrecy he needed for the operation.

Louise found a café on the second floor of a building one door down and on the same side of the street where she Henri and M. Mijoux would meet. The corner had been chosen for its convenience to the Minister, on his way to the Chambre from his apartment. There was a hotel on the corner and a small indentation in the curbing for the hotel guests to pull in and unload luggage. The Ministerial limousine driver would find it convenient to pull over there. From her vantage point in the café one flight up, Louise had a clear view of the hotel front and with her telephoto lens could take pictures without detection.

Louise was a little anxious. Not from any danger–she didn't anticipate any–but because of all the work that had gone into the preparation for the picture-taking and the many things that could go wrong. She carried a phony press badge to make her elaborate camera equipment more plausible and a half hour before the appointed time had ordered a café-au-lait and brioche brought to a table beside the railing. She had a clear view; her camera was prefocused. The waiter at the café was bored and possibly hung over. Once he'd brought the American woman her breakfast, he wanted nothing to do with her.

Charles had placed himself on the other side of the cross street with Henri. From his position, he could see both Louise and the place where the conversation would happen. Charles had instructed Henri in some farm issues, and told him that his role in the "reality movie" was that of a local politician who sought the farmers' votes and who was about to meet the Minister of Agriculture, whom he admired. The actor playing the Minister, Henri was told, would look very authentic. Henri knew where Louise (the "cinematographer") would be located and would try to position himself for a good take.

The time dragged. The limousine was a little late. Charles sent Henri across the street. A few minutes later, Charles saw the limousine with its Ministerial flags approaching. He gave a wave, to both Louise and Henri, that action was to begin. Henri looked appropriately anxious, peering down the street. The limousine crept along with the heavy morning traffic. Louise had her hand on the camera. A horn blared and brakes screeched. There was the unmistakable sound of crunching car bodies. Directly in front of the hotel one car had rear-ended another. The drivers climbed out slowly, their movements deliberate, resigned to the unpleasantness of arguing, or at least exchanging information. All traffic stopped. The Minister was three car lengths behind and in the same lane as the accident.

Charles and Louise waited to see what the Minister would do. If he got out and walked to the corner, all would be well. But he didn't. Instead, his chauffeur stepped out of the limousine, impressed the neighboring drivers with the importance of his passenger, and stopped the slow creep of traffic past the limousine. This created an opening. He gave an appreciative gesture informing the line of traffic to wait, and returned to the limousine. He then pulled into the space he had created and pulled around the cars that were blocked by the accident.

Charles couldn't tell what was going to happen. Louise, too, was frozen in uncertainty, her hands on the camera, unable to predict what would happen but sure that things weren't going well. Henri stared at the creeping limousine, looked back at Charles, but, getting no signal, looked again at the limousine. When the big car drew ahead of the two fender-bended cars, Charles saw the front wheels turn and realized that the chauffeur was going to pull around the corner and stop beside a newsstand. The car would be out of Louise's line of sight. Charles gestured for Louise to come down to the street. As soon as the little wreck occurred, she'd suspected that the limo might pull around the corner, and she was on her feet and running as soon as Charles signaled her to come down.

"Madame!" the waiter shouted, as he realized that the American woman might leave without paying her small bill.

"Catch you later," Louise yelled as she ran out of the café toward the stairwell.

"Cashew lateur?" the waiter queried helplessly, and then, realizing that she wasn't going to pay, "Salaude! Americaine!" It was hard to tell which of those two words he felt was most damning.

The Minister's car pulled in behind the newsstand, and Henri, following a second gesture from Charles, walked around the corner to meet him.

"Monsieur le Ministre," he said and gave a deferential little bow.

"You must be Henri," the Minister replied with a half smile and extended his hand, which Henri took. There was no sign of any autograph.

"I'm most pleased to meet you," Henri said. Louise had reached the street and paused to catch her breath and to dismount the telephoto lens and plug in a large, press-type flash attachment. She didn't know what was happening around the corner. She looked toward Charles. Just then he was hidden by cars moving across the intersection. She finished attaching the flash and looked again, just as the light changed, and in the brief break in traffic, she saw Charles signaling her to move around the corner.

"I'm grateful for this opportunity to meet you," Henri said.

"I understand you organize the farmers to the north," the Minister replied.

"Yes," said Henri, "we have the same problems as farmers everywhere–price fluctuations, weather–you know, of course, but we also have some special problems of our own."

"Of course, I understand. Why don't you write me a letter about it," the Minister suggested." This seemed so much more reasonable to Henri than trying to influence agricultural policy while standing on a street corner–he saw no way to refuse, even though he knew Louise couldn't see him and therefore he should stall for time. They couldn't film if the camera wasn't there. He glanced toward Charles, but Charles had wisely disappeared.

"I will do that," he said.

The Minister reached out to shake his hand again to say goodbye, and Henri hesitated to respond in kind, realizing that there had been no camera present to film the exchange.

"Monsieur, are you perhaps forgetting ..." Before he could finish his sentence, the minister said "Ah, yes, of course, the autograph, with pleasure." He drew forth from his coat pocket a small envelope containing a picture of himself, evidently pre-signed, and handed it to Henri. At that moment, Louise ran around the corner, and her flash went off just as the exchange took place. The Minister waved and smiled as he turned back to the limousine. Louise kept snapping pictures. Henri stood, looking confused, holding the picture, as the limousine pulled out into traffic and disappeared. Charles had crossed the street and came up to Henri with his hand extended. "Bravo! *Excellente!*" he said in Italian. Louise said nothing.

"I could find only this American woman to take the pictures," Charles explained to Henri.

"But where is the movie camera?" Henri asked.

"Ah," said Charles, "perhaps you don't realize that today, with special equipment that we've developed in Italy we're able to convert this series of still pictures into a clip of moving film. It should be fine."

Henri seemed to accept this explanation, although Charles realized that it wouldn't be long before Henri, talking to some of his colleagues, would discover that no such technology existed.

They walked back to the café where Louise had been sitting and climbed to the upstairs balcony. The waiter scowled at first but then realizing that now she would pay for her coffee and brioche, smiled unctuously.

"Did we get what we wanted?" Charles asked Louise in English, but preserving the Italian accent.

"I believe we did."

They concluded their business with Henri, paying him in cash, which surprised him. They also gave him a business card with the address of the hotel and the phony Italian film company's name, reminded him of the bonus for secrecy, and said goodbye.

After he left, Charles said, "He'll become suspicious. The still pictures were a surprise."

"He'd never have known if I hadn't had to come down to the street."

"We can only hope that the pictures are usable."

"I believe there's one good one. The first one I took."

Later, working with her computer, Louise altered the picture to make it appear that the Minister was handing Henri an envelope containing money. With additional computer work, she could create a completely fictitious person, fitting Henri's altered description, who could have some very incriminating connections, and since the Minister of Agriculture was MOLP's closest associate in government, it would be most helpful to have such a picture. There was still much work to be done to create the full scandal and involve MOLP himself. That, however, would have to wait until they had more information.

Before they went to bed that night, Louise took out her C harmonica and began to make up little tunes and riffs while Charles tuned his guitar. She began to play a Malvina Reynolds song called "The Little Mermaid," about finding love by the seaside and then losing it. Charles sang the words, and Louise shifted to a descant above the melody, bringing out the sadness. They ended with the plaintive "Perhaps on some far coast I'll find her–the spin-drift child of Camolie...," reminding Charles of his recent Italian persona. Then, they put their instruments away, took off their clothes, and fell into each other's arms, making love slowly, the musical after-effects still drifting through their minds.

Chapter 11
Marseilles

They decided to close down operations in Paris. It was best not to stay in one place too long–someone might begin to be curious about them. Besides, they'd accomplished two good things–a picture that would prove useful later on, and a clear idea of MOLP and all his relationships. It was time now to develop their plan more precisely.

Their research had produced a lead–one of MOLP's former mistresses, a girlfriend really, from his university days, lived in Marseilles. She wasn't doing anything illegal as far as they knew, but the fact that she lived in the city with the most unsavory reputation in France hinted at possibilities. So they decided to head for Marseilles, long a center for illegal activities, the point of entry for all the criminals and illegal products that Africa, Asia, and the Middle East could come up with. Little did they know that from Marseilles they'd travel on to Kazakhstan, where they'd face a cold night on the steppe, wondering if they'd survive at all.

The former mistress's name was originally Astrid Tuttlies. Born in Frankfurt before the war, her family had moved to Austria to escape the Nazi regime. They survived the war in Austria, even though the Nazis took over. But after the war, when life in Austria was difficult for everyone, Astrid's family left and traveled to Italy, where they stayed for a few years, and then to Marseilles.

By this time, Astrid was a young woman, tall and attractive. She found work as a waitress and attended the university. She met MOLP when he too was taking courses. During a philosophy class, he made a clever comment that challenged the professor. She looked back to see who the upstart was, and as she looked over her shoulder smiling a little, he was smitten. After the class, he sought her out, and they had coffee together, talking about the point he'd raised. After that, there was no stopping them. He was one of the few male students taller than she, and they admired each other's intelligence. It was a typical student romance–the excitement of new ideas spilling over into the bedroom.

Charles and Louise discovered that she was now called Tuttlies-Fourget. A decade after her university days, she'd married a M. Fourget, a local merchant, and stayed married for many years, until he died of liver cancer twelve years ago. Before she met Fourget, she'd worked as a German teacher for several colleges and institutes in Marseilles, but when they were married she stopped working to keep house and have his child. After he died, she didn't go back to teaching, but retired, and now she was living by herself in a small apartment in a pleasant part of the city.

None of this was particularly exciting, but to Charles and Louise it had possibilities. Living in Marseilles, married to a merchant, she might easily have been connected to bribes, smuggling, or corruption of officials, and if she hadn't been, it wouldn't be difficult to manufacture such a connection. They wanted to meet her, and that meant leaving Paris.

They rented a car from one of the larger Parisian agencies and drove it around to each of their hotels, picking up their belongings and checking out. The second hotel had been only for show and was no problem, but all of their luggage, the guitar, and equipment were in the first one. They filled the hallway with boxes and luggage as they waited by the door for the bellman to come up. His eyes bulged as he saw the extent of their electronics, and Charles explained to him that they were journalists from America, as if an elaborate computer layout was standard operating procedure for reporters writing for American publications. They had discovered long ago that if you were American and pretended to be rich, everyone bought it. As always with the hotel staff, he used American-accented French, although the effort offended his sensitive ears.

After three trips to the room and back, the car was loaded, and they began to find their way out of Paris, Louise navigating, while Charles drove somewhat nervously, behind the wheel for the first time in nearly a month. Paris was a driver's nightmare, with unclearly marked streets, sudden one-ways, and traffic–horn-blaring, creeping traffic–clogging the intersections with furious drivers. Gallic intransigence was expressed loudly and crudely whenever there was a slow-down, giving way only after considerable delay to the more widely known resignation of the French driver. They said little, concentrating on the traffic and the navigation.

In time, the noise and dirt of the city gave way to suburban propriety, better street signs and less traffic, and then they were out in the country, sighing in relief. The French farmland was picturesque, greening in the spring sunshine. They picked up some bread and sausage and stopped for lunch in a picnic area. In the distance, the fields were being groomed for planting with careful attention. Huge tractors pulling harrows raised clouds of dust in the distance, and everywhere they saw activity and eagerness to prepare the soil, get seeds in the ground, and fertilize.

The setting wasn't conducive to plotting, and it was only with some effort that they considered Mme Tuttlies-Fourget. In documenting her life, and trying to find something they could use against MOLP, they had identified a two-year period in her late twenties, before her marriage to Fourget, that was oddly blank, and it was ostensibly to identify her activity during this period that they had been rolling steadily southward toward Marseilles. In reality, they just wanted to move on, and Marseilles had the flavor of crime and intrigue that they needed to put meat on the bones of the story they were going to invent for MOLP. Actually, they didn't even have many bones yet.

"Let's stay in the role of American journalists," Louise suggested.

"It does simplify things," he agreed. "But I'm getting tired of speaking bad French."

"You can handle it," she said.

"We can interview Mme Tuttlies-Fourget as if we're writing a piece for an American magazine about MOLP's life."

There may have been some risk in playing a role so close to their reality, but they counted on their age making it unlikely that their interviewee would become suspicious.

It wasn't their first time in Marseilles, but they chose a hotel different from the one they had stayed in previously, a practice they followed routinely. They arrived, looking the part of aging journalists, working for a magazine read by older Americans. They kept their electronic equipment in the car trunk at first and brought in only their luggage, the guitar, and some of the photographic equipment. Later, they could bring in their electronics in small loads without arousing suspicion. As usual, Louise posed as the photographer. They checked in, found their room satisfactory (if a little seedy), took a nap, and then went out to dinner.

They found the restaurant. Although it had been several years, the place seemed not to have changed at all. They found a table with a view of the harbor, not quite the best but good enough, and examined the menu. At last, they had found something that was unique to the area–seafood of every imaginable kind cooked in the southern French style with hints of Italian and Spanish flavors.

"No, Monsieur, we don't have mussels this time of year," the waiter had said.

"All right, I'll have the trout with almonds and herbs."

After a number of questions, translated by Charles, Louise ordered a kind of crab she'd never heard of before. They declined the sommelier's attentions and ordered mineral water.

They were thirsty, but they didn't want to dull their palates with alcohol.

"Any other ideas?" Charles asked, finding nothing to comment on in their surroundings.

"Not really. Let's hope the old mistress will give us something."

"And what if she doesn't?" He looked at her directly for the first time since they had sat down. She looked as though she had been waiting for him to lose interest in the surroundings and take an interest in her.

"We may have to make something up."

"That would be business as usual."

"Right."

Charles sat back in his chair and folded his arms. "I think an old mistress would be an excellent way for a President to channel activities that he wanted left out of the public eye."

"Like what?" She sensed now that Charles was beginning to formulate an idea.

"Well, probably it would be something related to the businesses he was involved in before the election. How else could it be?"

"Yes, of course. He was involved in a number of things, but he made most of his money with oil." Louise had done a lot of research on MOLP and knew just about everything there was to know about him.

"Did he own wells?" Charles had done some reading on MOLP, but had forgotten many of the details. Nevertheless, the idea of the President owning oil wells didn't seem right to him.

Louise was quick with her reply. "No. In fact in all of his dealings he disdained anything tangible. He'd rather buy futures than commodities, options than products, easements than real estate."

"But with oil, was it futures?" Charles was trying to recall what he had read.

"Sometimes. Or the right to run a pipeline. He did own some stocks that included oil companies." Louise went on to clarify for Charles' benefit the nature of modern investing. "These days not many people hold any one thing. Everything is diversified in mutual funds. MOLP was trained originally in banking, you know, so he understood the value of the holding, the power of making money with money."

"Does that work for us?" Charles was starting to think in the way that often ended up with a plan they could work from, but he was also getting hungry and kept looking for the waiter.

"It certainly makes it easy to trace his activities. Everything is recorded."

Their meal came and as usual they stopped talking.

Back in their hotel room, they took out their instruments, Charles played a few French songs that he'd learned in college. Paris hadn't inspired them to sing French folk songs, but Marseilles did.

They sang "Perrine," which they knew from a recording by Theodore Bikel. Reminded of Bikel's wonderful music, they played "Ma Guitar et Moi," one of Charles' favorites. Then they put their instruments away and crawled into bed and went to sleep with the French tunes running through their minds.

Chapter 12

The Mistress

The next day they found Mme Tuttlies-Fourget's number in the phone book, called, and introduced themselves. She said she'd be happy to see them at four.

"We can have tea," she said with an eagerness that Charles didn't quite understand. He described this to Louise after the conversation was over.

"Maybe she thinks we're English," Louise suggested.

"I said American."

"Well, maybe she's lost track of the difference."

"She's not that old."

"We'll see."

Later that afternoon, they rang the bell to her flat, which was in a middle-class part of town, certainly unpretentious, but comfortable enough. She buzzed them in and they walked up the three flights.

Mme Tuttlies-Fourget was tall and thin and her skin leathery, but there was still some color in her cheeks. She wore her hair pulled back in a librarian's bun, which accentuated her large nose and made her look like a large, skinny bird. She wore a simple dress, but it was a little dirty and somewhat wrinkled. She was in a mild state of disarray. She appeared to be about ten years older than Charles, in her late seventies or early eighties, but there was an odd jauntiness to her and the color in her cheeks made her seem a little younger. Her voice, however, was a bit quivery.

"It's really very nice of you to have us for tea," said Louise, and Charles translated, making a few intentional errors in his French as he did so. If they were going to play the role of

American journalists, they might as well play the part thoroughly. He took out a small notebook and pencil.

They sat down around a low table, and Mme Tuttlies-Fourget poured each of them a cup of tea from a china teapot. For herself, however, she produced from a side table a bottle of beer and poured some of it into her teacup.

Charles struggled to bring his eyebrows back down. "As I said on the phone, we're doing a little story in our magazine about your old friend, now so famous, and our readers are quite interested in you and in him."

"Well, I can tell you plenty. He wasn't a very good lover, you know." She spoke in French but with a German accent.

"Let's get to those details a little later." Charles found it difficult to keep the laughter that welled up in him, from getting into his voice, and he didn't dare look at Louise, who was hiding her face behind her camera.

"Well, it's true just the same."

"We're interested in you, too."

Mme Tuttlies-Fourget's cheeks colored even more, and her large, beak-like nose twitched a little. The hand that wasn't clutching the cup of beer fluttered to her hair.

"What do you want to know?" Her voice quivered.

"When *Monsieur le Président* went back to Paris, what did you do?"

"I graduated too, of course. We were in the same class. I looked for work in the business sector–I wanted to make money, you see–and I got a few jobs. For a while I was secretary to one of the Vice Presidents of the Dutch Oil Company. I think they were later bought out by Americans."

"I think it was the Dutch who bought out the Americans," Charles noted.

"I don't know. When I worked for them, it was just the Dutch, but I didn't like that job either."

"Why not?"

"I worked for them for a number of years, and at first I liked them very much. They're very polite and yet also very truthful–an unusual combination, I think."

"Indeed."

She took a large gulp of beer from her teacup and continued. "But after a few years, I began to feel that they didn't really like me very much."

Mme Tuttlies-Fourget drained her cup and poured herself another cupful of "tea."

"I was German of course, and, yes, the war was over, but there were probably still bad memories."

"No doubt." Charles encouraged the topic, thinking it might bring out something that would help them embarrass MOLP.

"My countrymen didn't always behave very well."

She said this last sentence as though describing the schoolyard behavior of a group of small boys, and Charles, translating for Louise's sake, tried to get the flavor of it into his translation. There were so many different ways the Germans had of being in denial in those days.

Mme Tuttlies-Fourget had another hit of tea and continued, "So, it wasn't very comfortable for me."

"And what did you do then?"

"Well, I went to Kazakhstan."

"Kazakhstan?" The name of the Central Asian Republic had come out of the blue, and Charles couldn't keep the surprise out of his voice.

"Yes,I suppose it was a little extreme, but by this time I wanted to get away from the Dutch, away from the French, away from everyone." She fortified herself with more beer and went on. "I always had to explain myself, you see, show that I had been against the Nazis. But every German was doing the same thing, and most of them were lying. I wasn't lying, but everyone thought I was. It was most uncomfortable."

She drank more beer, this time directly from the bottle and emptied it.

"But why Kazakhstan?"

"I met someone who had been there, and he said they were looking for German teachers." She stood up. "Excuse me."

She went to the little kitchen and returned with another bottle of beer. She took a swig directly from the bottle. Charles thought that the tea party was probably over, but the interview was just beginning.

"So I went to Alma-Ata. It was of course still in the time of Stalin, and people weren't free to speak. Kazakhstan was a part of the Soviet Union. They sent political prisoners there. I stayed for two years, teaching German in the schools, but suddenly they didn't want to learn German. They thought that Germany would never recover its strength. Now, I understand, they want to learn German again, although English is more popular."

"You're still in touch with people in Kazakhstan?"

"Oh my, yes. I have a number of friends there. My son Werner was born there."

At the mention of her son, Charles wanted to pursue the topic. "And what happened with Werner?"

"Of course when I came back to Marseilles he came with me, and he went to French schools. He was a clever boy and did well in school and went on to study in the French universities, but when he finished his education, he went back to Kazakhstan to be with his father and his grandparents. I think he didn't feel accepted by the French."

"So he is still in Alma-Ata?"

"Yes, they call it Almaty now. He is happy there. He uses his father's name–Tatinan."

Charles wrote the name down in his notepad.

"And what does he do?" Charles sensed that the son might be an avenue for creating something that would embarrass the French President.

"He is an exporter."

"Of what?"

"Of many things, I believe. I'm not sure."

Charles and Louise sipped their tea, struck by the lack of information in this response. Mme Tuttlies-Fourget finished another bottle of beer. She was, by now, quite tipsy, and had they really been journalists interested in the young days of MOLP they'd most probably have had to quit for the day and come back another time, when they could be more sure of Madame's memory.

They were, however, quite interested in Mme Tuttlies-Fourget's connection to Kazakhstan, recognizing that something might be built up between the French President and a country that was a former member of the Soviet Union. They'd have to read up on the country, but their sense was that Kazakhstan was now struggling to recover from decades of exploitation as farmland for Russian bread, from being a holding pen for political prisoners, and a nuclear test site besides. They believed the well-known official corruption in Kazakhstan might also be useful for them. The recent discovery of vast oil reserves under the Caspian Sea might help, too, and, although there were virtually no Muslim fundamentalists in Kazakhstan, the country shared borders with Uzbekistan to the south and wasn't very far from Chechnya. These were all possibilities. A little farther away were Afghanistan, Al Qaeda, and opium poppies.

"May we have your son's address?" Charles worked hard to keep the excitement out of his voice. "We'd like to look him up." Had she been sober they would probably have needed to explain this interest in her son, since it didn't follow from their cover story as journalists, but they judged her sobriety as fully deteriorated, so they didn't bother.

"Of course." She rose, somewhat unsteadily, and retrieved a business card from a desk on the other side of the room, which she gave to Louise.

They stayed a while longer, letting Mme Tuttlies-Fourget ramble on about her university days with MOLP, and getting progressively drunker, and then they excused themselves. There was research on Kazakhstan to do, visas to obtain, plane tickets to buy. They had never been to Kazakhstan, or anywhere in Central Asia, and the prospect was exciting. And they seemed one step closer to their plan.

Chapter 13
The Smell

It took a week to make arrangements through the American Embassy in Marseilles. They had no difficulty, of course. They had only to mention a few specific words while chatting with the Ambassador, and he turned them over to an attaché who agreed to meet them in an out-of-the-way place.

The attaché was young. He'd probably never done anything like this before, but he was well trained and promised quick action on all their requests. He was curious about Kazakhstan, but knew it would be unprofessional to ask them. But back in his office, he looked up the CIA's Kazakhstan fact sheet on the Internet. Several facts intrigued him. Physically, it was a huge country–about four times the size of his native Texas, and for a Texan the comparison was impressive. It had a high literacy rate, but pervasive corruption in the educational system made it impossible to assess the actual competence of graduates, in reading or anything else. Certainly, they were less well educated than the numbers suggested. The population was about evenly divided between Kazakhs and Russians, with some other minority groups. The Russian population had declined rapidly as many ethnic Russians went "home" when the Soviet Union fell, and a slow exodus still continued. The attaché closed his computer, better informed but still curious.

On the other side of town, in their hotel room, Charles and Louise were discovering the same information on their computer. While they waited for their papers, they explored Marseilles, finding some parts interesting. But for the most part they were restless and eager to get on to the next phase of their work. Often, they simply sat in cafes sipping mineral water, Louise writing in her journal, Charles watching people go by.

Finally, a call from their embassy contact told them the papers were ready, and they would leave in two days for Almaty. They carefully packed up all their computer equipment, hoping they could convince any curious Customs agents that all modern journalists traveled with such an elaborate setup.

The competition among countries for pipeline routes to bring oil from the Caspian Sea to the rest of the world was a big story, justifying their presence. It wasn't a new story, but dwindling energy supplies worried many older Americans.

They flew first to Frankfurt, coincidentally Astrid's hometown, then took a Lufthansa flight to Almaty, arriving late at night. They slept off the flight in a small hotel near the airport, and the next morning they were still groggy, but alert enough to begin work.

After breakfast, they called Werner Tatinan, found him at home and arranged for a meeting the next day. He seemed glad to hear from someone who knew his mother.

After checking out of the airport hotel, and moving themselves and all their luggage by taxi to a larger one in the center of the city, they set about using the morning and early afternoon to explore. They went first to the main tourist attractions–the old Russian Orthodox Church, a pretty enough building but no cathedral, then to the Green Bazaar.

This was an extensive soukh with many different shops built up around a central area where fruits and vegetables were sold. They found it different from anything they'd seen in Europe. Charles, however, had been in a similar bazaar in Istanbul and wasn't surprised to have people call out to them in English as they walked past. Few people in Kazakhstan spoke English, but it was a certain attention-getter for the enterprising vendor, so most shopkeepers learned a few phrases to call out to any tourist who might walk by their little stand. Several shouts were in German, but mostly English.

They had lunch in a small place near the bus station, just a pastry shop with a few tables and chairs. The food was dull and far from nutritious, but they were still in the tourist's frame of mind, when almost everything seems interesting, if not wonderful, simply because it hasn't been seen before. When he was teaching at the university Charles had a colleague who took a trip to China and came back complaining that her index finger was tired from pointing and saying, "Look! Look!"

After a modest lunch, they lingered over a soft drink and watched people walk by. From differences in dress and bearing, and the occasionally overheard phrase, they began to realize that most of the people in the streets of Almaty were either Kazakh or Russian. Only a handful were not, probably German or French. They heard no English at all. After a while, they took a taxi to Werner's home.

The sign on the door said W. Narimanovich Tatinan. He greeted them at the door of his flat in one of the nicer sections of Almaty. He was a man in his fifties with the bronze good looks typical of many Eurasians. As they removed their shoes, he introduced his wife, Gulmira, and offered them tea.

They sat around a small table, loaded with cookies and candy. The room was large and well furnished. Brightly colored rugs hung on the walls. As Mrs. Tatinan poured tea–first a little milk, then very dark tea, then water–into small cups with no handles, they told Werner what news they had of his mother, leaving out her drinking habits.

Charles spoke to him in Russian, the lingua franca of Kazakhstan. "We're working on two stories here–our magazine is small and can't afford regular foreign correspondents. Your mother told us much about the French President's youth. That's our first story. Our second story is about Caspian oil and the debate over the pipeline route. Perhaps you know something about it?"

Like most Kazakhs, Werner disliked coming directly to the point, and he parried. "Your Russian is quite good. We don't have many Americans here, and those we meet don't speak Russian, much less Kazakh."

"It was my major in the university," Charles replied. Over the years he'd claimed many languages as his university major subject. "But I'm afraid I lack a practical knowledge of spoken Russian." As he said these words he reminded himself to make errors typical of an English-speaking person.

"Can you help us with our story about the Caspian Oil reserves?" Charles pursued.

"I know something, but not as much as some others. It's not much connected to my work."

"And what is your work?"

"I export. Mostly to France."

"What do you export?"

"It varies–with the market in Europe and with the availability of goods here."

"And what is available at this moment?" Charles knew his insistence on detail was obnoxious, but it fit his journalistic role.

"We're sending vodka and American videos to France, and a few other things."

The vagueness of "a few other things" made Charles suspect that there was more to the story.

"I'm sure there's always a good market for these things." Charles tried to bring out more information, but Werner changed the topic.

"Yes, there is, but I'm getting too old for such activities. I'm thinking of retiring from the business."

"Would you sell the business then?"

"In a way. My colleagues would take over."

"And would you get a pension from the government?"

"Probably not. Private businessmen don't get them. But I have some savings. We'd be comfortable. We might move to another country. South America, perhaps."

Charles decided to go with the free flow of topics. "Things are improving there rapidly. Brazil is of course doing very well. Chile is growing. Venezuela is strong. Even Colombia seems safer, and because of it the economy is booming."

"Kidnapping is no longer a worry?" Werner asked.

"The drug cartels are being marginalized, and the guerillas seem to be on the run. You should also consider Costa Rica, a beautiful place with a stable government and friendly people. Many Americans retire there."

At the mention of Costa Rica, Werner's eyes seemed widen a little, as if he'd been frightened. Charles and Louise both noticed the reaction.

"Can you put me in touch with someone who's familiar with the Caspian oil story?" Charles asked, not wanting to pursue a topic that seemed frightening to Werner.

"Yes, I can." Werner took out a small card case. "Here's a name and number. This man is a friend of mine, and he'll answer your questions, but you need to be a little careful, I think, with the oil people. There are huge amounts of money involved in this business, and many governments, including your own, are trying to get access to the oil. If they think you're trying to get useful information for your government, they may not like it, and you might be in some danger."

Charles' face registered the importance of the warning as he examined the name on the card. One side was in English and the other both in Russian and Kazakh. "Thank you for the warning. It's hard to imagine that someone would feel threatened by information published in our little magazine. But we'll be careful anyway."

"Yes. I advise it."

Charles allowed a look of discomfort to come into his face. "May I use your bathroom?"

"Of course. It's right down there." Werner waved his hand toward a hallway on the other side of the room. Charles rose and followed the moving hand, remembering that Kazakh people don't point with the finger; the gesture was considered crude.

Charles' research had also told him that squat toilets were used here and that tourists should bring their own toilet paper, so he was relieved to find both a toilet seat and paper. He hated squat toilets because his knees rebelled at the position. And when he went to wash his hands in the separate room, the actual bathroom, he looked in the medicine cabinet–as he always did– but found nothing unusual. Earlier he'd detected the faint odor of a chemical used in the manufacture of heroin, yet it was obvious that neither Werner nor his wife were users. This made Charles suspicious about Werner's "export" business.

After a short while, they thanked their hosts, particularly Gulmira Tatinan, who hadn't said a word, and left. Walking slowly back to their hotel, they discussed the visit. Charles told Louise about the odor. He was quite sure about it, and he thought it merited further investigation. It was possible, but most unlikely, that the odor resulted from some innocent brush of the clothing against someone else. It was more likely that Werner was connected to someone who made heroin.

They walked back to their hotel, glad for the exercise. Their hotel was large, rather expensive, and westernized, appropriate for the role they were playing. Louise had set up the computer when they'd arrived, so it was easy to email Henderson and tell him that Werner was probably manufacturing heroin.

Henderson's answer came back immediately–it was early morning in American and he was already hard at work. "Follow Werner," Henderson wrote, "and get the addresses he visits, then systematically watch each one and take pictures of the people who go in and out. If any of them are known to Interpol, you'll have a scandal tying the French President to drug manufacturing."

A look of accomplishment flashed between them as Louise shut down the computer with a flourish.

Chapter 14
The Korean

The next morning, Charles and Louise waited in a rental car outside Werner's building, and when he came out they followed him, driving slowly through the streets. Almaty was bustling with people hurrying to work, much like Paris. It didn't seem exotic or remote enough to be Central Asia. The people were well dressed and businesslike, and the modern buses and cars gave the city a European atmosphere. A few modern buildings sat next to older Soviet era ones with crumbling concrete steps, the rebar showing through, and peeling paint on the exterior window frames.

Werner walked briskly and soon boarded a bus. Traffic was heavy, and Louise, driving, felt an absence of traffic regulations–every driver seemed out for himself. Each time the bus stopped, they pulled to the right and watched to make sure Werner wasn't leaving the bus. Eventually, in a residential part of town, Werner emerged and walked to the next corner. They kept back, inching along next to the parked cars, ignoring the blaring horns of the drivers who found it difficult to pull out and pass them. He entered a building with no name on the door, and they stopped to wait and watch, waving the impatient drivers around them. Louise unlimbered her camera and attached the telephoto lens. She took pictures of all the people leaving and entering the building. None looked familiar, but later, just to be sure, she'd send her digitized pictures back to the States to be checked against FBI and CIA records.

Werner emerged at half past twelve, and they trailed him to a restaurant.

"He's getting his lunch. We've probably got most of his associates. We know where he works. I'm hungry. Let's have lunch too," Louise suggested.

"You're on," said Charles, his stomach already rumbling.

They parked the car in a spot that miraculously appeared in front of them, and Louise slipped into the back seat, made some connections, and sent the pictures off. Then they got out to inspect the menus posted outside the restaurants.

Louise stopped at a shop window displaying fashionable clothing for women. "See how low the prices are," she said. "No wonder exporting is a good business."

"And most of the goods are made in China or Korea, where they're sure to be even cheaper at wholesale prices," Charles replied.

"Do you mean they import from China and Korea and then reship the goods to European countries? It doesn't seem very economical."

"I doubt there's much of a market for these goods in Europe. They're not very well made," Charles said. He'd stopped earlier to look at goods displayed on the street.

"Maybe it's a cover for something more profitable," Louise said, looking up at Charles.

"Drugs, you think?" he asked.

"Maybe. Or a way to launder money."

By this time, the temperature had risen considerably, and they needed shade, water, food, and rest, all of which they found in a small bar with a name printed in Cyrillic characters but pronounced Bella Napoli. After a lunch that mixed Kazakh and Italian flavors, they sat back and reflected on their progress.

"We really don't have anything," Louise said.

"I know. But there was that smell in Werner's apartment. He's been around heroin manufacturing."

"And the Feds might recognize one of those faces. I'll check back this afternoon."

When they got back to the hotel, Louise logged on and whooped almost immediately, "A hit! We got a hit! Shen Guo, a Korean gangster, mostly into drugs, born in Seoul 33 years ago." She rattled off a list of other characteristics, including "should be considered highly dangerous," and "wanted in Korea, Japan, Mongolia, China, Uzbekistan, and Russia."

"Isn't it odd that he isn't wanted here in Kazakhstan?" Charles wondered. "It's like they skipped over it."

"Maybe someone's getting paid off to keep Kazakhstan a safe haven for him," Louise suggested.

"He must have lots of enemies, though, even here," Charles said, his eyes gleaming with interest. Maybe we can give some of them a helping hand."

"I'll look a little deeper on the Internet and check out the drug scene here, but we have to keep our eyes on the prize," Louise said as she closed down the computer in her lap.

"Sure," said Charles. But now that we have a warm, even hot, body, it shouldn't be difficult to make connections. I'll try to follow Mr. Shen. Maybe something will turn up."

Chapter 15
The Tail

With the application of skin bond to alter his eye shape, a little darkening make-up, and careful attention to his clothes, Charles passed for an old Kazakh "ata," or grandfather. As he made these preparations the next morning, his heart beat a little faster. He didn't speak Kazakh, although he'd been doing his best to pick up words and phrases. He did speak Turkish, a related language, and had begun to work out some of the "conversion principles" so that he could apply his knowledge of Turkish to Kazakh, but he still didn't feel comfortable speaking Kazakh. This made him nervous. He figured that Shen, if he was based in this country, had surely picked up some Russian and wouldn't need Kazakh. But Shen might have cohorts who spoke Kazakh, and Charles was trying to pass for Kazakh. With a start he realized that he could've made himself up to be Turkish, but he didn't want to start all over again; he might miss Shen's arrival at the "office."

So he was uncharacteristically ill at ease, squatting across the street, looking like a down-and-out Kazakh grandfather, and finding out quickly that he couldn't squat for very long. He was careful to look sober. A drunk old man could get beaten and robbed. Shen came soon went in the building. Charles waited. In less than half an hour Shen came out again, carrying a different briefcase. Charles followed him, and while walking along dove into his blue shopping bag and quickly exchanged his dirty jacket for a cleaner one of a different color, put on a pillbox style hat he'd bought because he'd seen older Kazakh men wearing them. He also took a red plastic shopping bag out of the blue one, and repacked his gear into it, including the blue bag.

Approaching the commercial area of the city, Charles felt Shen was probably heading for the Green Bazaar.

It wasn't difficult to follow him–Shen was quite tall–and Charles stayed well back. From time to time, he'd let Shen get out of sight for a moment. Charles then quickly changed some aspect of his appearance–a hat, glasses, or a coat. Sometimes he'd change his gait or stature by straightening or stooping, all to avoid a constant image that might tip off Shen that he was being followed. At a kiosk, Shen stopped and bought a can of soda, then searched his pockets to pay for it. Find nothing in his pocket, he reached down and opened the briefcase, extracted a bill and gave it to the vendor.

So it's money he's carrying, Charles said to himself. *And he doesn't mind if someone sees him taking money from his briefcase. He feels confident.* Charles quickly scanned the street, expecting to find a bodyguard or two not far off and hoping that he hadn't been spotted. He hadn't been trying to stay out of the view of anyone except Shen. He saw no one but still felt uncomfortable.

Shen walked on, taking sips from the soda can. He turned a corner and went out of sight. Charles hurried, but when he reached the corner Shen was nowhere to be seen. Charles waited, adopting the pose of an old man enjoying the warmth of the spring sun. Shen emerged in a few minutes from a building only a few feet from where Charles had stationed himself, a building with a small sign over the door in the shape of a bottle. Charles, afraid that Shen might've gotten a good look at him as he came out of the building, held back, to put some distance between them. Shen was heading for the Green Bazaar, a partially covered soukh that sold everything at bargain prices. It would've been prudent to abandon following Shen at this point. The risk of being found out seemed high. But Shen might lead him to valuable information, possibly an important contact. So, he once again changed his appearance, this time more radically, straightening up and donning sunglasses to make himself look younger.

Apparently he hadn't been "made." At least no dreaded heavy hand fell on his shoulder, and he continued to follow the tall Asian, although his caution increased. As he'd suspected, Shen went to the Green Bazaar. Charles could easily have lost him there, but Charles entered the bazaar just in time to see Shen turn a corner. Quickly trying to orient himself, and wishing Louise was with him to help, Charles thought Shen was headed toward the large central area where fruits and vegetables were sold. Charles headed straight for it. When he arrived, he could see Shen, just leaving a stand displaying cases of strawberries and raspberries. He no longer had the briefcase. A man behind the fruit stand was, however, just straightening up, and Charles thought he'd probably just tucked the briefcase away under the counter. After making sure Shen was out of sight, Charles went up to the stand and took a good look at the vendor while pretending to examine a box of strawberries. He was dark skinned and foreign-looking. Not Kazakh. Charles turned and walked away, relieved that the stress of following Shen was over.

He stopped and looked around. The central area was a large and open square with a main walkway around the perimeter and several aisles crossing from one side to the other. The vendors stood on a platform that elevated them a foot or more above the customers–probably, thought Charles, to give them a psychological advantage in the inevitable bargaining. The scene was energetic and loud with the voices of vendors and customers engaged in the rituals of haggling: the false shrugs of feigned disinterest, the pretended protests at exorbitance, and the vendors shouting out lowered prices just before a customer walked out of earshot. It was an elaborate game, and those who played it well came out ahead. Customers unfamiliar with the game paid more or ended up with goods that were inferior or weighed less than the scales seemed to show. Subterfuge was common, and Charles could see how, in this atmosphere of chicanery and deceptiveness, business of a much more sinister nature could be conducted without arousing comment or suspicion.

Later that day, Louise, looking like an American tourist with her camera at the ready, returned to the Green Bazaar to take a clear picture of the man Charles thought had taken the money and send it to Washington. But it turned out that he wasn't known to the federal authorities. Either he hadn't yet been identified as a drug dealer, if that's what was going on, or Charles had been wrong about who received the briefcase.

* * *

Sweltering in Almaty's summer heat, and closing in, they felt, on some major skulduggery, Charles and Louise couldn't have suspected that only a few weeks later they would be huddled together for warmth in a shallow trench on a cold steppe hundreds of miles to the north.

Chapter 16
Raisa

An encounter in the Almaty library led Louise to consider that the Russian mafia might be useful to them. She'd been reading all morning in a library carrel nestled up against one of the outside walls. A grimy window looked out on not much of anything. The library was quiet, nearly empty, and it had the smell of old books she loved. Occasionally the sound of high heels echoed on distant marble. She thought about those high heels and the shoes they elevated. The thought made her back ache; she couldn't understand–could never understand–the point of high heels. And here in Kazakhstan she'd noticed something else–both the men and women wore shoes with exaggeratedly pointy toes, like so many elves.

She liked the atmosphere of the library–nostalgic of schools and colleges, of other research jobs in far off cities. The sounds and smells made her heart beat faster.

She'd gone first to the Internet and found out all she could about heroin production. It began with poppies. In the spring, before the seeds formed, the poppies were full of narcotic juice, actually a toxin the poppies had evolved to protect the flowers from foragers at a crucial stage of development. The growers slit open the immature seedpods to drain off the milky juice, the raw material of opium. With a little drying to concentrate the drug, it could be smoked or eaten. The heroin makers, however, went further. They dissolved the poppy juice in alcohol, then added certain chemicals (one of which Charles had smelled in the Tatinans' house) to further refine it. Finally, they boiled off the alcohol, leaving a powder that could be heated and liquefied, ready for injection.

Only the final stage of manufacture took place in Almaty. The poppies grew in Afghanistan or China. The milky juice was extracted there and the opium rendered. Opium could be sold in some parts of the world, but heroin was much more valuable. In spite of its expense, the innocent-looking white powder had blighted many urban neighborhoods. Charles and Louise were sure this final process occurred in the building they'd seen Mr. Shen visit. Maybe he was visiting his mother, who gave him a briefcase full of money, but they thought this unlikely.

In the library Louise searched for more information in the limited number of books in English. Poking around, she found a collection of books in English about Almaty and other cities in Kazakhstan, which sent her off on a sidetrack. She read about the city's economy, particularly its slow decline during the long Soviet era, followed by the current beginnings of recovery. Some books claimed that Kazakhstan would soon be a world leader. Others described the history of cities along Great Silk Road, a conduit for silks and spices bound for Europe during the Middle Ages and Renaissance, and probably during even earlier centuries.

She read about cave-like drawings deep in the vast Kazakh steppe, which suggested that the land had been inhabited from the earliest centuries of human existence. After they left Africa, the earliest humans spread in many directions, including north. After a time in Central Asia this group separated, some going east to begin the East Asian ethnic group, others going north and west to begin the European group, and a third group going north, farther and farther, until they reached the land bridge to the new world, and thence down through North America, creating the Native American populations to the East, and then on farther south to South America. So, Louise realized, it was after leaving Central Asia that the current racial groups developed. No wonder the people of Kazakhstan looked so much like all the different populations of the world.

She read too about the country's long domination by Russia, first under the Czars, who were invited in by the Kazakh nomads to protect them from the Mongols and Chinese to the East and from the Turks to the west, and then, later, under the Soviets. From the beginning, the Russians saw Central Asia as a source of goods to be sent back to Mother Russia. They took cotton and other products from Uzbekistan, Turkmenistan, Tajikistan, and Kyrgyzstan and assorted minerals from Kazakhstan. In more recent times they used the vast steppes of Kazakhstan to test nuclear bombs, polluting a huge desert area with radioactive contamination that would remain for decades, if not centuries.

And Zhezkazgan, to the north and west of Almaty, housed one of the infamous gulags, at first a source of free labor for the local copper mines, but with the advantage of an extremely remote location. It was so far from anything, surrounded by the immense uninhabitable steppe, that political prisoners could be kept there without the need of walls to prevent their escape. These prisoners, in the middle of a vast emptiness, might as well have been on an island in the middle of an ocean. The Kazakh steppe made up most of the country, and Zhezkazgan was right in the middle of it, surrounded for thousands of miles by nothing but dry, flat, windy desert–home of a few small antelopes and the ferocious desert eagles that preyed on them.

* * *

As Louise read about the gulag system, she saw a woman she thought could be about her own age, quite stout, with grey hair and sad eyes set in a jowly face, also reading in the same area, but in Russian. After smiling and acknowledging their common activity, they began to talk. Her name was Raisa, and her English was accented but quite good. They talked easily, instinctively trusting each other, and shared a number of personal facts. Among these, Louise learned that Raisa's husband had died in the camps toward the end of 1975.

"In 1975? So the camps were still in operation then?" Louise asked, holding her own book on the gulag.

Raisa nodded slowly. "Yes. Some were closed down during the 'thaw' under Khrushchev, but many remained open until the '80s when Gorbachev came into power. In Zhezkazgan, where my husband was, the camps were kept running as long as possible for cheap labor in the copper mines." She shook her head sadly, and her eyes glistened. "He was sent here in 1961, when we were young and very much in love. It took me two years to find out where they'd sent him, then an additional three years to get permission to come myself."

Louise hesitated, looking into Raisa's face, then asked gently, "What had he done?"

Raisa didn't hesitate to answer. "He was journalist, and he made a decision to write truth when truth was dangerous. There were many others like him."

Louise realized that she liked this woman. Her voice and words conveyed an emotional honesty. She'd suffered and learned from the suffering, an unusual quality, Louise thought.

"So you came here to be with him?" Louise asked.

Raisa nodded. She wasn't afraid to remember. "Yes. At first they wouldn't let us see each other. But we found ways to meet." She smiled at the memory. "Eventually, we could even live together, although in very miserable conditions."

Louise moved closer to her. Her voice softened even more. "And why are you reading about the camps now?"

Raisa smiled a little. "At first, it was just way to be near him. I didn't expect him to die, of course, although mines were very dangerous. I don't know why but many men who worked in mines became sick, coughing always, and becoming very weak. Then they died. But now, I no longer read to be near him. I read now because I'm angry, angry with men who ran camp. I don't know their real names. They were called Josef, Pyotr, and Aleksei, which we all knew were false names. I want to find real name of man we called Josef–I think he named himself after Stalin. It was he who decided that my husband, this sweet man who loved words and truth, should die for his sweetness."

By now, tears were flowing down Raisa's cheeks, although her voice was steady. "Sergei was, in my memory, like single flower in garden of flowers, more beautiful than the rest–at least to me–and this Josef decided that beauty in him didn't matter, that his sweetness could be spent and his beauty extinguished so that few more pounds of copper could be extracted at cheap price. I'm angry at that man, and I want to find out who he really was."

Louise found that her tears, too, were beginning to flow. "There must be many others who are angry like you," she said, her voice husky.

Raisa shook her head with resignation. "Not so many. I thought at first, like you, that there would be many. But some have found new lives, new husbands or wives. Some have just tried to forget."

"What about the Kazakh people?" Louise asked, her voice rising. She felt herself joining in Raisa's anger. "Aren't they angry over the exploitation of their land?"

Raisa's head again shook in that same slow denial. "No. I thought too that I'd find them angry, and that together we, Russians who were injured and Kazakh people who were badly used, would find a way to say we're angry."

"But you didn't find them?" Louise felt frustrated at the apathetic response to an obvious injustice.

"No. They not angry. Well, maybe few, but even those few only little angry. Most just accept it as story of their history. They're proud now to be recovering, as they should be, but not much anger over reason why they must now recover."

"But why?" Louise asked, anger in her own voice.

"I don't know exactly." Raisa shrugged her heavy shoulders. "Maybe it because they were exploited for so long. It began long before Communists took power, in time of Czars."

She straightened up, and there was more energy in her voice. "They tried rebellion, but authorities put down very quickly and ruthlessly. They realized then that rebellion was not option, and so now today they have complacency." Raisa set the book she'd been reading on a small oak desk.

"Hmm. Maybe so," Louise said.

Raisa leaned against a bookcase, and her body sagged a little. "They also, how do you say, fatalistic, and this reduces ambition. Same could be said of us Russians."

"I see." Louise began to see more clearly the complex relationship between history and culture, something she'd spent little time on in her studies.

Raisa straightened up. "But there are few who share my anger–those who have suffered personally. I have met some of these women."

Louise then asked what she thought was the most important question of all. "And what will you do if you identify the person whose decision it was to send your husband into the mines?"

Raisa had no hesitation in answering. "I don't know. To be frank, I'd like to kill him." She turned away just a little, as if the thought had come too easily and she wanted to send it off in another direction.

Louise felt herself slipping into a problem of professional ethics. She'd have to report any real threat to someone's well-being; her training as a therapist was specific on this point. "I can understand your feeling. But is it possible?"

"Maybe." Raisa spoke as if she were talking about a more mundane topic, like what she might cook for dinner that night. "The Russian mafia is here, as they are everywhere. But I don't know how to contact them, and maybe, when time comes, and I find 'Josef', I may be able to–not forgive, no, never forgive–but maybe forget. I don't know."

Louise decided that Raisa posed no immediate threat to anyone, but she wanted to stay in touch with her. She really liked her, and there was this ethical question, which Louise left pending. There was another aspect too. Their conversation had ended, and Raisa was again reading from the book she'd set down, but when Louise turned back to her own research, she thought about the Russian mafia. Perhaps they might fit in Charles' and her mission. Louise didn't want to read any more; she wanted to think. She spoke again to Raisa.

"I have to leave now, but I'd like to stay in touch with you." She took a notebook out of her purse, tore off a slip of paper, and wrote down the name of the hotel where she and Charles were staying. She handed it to Raisa.

Raisa then gave her a small card, like a business card, with her name—Raisa Ivanova Kolokov—and address and phone number on it, English on one side, Russian on the other. "I sometimes teach people who want to learn English," she explained.

"Will you be staying in Almaty for a while?" Louise asked.

"No. I want to go back to Zhezkazgan. I think there may be some more records there in museum or perhaps in Akimat, town hall I think you call it. But I'll keep your number." She slipped the piece of paper Louise had given her into her pocketbook. "I'll leave a forwarding message in English on my answering machine. I'd do this anyway for my students."

"I wish you luck in your search. I'm thinking my husband and I might also go to Zhezkazgan, so perhaps we'll meet again," Louise said, smiling.

"I'd like to see you again. So *do svidaniya*, as we say in Russian—it means until we meet again—rather than *proschay*, which is goodbye." She reached out to shake Louise's hand, and Louise was surprised by the strength of her grip. Then with a last brief wave, Louise left the room and walked back downstairs and out the door into the sunshine.

Chapter 17
Almaty

That night, Charles and Louise ate dinner in an outdoor café on the sidewalks of Almaty, giving them an opportunity to indulge in one of their favorite pursuits–watching people going by. The city wasn't much different from Paris in the bustle and the afternoon spring sunshine still filtered through the trees lining the streets. But, looking more closely, they could see that about half the people were Asian of several different looks. The other half had the various faces of Russians. The Kazakhs, those with the different Asian looks, were different from Chinese or Japanese or Koreans. Many of them looked, to Charles and Louise, more like Native Americans, particularly those who lived in Canada.

Charles and Louise were discovering that Kazakh and Russian food wasn't very interesting. Tonight they were having shashlik, apparently Kazakhstan's answer to the American hamburger. It was simply four or five small pieces of meat on a skewer, grilled over an open fire, and served with bread and raw onions. There were several kinds of meat used–chicken, beef, liver, and most often mutton. They tried a couple of possibilities. It was tasty, and they enjoyed it, but they thought not worth the adulation it seemed to receive from the locals. And they missed green salads and veggies.

Over their meal, their plotting continued.

"I met a Russian woman today who's interested in avenging her husband's death in the camps and might hire the Russian mafia to do the job."

"The Russian mafia? Are they here then, in Kazakhstan? Charles sounded skeptical.

Louise took her eyes off the passing crowds and looked at Charles. "This woman, Raisa, says they are, although she doesn't know how to get in touch with them."

Charles returned the look. The conversation had become more interesting than the passing people. "Just knowing that they're here might be useful to us."

"That's what I thought." Louise's eyes brightened, and her voice became more animated as she changed the subject a little. "You know, I think I can get into the records of the camp in Zhezkazgan. Most of the gulag records have been digitized. People in Russia have been working on it for several years. Do you think it would be helpful?"

"Well, we could find out who was in charge, the guards and officers. If the Mafia's here, they're probably blackmailing people who have something to hide," he suggested.

Louise quickly corrected his impression. "They didn't really have guards. They weren't necessary in the middle of the steppe."

Charles nodded. He was beginning to get a handle on the vastness of the steppe.

Louise went on. "But there must've been people making decisions. I'll work on that. I think we can find out who they were."

Charles had another thought. "We should find out about the Mafia types who might be here too. We'll want to steer clear of them."

Louise made a mental note. "OK. I'll see what they know in Washington."

Charles had a sudden idea. "Our main connection is that house Shen went into. I need to get inside."

"Now I'm a little worried." Louise wasn't a worrier–certainly not about her own safety. But sometimes she worried about Charles.

He tried to reassure her. "I don't need to get far inside. Just inside the front door. It shouldn't be hard."

"The repairman thing."

"Yeah."

Chapter 18
The Stakeout

Charles found a store in Almaty that sold uniforms and bought a set of used blue coveralls. He found some used boots in a kind of consignment store. He put together a fake ID for the city heating system and picked up a clipboard. In Almaty, as in many former Soviet cities, steam was generated by huge plants outside the city and sent through large pipes to all apartments. It was a cheap way to provide heat, but it left the cities vulnerable when the system broke down during the harsh winters.

He let his beard grow for a day, doing what he could to look like a Russian worker, donning the overalls and boots. Clipboard in hand he looked like a workman who'd been asked to survey the neighborhood.

When he walked up to the small vodka plant on Dyenuskova Street and knocked on the door, it was opened immediately by a young but huge and rough-looking Kazakh. He wore a drooping moustache that accentuated the downturn of his mouth. *Trying to look like Genghis Khan*, Charles thought, and he did. He answered Charles' knock so quickly he must've been sitting right by the door. But only enough to poke his head through.

"What is it?" he said in surly Russian.

Charles spoke in his best Russian, which was very good. "We're using our summer time to check on how the heat was during the winter. May I come in?"

Charles pushed the door open and stepped inside without waiting for an answer, and the young man stepped back. Years of training to respect the elderly had momentarily made him hesitate and give way, but only briefly.

"You can't come in here." His manner was abrupt, and the hesitancy was completely gone.

Charles persisted. "I just need to ask a few questions. Was the heat adequate last winter?"

"You have to leave. Our heat was fine." The man was doing whatever he could to terminate the conversation, and he was beginning to push Charles toward the door.

"OK. I see. You don't have to cooperate. We're a free Republic now."

"That's right. So scram."

Charles left quickly. But he had what he needed, and he hurried back to the hotel where Louise was busy printing out Russian files. In his haste to get home he tripped over a pipe running along the sidewalk from the side of the road to the house and flailed his arms around for a second to keep his balance.

When he came in, Louise was too excited about what she was working on she only acknowledged his presence and then used him as a sounding board. "I think these are the records of the Zhezkazgan prison camp, but I need your Russian. Take a look."

Charles shelved his own excitement for just a minute. "That's what it looks like. See here they wrote down the names of the prisoners, why they were sent, and the towns they came from. This column looks like cabins or dormitories they were assigned to. Print it all out. We can take a close look at it later."

Louise remembered where he'd been and grabbed his arm. "Did you get in at Dyenuskova Street?"

Charles had much to tell. "I did, and I'm sure they're manufacturing heroin there. I smelled the poppy juice, the acid, and the ammonia. The smell was strong. You probably could have smelled it. There was lots of alcohol too, as would be expected in a place that produces vodka, and oddly a clear smell of sour milk. But I smelled something else that I didn't recognize."

Louise was curious about the odd smell. "What was it like?"

"It was chemical, but not a chemical usually used to make heroin."

She pursued. Sometimes, at times like these, when Charles was trying to place an odor, it helped if she quizzed him. "Could it have had something to do with the production of vodka?"

"No." Charles chuckled. "Vodka is nothing. It's just distilled spirits, which you can make from anything. Then you add water to it."

"Water?" Louise found it hard to believe, so Charles explained.

"That's what the word vodka means–little water. There may be some irony in the diminutive." There was, in fact, more than a little irony in giving a nickname to the substance that Stalin had purposely made cheap and plentiful so that the population would remain complacent in the face of economic shortcomings. Workers might not get paid on time, but if they could get drunk then it didn't seem to matter.

"I thought it was made from potatoes."

Charles clarified. "It usually is, but only because they're the cheapest source of starch, which turns to sugar, which ferments and can be distilled into spirits. Then they just add water to make it the right strength."

Louise was satisfied and wanted no more of the vodka lecture. "Well, what do we do?" She really knew the answer, but it seemed best to let Charles spell it out.

He took the lead. "We have to find out more. Where do the raw materials come from? How are they brought to the little vodka plant? When the heroin is done, how do they ship it from there, and where does it go? We should get pictures of all the other people involved in the operation too."

Louise had reached a decision. "I guess we should rent a place across the street."

"If we can."

They couldn't. The best they could find was a two-room apartment. It was on the other side of the street, but at least half a dozen houses farther up toward the milk factory at the end of the block. The milk factory was, in fact, why they couldn't find a place closer to their target address. It seemed odd to them that a factory would be right in the middle of a residential area, but Kazakhstan didn't have zoning regulations, and if someone wanted to build a factory in the middle of a residential area, they just did it. The lack of zoning regulations gave certain advantages. The employees could live close to where they worked, and many rented apartments on the same street. So Charles and Louise settled in, bringing their luggage, musical instruments, and all the computer equipment into the new apartment. They mounted the camera, and trained the telephoto lens on their target down the street. At least they were less liable to be discovered in this location, but they'd have to spend a little more time and take more shots to get high-quality pictures. It would be a while before they discovered how lucky they'd been to end up there.

* * *

As she looked through the telephoto lens for a last time to make sure it was lined up and focused, she asked, "Do you think we could get a mike in there?"

Charles shook his head. "I don't think so. The goon at the front door knows what he's doing. It was hard for me just to get in long enough to get a sniff."

She had another idea. "Maybe we can get into the house where Werner works."

Charles shrugged his shoulders. "Maybe. That's probably where they do the paperwork, make phone calls, keep records. They're trying to make it pass for a legitimate operation, so they didn't have guards posted at the door."

She had another idea. "If we could get a mike onto Shen, or his briefcase, he'd carry it in for us."

Charles negated that idea. "I don't know. He won't let the briefcase out of his sight. And the payoff would be small anyway. He's only in the building on Dyenuskova Street long enough to pay the workers. Then he leaves. We wouldn't hear very much."

She gave up this particular line of thought. "OK. Maybe that won't work. But let's keep thinking about it."

The manufacture of heroin was not their mission. It wouldn't be the first time they'd gotten involved in something tangential. Some of these side tracks had been productive, and a few had paid off in spectacular accomplishments, but others had made it harder for them to accomplish their goal.

"Remember that breaking up the drug ring isn't really our mission. It's just a fun project," he said.

Louise agreed. "Yeah, fun. Right. Of course. But let's check with the boss."

They sent a quick email on their secure connection, and Henderson said that since they were right on the scene, they should make the decision themselves.

"We could put the main elements together, get some evidence, and then call the local authorities to finish the job," Louise suggested.

Charles wasn't so sure. "Let's not be too hasty to do that. Someone higher up could've been paid off to keep the heat off this crew. Calling the authorities might just tip them off."

Louise recognized the wisdom of this advice. "I'm sure you're right. I'm remembering that Shen is wanted everywhere but here."

They'd reached a joint decision. It was the way they typically worked–half argument, half brainstorming.

"OK, well, let's get what we can with the camera." Louise was eager to get started.

The new apartment became a small center of activity. They took turns watching the house, and alternated with time on the computer. They explored a number of things on the Internet—more details on heroin production, the history of organized drug manufacturing and trafficking, possibilities of the Russian mafia in Kazakhstan, more details about smuggling operations in Asia, and the records of the old camp in Zhezkazgan. When they could take a break, they played and sang folk music.

Chapter 19
The Pipe

One day while they were watching the house, a small truck parked in front. Six men came out of the house carrying cartons marked with the vodka logo and loaded then into the truck. From the way they handled the cartons, Charles and Louise could tell they were heavy, packed with full bottles. With six men loading, it should've taken only a few minutes, but the loading stopped three times while the men asked someone inside the house a question. It seemed odd to Charles and Louise, watching through their telescope, that the men were so unsure of what to do. By the time the operation was finished and the truck had left, Charles and Louise were convinced it was the first time a load of vodka had been taken from the house. It was a new operation.

After two weeks, the routine at the little vodka plant was evident. Shen came once a week with money. Six other people came and went every day. The front door guard spent the night there and left for only a few hours in the middle of the day. But two important elements were missing. The spying couple couldn't figure out how the most important raw material–the opium itself–came into the house or how the finished heroin left. They'd seen the truck being loaded, but they couldn't figure out where the heroin was. From the way the men handled the cartons, they could tell the vodka bottles were all full, and no other packages came out. Was the heroin hidden somewhere in the bottles? If so, they couldn't see where. And how did the opium get in? Shen went in with a briefcase, but it wasn't big enough to have both money and opium.

One day they were walking to a restaurant they hadn't tried yet, when Charles tripped again over one of the many pipes that went across the city sidewalks from the street directly into houses.

He complained about it for the umpteenth time. "Isn't it crazy that they put these pipes down right over the sidewalk?"

Louise couldn't really explain it either. "Maybe it's just too much trouble, or too much money to dig up the concrete and lay down new pipes."

Charles couldn't believe this explanation. "Maybe the pipes get installed in the winter, when the ground is too frozen to dig."

Louise seemed to accept this. "Hmmm, maybe. What's in them, anyway?"

Charles thought about it, puzzled. "It can't be water. It would freeze solid in the winters here."

"How about hot water?" she asked.

He was emphatic. "I don't think so. If demand ever slowed, at night for example, it would still freeze in the dead of winter, then all the pipes all over town would burst simultaneously. It would be a disaster." They stopped and waited for a traffic light to change.

"Natural gas?" she wondered.

He shook his head. "No. I read just the other day that they don't use natural gas here. They consider it too dangerous."

Louise remembered some news stories from New York City. "It does cause big explosions from time to time."

He was still puzzled. "What then?"

Louise suddenly got it. "It must be wires. As I think about it, there are some places where the power lines come in overhead, from telephone poles, but in some houses they don't. They must be the ones with the pipes."

Charles looked up and around to find confirmation for the theory, but couldn't see any houses near them with pipes but no wires. Nevertheless, he thought her explanation likely. "It makes sense. Maintaining overhead power lines with temperatures going down to 30 or 40 below zero would be very hard." The light changed and they crossed the street. They felt good that they'd "solved" at least one little mystery about this odd country and walked in silence the rest of the way to the restaurant.

The new restaurant, however, was a major disappointment. They'd already discovered that most of the restaurants served the same food, although the atmosphere might change. Still, here and there in the city, some restaurants served different cuisines–Chinese, Turkish, Lebanese, even French at one–but mostly it was the familiar combinations of borscht, various forms of poor-quality meat wrapped in pasta, stroganoff, stuffed cabbage or peppers, and the ever-present Kazakh favorite–bishparmak, boiled horsemeat, beef, or mutton on a bed of rice or pasta. They tried everything at least once, and some were OK, but there was little variety, and soon they found the food boring.

Charles was working his way through "beef stroganoff," but it didn't look like any he'd ever had, since it lacked sour cream and didn't have that much beef. Suddenly, he said, "That's it! That's how they get the stuff into the house!"

"How?" Louise didn't need to be told what he was thinking about.

"Through the pipe. It doesn't matter what its original purpose was. If it's there, it can be a conduit. And it should show us where the opium comes in. I'll follow it this afternoon, and we'll see where it goes."

But Louise had an objection, and she grabbed his arm across the table to get his attention. "But opium is dry."

He brushed her complaint aside. "That's easy. They wrap it up in small waterproof packages and pump it in with water."

Louise continued to play the lead prosecutor. "But it's too cold in the winter to run water through the pipes, so they'd have to stop production in the winter. That doesn't sound like drug dealers to me. They're out for every nickel they can get."

He was still excited. "But they'd have to stop in the winter anyway. The poppy juice is only narcotic in the early spring. As soon as the pods mature, the narcotic is lost. That's why we can eat poppy seeds without getting high."

Louise remembered something she'd read that confirmed Charles' contention and capitulated to his argument. She wanted some actual evidence that would either bear out or refute his theory. In fact she thought his idea was far-fetched. She thought it more likely that they just brought it in paper bags or with the groceries.

In spite of her doubts, they were excited enough to leave the rest of their boring dinner and go back to the apartment, walking across the street from the house they had under surveillance. They looked closely at the pipe. After leaving the house and crossing the sidewalk, it made a 90-degree turn downwards into the gutter, then another one sideways to head up the street. They walked along on the opposite side, following the pipe with their eyes, past their apartment, all the way to the end of the block where they saw the pipe make another set of elbow turns that took it up over the sidewalk again and then into the back wall of the milk factory near the garage door where the milk trucks came and went so often.

"I'll be damned," said Charles, pleased with the correctness of his deductions and admiring the drug dealers' ingenuity. "That's a really good cover." The opium came in milk trucks, was transferred inside the milk factory to the pipe, and pumped down the street to the vodka plant.

Back in their apartment, they swiveled their telephoto lens around, training it for the first time on the milk factory. The sign on the front door said in handwritten Cyrillic characters "Bawnlay Milk Products."

Charles was quick with a linguistic analysis. "Bawnlay isn't a Russian word. If I'm not mistaken it's a corrupt form of the French for 'good milk.' That's ironic. But why'd they use French? The Russian *Kharashow moloko* would make better sense in a Russian-speaking country."

They watched a number of milk trucks come and go.

"So they bring the opium into the milk factory, pump it through the pipe to the place down the street, where it's made into heroin and shipped out in the vodka trucks."

Louise's brow wrinkled and the corners of her mouth turned down. Charles recognized that she had an objection.

"You don't agree?"

"It's not that I don't agree. I'm just puzzled."

"About what?"

"Well, I can see why they use the pipe: it reduces the time they need unload the opium, which reduces the risk of their being discovered or bribing another official."

"Right."

"But I don't understand how they ship the heroin out in the vodka trucks." She rested her chin in her hands and looked at Charles, waiting for an explanation.

"I take your point," Charles said. His years as an academic led him from time to time to talk as if he were debating some minor point of metaphysics with a colleague. He went on. "Vodka is clear, colorless, and there isn't any obvious place, in a carton of vodka bottles to hide a package of heroin."

Louise thought. "How about false bottoms on the boxes?"

Charles shook his head. "I don't think so. They'd have to be about three inches thick. Inspectors at the borders would notice that, which would mean another big bribe, and not just one, but one every time a truck crossed a border. It would cut into profits."

Louise had another objection. "Why can't they just fly the stuff out?"

Charles considered carefully. "Possibly. Fewer borders to cross, of course, but the customs officials at airports are less corruptible, so the bribes have to be bigger."

Louise pursued. "Unless they land in some remote area and transfer the cargo. That's what they do with drugs being smuggled from South America into the U.S." She sounded sure on this point.

129

Charles lip stiffened as he shook his head, reaching a conclusion. "But the whole point of using the vodka trucks is to conceal the true nature of the cargo. Vodka is heavy. A carton probably weighs 50 pounds. That makes it too heavy to fly any real quantity. Besides, the whole point of concealing the heroin in a legitimate cargo is to send it by ordinary, legitimate channels, so as to reduce the bribery and minimize cost."

Louise conceded. "So, we're back to the first question: Why use vodka? It seems like a poor choice. Whiskey would be better."

Charles jerked his head back in surprise. "What do you mean?"

Louise explained. "Well, if you had a small packet of heroin in a whiskey bottle, it would be at least partially hidden."

Charles wasn't buying this line of thinking at all. "But not hidden enough."

Louise gave him that look that meant he had said something stupid. "I know that. I'm just saying vodka's clarity makes it a particularly bad choice."

"Unless…" Louise's eyes widened for a moment, and a slow smile spread across her face. "Maybe they aren't making heroin at all but laudanum, just dissolving the opium in the vodka."

Charles picked up on her excitement, but registered an objection. "It would make it cloudy." Then he had an objection to his objection. "But I'm not sure how cloudy."

Louise raised her eyebrows and looked hopeful. "Maybe they have some way of making it clear. Isn't it some kind of resin particles that make it cloudy?"

Charles seized on the idea. "Of course! They just need to precipitate out the particles–they would be waxes I think–which would leave a liquid that looked just like vodka. But it would be potent enough to knock out a horse."

Then it was Louise's turn to object. "It still wouldn't be heroin though. The junkies wouldn't be able to inject it. The high would be poor by their standards."

Charles thought for a minute. "I have two answers for that."

"Go on."

"First, it wouldn't be difficult to boil off the alcohol and water at some place nearer the market and produce genuine powder heroin. Even the junkies could do it, but they probably wouldn't have the patience."

"And the second answer?"

He got serious. "It's more sinister. They could be trying to broaden the market by getting people addicted to laudanum as a first step, easy to do if it's already in vodka, then when the laudanum doesn't work well for them any more, they can sell them heroin."

Louise nodded. They had another theory to test. "That's a real possibility. It's just the way drug dealers work."

Charles agreed and added another thought. "It's a way for the Korean distributors to get back in the market."

Louise was puzzled. "Back in?"

Charles explained, "I read on the Internet that they were shut down by a coalition of governments several years ago. The Colombians took up the slack and started producing, and the Koreans couldn't make a go of it. Now the Colombians are faltering because of government crackdowns, and the street price is rising, so the Koreans may have seen an opportunity for a comeback."

She was thoughtful. "It sounds as though this might not be a small operation after all."

Charles had to agree. "Maybe not."

"I have another question," Louise said.

"What's that?"

"A milk truck carries milk, a liquid, and they can pump the liquid into the pipe and then to the house. But opium is dry and not easily dissolved."

Charles was quick to answer. "We've already talked about this. They have to put it in small waterproof packages."

She wasn't convinced. "But then how can they pump it?"

He wasn't deterred. "As long as the packages are small enough to pass through the pump, it would work." He paused for a minute. "But they can't be that small."

"Why not?" Louise wanted to know.

"The pipe is only about three inches in diameter, so the propeller that drives the fluid has to fit inside it, and that means that the spaces between the propeller blades would be no more than a half inch wide. That's just too small to be practical." He stopped and a slow smile spread across his face. "I know how they do it."

"How?"

"They don't use a pump at all. The truck's tank is three or four feet off the ground. The pipe is at street level, and the house surely has a basement. If the pipe goes into the basement, all they'd have to do is connect the truck tank to the pipe, and the milk would drain directly into the house. No pump, no problem. The packages would have to be small enough to pass through the pipe, that's all."

Louise was still not convinced. "I don't think they would want to take the time in the milk factory to pack the opium into so many little packages."

Charles agreed with this, but stuck to his theory. "No, it must be done at the source–right in the fields, probably in Afghanistan."

Louise asked, "What about those small waterproof packages?" But as she posed the question, Louise knew the answer as soon as Charles thought of it.

"Condoms. Just like they smuggle heroin inside a person. And with the U.S. military presence in Afghanistan, I'll bet there's a ready supply."

"Probably, with all those horny guys."

Charles elaborated. "They would pack small amounts of opium in condoms, seal them shut by tying a knot, toss them in a milk truck full of milk, drive it across a few borders–and they're easy borders to cross: Pakistan, Turkmenistan, Uzbekistan, maybe Kyrgyzstan, or maybe the other way, around the Caspian through Russia to Turkey. At this end the milk, plus opium-packed condoms, drains directly into the little vodka plant. The milk is discarded. The opium is dissolved in the alcohol, bottled and labeled as vodka, and shipped out in trucks to wherever."

Louise added, "We need to find the wherever."

Charles thought he knew. "I'll bet you anything it's Marseilles."

"Why?"

"That's where the old Korean distributors used to ship to. And Werner would have contacts there."

Louise feigned mock horror. "His mother?"

Charles laughed. "No. I doubt it. She is a little too old and a little too much into her own bottles to be useful. But he'd have boyhood friends. He grew up there. That explains the French name."

Louise now agreed. "OK. Now we need to verify this theory. If it's laudanum, the first shipment we saw them loading should be already hitting the streets. The police should be on to it pretty soon."

Charles got very serious. "Overdoses would be a real problem. Anyone who's used to drinking vodka could easily take in way too much laudanum and die in their sleep."

Louise saw the problem as even bigger. "The police might not even recognize it. It would look just like alcohol poisoning, with the bottle nearby and a guy dead in a ditch."

To get the information they needed, Louise turned her attention to the computer, while Charles kept up surveillance on the two buildings. In a few days they had answers.

Chapter 20
The Drug

Charles and Louise had to prove or disprove the theory they'd come up with. At the same time, they wanted to find out more about the Russian mafia in Kazakhstan and any connection they might have to the Soviet camps. They hadn't formulated a clear plan yet with regard to MOLP, but they felt that in anything as unsavory as the gulags, there should be something that would suit their purpose.

The surest way to verify their laudanum theory was to find out that the opium tincture was being used on the streets, probably by young people. This was a much more serious line of investigation because if their theory was correct, overdoses would be likely, and people would be dying from them. So they put the other ideas on the back burner, and pursued the laudanum theory vigorously.

Louise had previously set up an encrypted email system with Henderson, and she sent him a note.

"Please check to see if police in French or Russian cities are seeing an increase in alcohol-poisoning deaths among young people. We suspect that vodka laced with laudanum is being made here and distributed to Europe."

Henderson acknowledged the message and within the hour fired off messages to the police in Paris, Marseilles, Rome, Madrid, Amsterdam, Brussels, Moscow, Kiev, St. Petersburg, and just to see, Beijing, Hong Kong, and Bangkok. Sometimes Henderson overdid things.

They also asked him to check on activities of the Russian mafia in Kazakhstan. He in turn, sent a note to a man in the Defense Department whose job it was to coordinate intelligence on the Russian mafia. This man's identity was kept a closely guarded secret, and even Henderson didn't know it. He had only an email address, which wasn't even the right one, but an address that alerted an associate that someone wanted to contact the agent. The associate carefully checked out the message and its sender before forwarding it to the correct email address for the Russian mafia intelligence coordinator, known professionally as the RMINC, or "Armink."

Russian organized crime was different from its Sicilian predecessors in several ways–more ruthless, for one thing, but also more corruptible. The U.S. intelligence organizations hadn't found it difficult to get information about organized crime in the former Soviet Union. All it took was money. The problem was that Russian mafia activities were widespread and there was a huge amount of information to deal with. Also, they had to choose very carefully what information to act on, because it was dangerous to do so. So they focused on important issues, like the sale of nuclear material or biological weapons. Drug smuggling was a little farther down the list.

Nevertheless, they honored Louise's request, and gave her a small list of names, mostly Russian, but a few Kazakh, with their last known addresses, descriptions, suspected activities, a "résumé" of previous convictions, and much more. All but one of these known mafiosi based their operations in Almaty–that's where most of the money in Kazakhstan was. The one exception was a man in Zhezkazgan, a fact that perked up their ears because of the former camp there, the continuing copper mines. They also noted that his criminal activities were extortion and blackmail. They guessed that he was blackmailing former camp officials and turncoat prisoners who wanted their pasts kept secret.

Chapter 21
The Batch

Friday morning came quickly. In spring, the sun appeared earlier and earlier, and in this northern latitude, the change took place rapidly. It was only 5:00 a.m., but it was bright enough to see. With the window open, they could smell some neighbor's flowers scenting the air, a rarity in the arid climate. They'd had only a sip of morning coffee when a truck, with the word "moloko" (milk) in big Cyrillic letters written across the dirty yellow tank, pulled into the factory's back entrance. The driver climbed down from the truck and pressed a button next to the garage door, but nothing happened. He turned away. Tired and disheveled, he rubbed his eyes and scratched his head. He looked as though he'd been driving all night, and he looked frustrated at not being let in. Charles and Louise watched with interest.

He sat down on the truck's running board with his head in his hands, as if he wanted to sleep even in that awkward position. He was rather tall by Kazakh standards, dark skinned and lean, probably in his forties. He could've been Afghani, Turkish, Iraqi, or Persian, but he didn't look like a Kazakh. Charles looked hopefully through the lens, took some pictures, and kept up a running commentary to Louise, who was already up and on the computer.

"This could be an opium delivery. Guy arrives early in the morning. Been driving all night. Could be Afghan. He's pissed that nobody's there to help him unload." Charles had forgotten about his coffee.

"Did you get a good picture?"

"Oh yes." He didn't take his eye away from the lens.

"License number?"

"Yup."

"Is anybody down the street making vodka?" Louise's voice dripped with sarcasm on the word vodka, and she took another sip of her coffee.

"Two came in earlier, plus the door goon."

"That would be enough to handle a delivery. There isn't much to do."

Charles' voice suddenly picked up energy. "OK, the door is opening. At the milk factory. He's going to drive the truck in. Too bad they're going to close that door. But I can see them uncapping the pipeline and connecting a hose from the truck. OK. The door's closed. But they're definitely going to drain the truck into the pipe that goes directly to the vodka plant."

Louise was looking toward the vodka plant. "A light went on in the basement."

"Probably where the drain is."

Now it was Louise's turn to get excited. She almost jumped up from her seat. "Look, the pipe's vibrating a little. Something's flowing through it."

Charles had taken his eyes off the milk factory. There wasn't much to see anyway. He nodded rapidly. "OK. That confirms one part of the theory."

"An important part. There's no other good explanation for why the contents of a milk truck would be pumped through a special pipe, away from the milk factory and into a vodka plant almost a block away."

"Right."

They sat back, basking their success. It was now certain what was going on in the vodka plant, even though they couldn't see it.

* * *

The day was getting warmer. It would be hot today. Foot and car traffic moved slowly through the waves of heat rising from the pavement. The milk factory's smokestack spewed a thin, black plume that streamed away slowly to the east. In the vodka plant, beyond the reach of Charles and Louise's telephoto lens, five men worked steadily. Inflated condom packages lay in a heap around the floor drain. Traces of milk puddled around the little rubber sacs, missed by a final wash of water that came through the pipe to wash away the milk.

The men were all Koreans, three brothers and two cousins. They worked steadily, washing each condom packet off in a nearby sink, then cutting them open and dumping the opium into a large metal pot that stood in the middle of the room.

In an hour the pot was a third full, and the packets were gone from around the drain. The cut condoms were collected, stuffed into a shopping bag, and tied up with string. One of the brothers–taller than the rest and younger–took charge of the package.

Two others produced a large glass bottle, like the ones that supply office water coolers. This one, however, was full of pure alcohol. They poured the entire bottle into the big vat, filling it. They spoke only briefly, and in Korean, as they carried out these tasks in the basement of the building on Dyenuskova Street.

Outside, birds were chirping, a few flowers were poking their heads above carefully tended soil in window boxes. A few women walked by, their high heels clicking on the sidewalk. Two women met on the street and kissed each other in greeting. A gentle breeze made the sparse leaves of a city tree waggle back and forth.

In the basement, a kind of wooden cradle held the vat in place over a metal heating element, and an electric cord connected to the element to a wall outlet. The men squatted on their heels and waited. One of them, with a soul patch decorating his chin, looked at his watch from time to time. Fifteen minutes passed this way, and Soul Patch looked at his watch again and then grunted monosyllabically, jerking his head toward one of the others. One got up and went to a cabinet, opened it, and took a long glass thermometer out of a wooden case. He lowered it into the vat for a few minutes, then pulled it out and, turning his head and squinting, read out a number. Soul Patch grunted again, and a long aluminum spoon was produced with which the mixture was stirred slowly.

They continued stirring and checking the temperature. If it got too high, they pulled the plug. When it came down to a certain level, they plugged it in again. This operation continued for nearly an hour, until the man wielding the oversized spoon withdrew the spoon. The plug was pulled, but they continued to check the temperature for another twenty minutes, after which, more grunting monosyllables from Soul Patch, as he dumped a packet of white powder into the vat, and stirred the mixture briefly. Then they all squatted again and waited. No one spoke. Soul patch consulted his watch from time to time. After half an hour he got up, chose an empty pre-labeled vodka bottle from the cartons that lined the wall, and carefully lowered one end of a piece of rubber tubing into the vat. He sucked on the other end until the liquid flowed, spat some out on the floor, and put the spouting end into the bottle. As it filled, he inspected it, and his voice rose in satisfaction as the others crowded around. Heads nodded. Smiles appeared. Backs were slapped.

They drained the vat, filling six cartons, each with 20 pint-sized vodka bottles containing clear laudanum. These they stacked against the wall opposite the cartons of empties, sealing each bottle with a hand-held device. They were finished by late afternoon. The street value of the product they'd produced was close to a million dollars.

Chapter 22

The Milk Truck

Across the street and up a few houses, Louise watched as the six Koreans came out of the house and walked together down the street.

"They must live together," she said, curious about them.

"Probably."

"Should we find out where?" She liked the idea and turned away from the lens to look at Charles.

But he was opposed. "There's no need to go downstream. We need to go upstream and find the source of the money."

"Where Werner works." Louise quickly saw the value of the approach.

"Yes. And then further up." He paused for a moment. "If we can."

Louise could see that they were going to end up looking at bank accounts, email correspondence, and maybe official records. "I think the stream will become digital."

"I'm sure."

They sat still for a while, trying to imagine the whole operation, now that they were clearer about this one part of it. Their empty coffee cups, now only cylinders of stained paper, sat on the table lined up like gravestones.

They'd seen only one "vodka" truck leave the building, and so far there'd been no unusual police reports, so they still knew nothing about the delivery system, the routing, not even the destination.

Louise started their debate. "Do you think they transport the bottles by truck the whole way?"

"We know air is out. It has to be by land–so train or truck."

"I'm guessing truck, at least through Asian Turkey. Then maybe a boat to wherever." She tried to imagine locations beyond this point, but there were too many to narrow down.

Charles raised his eyebrows with a new idea. "They could drive all the way to Marseilles."

"I know. There are advantages to that."

"But disadvantages too."

Louise had an idea. "If we could mark the truck in some way, they could be tracked from the air."

Charles agreed and expanded her suggestion. "Or maybe we could attach a transmitter."

They quickly agreed on this idea. "We can have one sent from the states to the U.S. embassy by diplomatic pouch. It could be here tomorrow," Louise noted.

Charles put in a request, "but Henderson should know we don't want local authorities in on it."

Louise began to make the transition from strategy to logistics, as if she were a general. "We'll have to move quickly. That last truck was here only for an hour while they loaded, and that was the first time. They'll be faster next time."

Charles knew what he had to do. "I'll get an outfit ready so I can be out there quickly."

They didn't know when the next milk truck would pull in, so they watched closely. With luck, they'd be able to track the next load out. Meanwhile, they had to get on the computer and follow the money trail upstream. A week ago, Shen had left Werner's office with a suitcase full of money, but they couldn't be sure if he'd picked up the cash there or brought it from somewhere else.

Chapter 23
The Money

The next morning, Shen arrived at the vodka plant with the now familiar black briefcase. He stayed only a short while and then headed up the street. They watched him enter the milk factory, which wasn't something he'd done the previous week. He came out a few minutes later, and they waited until he'd gone out of sight, then they both took a taxi straight to the Green Bazaar. Once there, they acted like tourists for fifteen minutes until he arrived and left the briefcase with the same vendor as the previous week. They confirmed that the man who received it was the same one Charles had suspected the week before. When Shen left empty-handed, Louise followed him this time–to minimize suspicion. Louise used the same careful tricks Charles always used to avoid detection. Shen didn't go far, however. He entered a hotel just a few blocks away.

Louise ran to the hotel entrance as soon as he was out of sight and was relieved to see him waiting in a line at the reception desk. She positioned herself carefully, and when the desk clerk gave Shen his room keys, she noted exactly which cubbyhole they'd come from. After Shen got on the elevator, she walked up to the desk and asked if anyone could speak English. The desk clerk, an earnest looking young man with straight black hair, went into a back room, but by this time she'd located the cubbyhole and memorized the room number–318. When a young woman appeared who could speak English, Louise explained herself.

"I'm an American journalist," flashing her fake ID, "and I understand that later today Mr. McComber, CEO of the California Manufacturing Company, will be checking in. I'm sure you've already been told about it. My partner will interview him."

"I know nossink of zis," said the woman, a little flustered.

"Well, it's coming up," Louise said, glancing at her watch. "Around three they tell me. Anyway, I just want to get myself set up to take some pictures when he checks in. I'll try not to get in your way."

"Of course, of course. Do eet," the woman said, eager to get the bothersome American journalist out of the way so that the hotel guests wouldn't be annoyed. Then she disappeared back through the inner door. The regular desk clerk returned to his post and began checking in guests.

Louise bustled around the reception area pretending to try various angles, setting up a small tripod, and positioning her camera for a shot of the registration book. Finally, she took one, and the people around the desk jumped a little at the flash.

"Just testing." She smiled at them charmingly, but two men in the line scowled and muttered in Russian.

She kept up her activities, until she saw the desk clerk flip the pages of the registration book back a few times. Timing her shots, she got decent images of the last half dozen pages of the registration book, showing the room numbers of everyone who had registered at the hotel for the last month or so. Then she packed up her equipment, thanked the desk clerk, and left with a final thought, "Don't forget, Mr. McComber, three o'clock, I'll see you then."

The desk clerk smiled wanly, and tightened his tie. He must've understood a little English after all.

She hurried out into the street and started walking briskly toward the apartment. At the first corner she came to, a large crowd had gathered, and Louise pushed her way through, brandishing her press badge. A large, recent-model black Audi was nose-on to a small yellow Lada that had rolled over completely and was resting on its roof. The roof hadn't collapsed and from the easy way people were standing around the vehicles, she guessed no one had been hurt. The sturdy little Lada must've rolled slowly over and the driver crawled out the window. Once a photojournalist, Louise took a series of pictures out of habit, then packed up her camera and moved on. A good wreck was always worth a few shots.

Charles, working on the computer, hacked into the records of the Ministry of Commerce. He wasn't as adept as Louise, but she'd taught him the basics, and after a number of unsuccessful attempts, he'd gotten in. There, in the Ministry's official records, he'd roamed through licenses and registrations and found three different things–the vodka plant was a former residence, owned by a local Kazakh man and currently rented to Werner Tatinan. Werner owned the other building, where he went to work every day.

Werner was obviously up to his eyeballs in the drug trade. With a history of legitimate exporting, he made an excellent cover for the operation. And since Werner was the son of MOLP's former lover, they now had a loaded gun with which to shoot down the French President's reputation. Portrayed to the press in suggestive wording, the President would look as though he were connected to the drug trade. A loaded gun was fine, but they had a lot to do before pulling the trigger.

The third piece of information Charles found was the licensing records for vendors at the Green Bazaar. The Ministry had a map of the entire Bazaar, with little numbered areas corresponding to each shop location. It wasn't hard to find exactly where Shen had dropped off the briefcase and the name of the man who had accepted it–Azamat Ahmedovich al-Ryadi.

"If that isn't a reflection of the times, here in Kazakhstan," Charles said to Louise as she walked in the door, a little breathless.

"When are you going to be finished with the computer?" She ignored his comment, eager to find out more about the man she'd followed.

"Soon," he answered, but then continued on with his original idea. "He's got a Kazakh first name, a Russian patronym, and an Arabic father with a Saudi surname."

"I know. Languages are fascinating," she said dismissively. "Can I get onto the Internet now? I have the name our friend Shen used to register at the hotel, and I want to check some back records."

"Sure. What's the name?"

"Chung Tien."

Charles thought for a minute. "That could be either Korean or Chinese."

Louise was impatient. "But we know he's Korean. I'll check the Korean bank first." Charles disentangled himself from the city records and stood up, relinquishing the computer chair to Louise. "You'd think we'd have two computers, wouldn't you?"

She didn't bother answering his complaint, since he knew why they limited themselves to one. She began massaging the keyboard and found the Korean bank records without difficulty, but the encryption was complex, and it took several hours of work before she got in. Once she did, Charles helped her with the Korean characters, and the account of Chung Tien was right in front of her, with a withdrawal of $100,000 this morning and another just one week before.

But the most interesting item was the money coming in. A transfer of more than $2,000,000 from a bank in Marseilles had arrived just a few days ago.

"That would be payment for the first shipment," Charles said, counting the days.

"It's a lot of money, but pretty small potatoes for heroin trafficking," Louise commented.

"Sure, but they're just opening up new markets," Charles countered. "The deposits will get bigger in a month or two." He paused for a minute. "And then it'll stop, and the account will be closed to avoid detection."

Louise's anger rose as she thought of the destruction these criminals could wreak on young people around the world. "Maybe we can stop it sooner than that," she said. Her mouth closed with a snap, and her lips got thin and pale.

Charles felt the same way. "I hope so."

He felt a rising affection for Louise, recognized it as a reaction he'd had before as they worked together on a project. How odd, he thought, that shared anger at cruelty and chaos could bring out tenderness, but he'd seen it in Louise and in himself on earlier jobs. He put his hand on her shoulder, and she reached up and put her hand on his hand and smiled at him. They didn't have to say anything.

Louise looked again at the computer screen. "Before that, there's only an initial deposit of a little less than a million dollars, dated one month ago."

A look of understanding came across Charles' face. "This is a new operation we've discovered here in Almaty."

They both sat with this information for a few minutes. It meant that what they were doing was even more important. If they didn't stop it, a whole new international drug trade operation would begin, fueling the poppy farming in Afghanistan, which was already supplying funds for terrorism in many parts of the world. If a new market for heroin were created, the farmers would plant larger crops, and more heroin would be made. The price would go down, and that would lead to a wider market, which would in turn lead the farmers to plant more poppies. It was a process that deserved the term "vicious cycle" like no other, for there was no question that once the process began in earnest and began to fuel its own growth, more and more young people on the streets of cities all over Europe and Asia would become addicted, and many would die, either from overdoses, from AIDS-infected shared needles, or from the violence that seemed inevitably to spread around drugs like a fungus growing on decaying offal.

Louise opened up another aspect of the operation for them to consider. "What do you make of Nicolai Ivanovich Lobachevksy?"

Charles looked puzzled. "You mean Azamat Ahmedovich al-Ryadi?"

Louise smiled. "Yes, but I was thinking of that old Danny Kaye song." Louise sang a little of the chorus, ending with the wild "hey!" at the end."

Charles nodded slowly. "I remember the song." But he went back immediately to the business at hand. "I'm guessing that al-Ryadi is getting protection money of some kind. It has to be the very first thing you do in this kind of operation."

"What kind of protection? Shakedown?"

"No. That comes later." Charles thought for a minute. "Al-Ryadi probably has contacts in the Ministries and pays them off to let Shen and Werner do their thing."

Louise nodded. "That would be my guess too."

Charles had another idea. "While you're looking at banks, see if there's one with Saudi connections."

There was and there she found al-Ryadi's complete account, an old one going back many months, with many deposits and withdrawals, most of them modest, probably the revenues and expenditures of his fruit-selling business. But some of the deposits from Saudi Arabia were anything but modest, and there were dispersals to accounts in Afghanistan that stopped after the American invasion, and some to Pakistan that started up not long after the invasion. They also found a substantial flow of money to Turkmenistan. With further study it was hard to escape the conclusion that money from Saudi Arabia was coming in to al-Ryadi's account, and that he was sending money out to help fund terrorist groups.

"Wow! I think we've hit the jackpot. And the feds don't know this guy?" Charles exclaimed.

"Nope. His face didn't ring any bells in the FBI. Now, of course, they'll have some more information, and they may recognize him from some previous activity," Louise answered.

As they looked closely at the history of the account over the past several years, they noticed that it would grow for a while, and then there would be a large transfer. This happened three times. The first transfer was to a bank in Jakarta a few years back, a little more recently there was one to a bank in Yemen, and a third transfer, a more recent one, to a bank in Australia.

It didn't take more than a few moments of thought for Louise to figure it out. "If I'm not mistaken, these large transfers coincide with suicide bomber attacks, don't they? At least the first two."

Charles agreed. "I think they do. And the Australian one is around the time they stopped a suicide bomber from attacking a hotel in Sydney."

Louise was now on the edge of her chair. They had discovered something very important, a missing link in the war on terror. Of course the antiterrorism guys had a lot to do, and it wasn't so surprising that they'd overlooked this country that had no record of terrorist activity. In fact, many of the anti-terrorism experts had assumed that the money used to fund terrorism was transferred via the ancient *hawala* system, which was based on mutual trust and memory rather than bank vaults and computerized records. If the terrorists were using regular banks, Louise thought it would be easier to trace their activities, even anticipate it.

She went on, "So this guy is sending money to different banks around the world, where people withdraw it to pay off suicide bombers' families."

Charles was somber. "That's what it looks like."

"What worries me," said Louise, squinting at the monitor through her special computer glasses, "is that the account has been building up for quite a while." She paused to think it through, but she couldn't avoid the conclusion. "He's ready to fund another attack."

Not only was this bad news, they had no way to act on it.

"But we don't know where," Charles said. He sat back and rubbed his face hard with both hands.

"No," said Louise, "but we will." While they'd been talking, she'd called up past issues of the *New York Times*, and written down the dates of the bombings they had been discussing. The timing was evident. "With the past transfers there has usually been a week or more between when the money moves and the attack itself."

Charles thought about it for a minute. "The attacker wants to make sure his family is going to get wealthy before he does himself in."

Louise added, "Or she." Women's liberation now required equal time for female suicide bombers.

Charles went the next step. "Well, we can get Henderson in on this and then, when we see what bank the transfer goes to, he can put a watch on the account and pick up whoever comes in for the money. It might even be possible to prevent the attack."

"Good," Louise said. "That could save a few lives–one, certainly."

Charles summed up for them. "So al-Ryadi makes his money by selling protection along with fruit, which costs him only a little to bribe officials, and then when the profits have built up, he treats himself to a suicide bombing."

She sat back in her chair. "That's about the size of it. And he also gets money, big money, sent to him from Saudi Arabia."

"A compendium of donations perhaps," Charles said, building up until there's enough for an attack. That connection may be the most important of all."

"How are we going to stop this guy?" Charles saw that Louise was getting very intense about the mission.

"I haven't figured that out yet," Charles had to admit.

Louise felt productive, and she waved her arms around a little as she talked. "He's important enough that the U.S. government can outbid all the bribes and bring him up before an international court."

Charles, feeling the need to rein her in a little, said, "But our job ends with identifying him."

Louise wasn't going to be deterred. When she got like this, she thought about little else, slept poorly, pushing herself to make things happen. "We'll have to see what Henderson says." She thought probably she could, by presenting the facts to Henderson in the right way, get carte blanche for them to work on this particular project, even if it meant setting aside for a while the task they'd been given to do.

They sent their report off to Henderson and got back an appropriate number of wows and holy smokeses. They were to keep monitoring al-Ryadi's account, watch-dogging for the next attack, which pleased Louise. It was as much as she'd hoped they could get in the way of an add-on to their mission. Besides, as soon as Henderson told the antiterrorism people what Charles and Louise had discovered, a team would be assembled, brought up to date, and given responsibility for watching the account. Once that team was in operation, Charles and Louise could, if they wanted, go back to their original mission. They were hoping, however, that they could continue on this one. They were on site, and that might make a difference. Meanwhile, they would make sure that nothing was deposited or withdrawn from the account without them knowing about it immediately.

Henderson, in his email, also told them to figure out a way to shut down the laudanum operation, but not to execute the plan until it was known who the distributors were and to whom they were distributing. It was the same game that narcotics police always followed, getting as much information out of each discovery as possible before shutting anyone's operation down, going "upstream" as Charles had put it just the other day.

Henderson also told them that the police in Marseilles had reported four deaths by alcohol poisoning in one week. Usually, they had only one per year. Autopsies would be performed to confirm the presence of opiates, but Charles and Louise didn't need the confirmation. They knew what the cause of death was. There was also a spike in alcohol-poisoning deaths in Moscow, but the usual number was so high that they couldn't be certain if it was due to vodka laced with laudanum or just straight vodka.

And then, when they didn't need any more confirmation at all, Louise found a news story in a daily paper distributed in Dubuque. An Iowa Senator, touring the area around the Caspian Oil fields, had come to a checkpoint on the border between Russian and Kazakhstan. All six of the guards were asleep, and a bottle of vodka, only one third empty, rested on the windowsill of the customs building.

"These guys can't hold their liquor," the Senator had wisecracked. And the quotation, accompanied by photos of the sleeping guards, and the vodka bottle up close, were shown on the Op-Ed page of the Dubuque paper. The logo of Werner's fake company stood out clearly in the enlarged photo of the bottle on the sill. They're easily amused out there, thought Louise. The winters must be long.

Chapter 24

The Interview

"Would you like some tea?" Mrs. Tatinan asked with a gracious smile, and Charles and Louise both wondered if she was completely innocent of her husband's work or a superb actress. A woman of average height, in her late forties, with medium-short black hair, permed in a '50s style, she looked half European and half Asian, as did many Kazakhs. In the part of Asia that gave birth to the European as well as the far eastern peoples of China, Korea, and Japan, plus the natives of North and South America, why wouldn't they look universal? She wore loose-fitting black slacks and a generous red sweater–a dramatic combination that accentuated her black hair and black eyes. It was the first time they'd heard her speak; on their previous visit she hadn't uttered a word, in deference to her husband.

"Yes please, if you don't mind." Charles was back to speaking Russian with the occasional American mistake–mostly using the wrong case ending, omitting articles, and saying "this" too often because the Russian word for it sounds like "is" in English. He also translated for Louise. They were still in their roles as American journalists writing for a Florida magazine read by retirees.

"We're working on a story about the new Caspian Oil discoveries," said Charles.

"I see," Mrs. Tatinan said, "many foreign journalists are interested in it. But why do you want to talk to my husband? He's not in the oil business."

"No, of course," said Charles. "We learned of your husband from his mother. She's an old flame of the French President, whom many of our readers remember as a much younger, and more passionate, man."

She smiled. "Yes, I've heard the story from Werner." But then a blank look came over her face as she realized they hadn't really answered her question, but she was too polite in the Asian way to challenge their explanation.

And, in fact the real purpose of their visit was to plant a listening device inside the Tatinan home, to try to get a clearer picture of Werner's role in the newly set-up drug ring.

Werner was expected home soon, and they were eager to plant the device before he arrived, so Louise, using gestures, asked Ainahan, as she was now calling Mrs. Tatinan, if she could be shown the rest of the apartment. It was remarkable how well they could understand each other. Ainahan gestured graciously for Louise to follow her, and while they were out of the room, Charles, pretending to look for something in his briefcase so that he could stay behind, slipped a recording device the size of a large button under the tea table and pressed it against one of the legs, high up and out of sight under the overhanging portion of the top. The gum-like adhesive immediately stuck to the surface, keeping the device there long enough for the epoxy, which was the actual adhesive, to take hold. The tiny battery in the device would be alive for several days, maybe a week. Charles pocketed the small piece of treated paper that had kept the adhesive from sticking to his pocket, straightened up and walked toward the bedroom, where Ainahan and Louise were looking mutely at the furnishings. As he was approaching them, the door opened behind him and Werner walked in and bent to remove his shoes and put on slippers.

Charles' heart beat just a little faster at the close call, but he turned, smiled broadly, and greeted Werner with the two-handed Kazakh handshake.

"*As-salaam alaikum,*" Charles said giving the traditional Kazakh greeting in Arabic.

Werner shook his hands warmly enough but didn't respond with "*Wu alaikum as-salaam,*" which puzzled Charles. Perhaps he was simply surprised to hear Arabic come from an American and didn't know what to say. Or, more likely he'd become far removed from the Islamic customs of his countrymen.

"It's very nice of you to talk to us again. As I said on the phone, we just have a few general questions about Kazakh energy systems, for background to our story. You are, I'm sorry to say, our main contact in Almaty."

"Well, I'll tell you what I can, but first let's sit down and have some tea." It wasn't the Kazakh way to come directly to the point.

Charles quickly sat down. "Sure, sure."

The women came back to the table too at that point, and Ainahan poured Werner a cup, again in the Kazakh manner–first some milk, then dark tea, then hot water to adjust the strength. She knew exactly how he liked it. Charles noted the grace with which his well-practiced hand held the teacup by the edges. For no reason but the oddities of culture, it was the Kazakh custom to drink tea from cups that had no handles.

Werner began, after everyone had been served. "Did you talk to my friend about the Caspian Oil reserves?"

Charles was a little apologetic. "I did not. I was a little nervous after your warning about the possible dangers of asking about this very sensitive issue. Also, we plan to go to Aktau to see things first hand, but Almaty is so pleasant that we're delaying our departure."

Werner smiled in agreement. "I can understand that. It's a lovely city. Later in the year, however, it will become unpleasantly hot."

Charles pursued his stated line of interest. "We wanted to find out some more information about energy in Kazakhstan. There seems to be abundant electrical energy."

Werner was very comfortable in his answer, something Charles took note of. Both Charles and Louise always paid close attention to the nonverbal side of communication, and at times could learn more from it than from the words. "Yes, there is,"

Werner said. "Every home in Kazakhstan is electrified, excepting perhaps some very poor, rural areas."

Charles raised one eyebrow inquisitively, "Where does it come from?"

"Many rivers pour down from the snowy mountains in the east." Werner gestured broadly eastward. "They provide enough electricity for the whole country."

"So you don't need to burn any fossil fuels to get electricity?" Charles continued to pretend that the Russian language was difficult for him, and he hesitated over the word for "fossil fuels" as though he were trying to recall the Russian.

"No, only for automobiles, and even for that the demand is small. In the country many farmers still use horses and donkeys for transportation." Werner's answer was unapologetic, and Charles wondered why. Perhaps he wasn't particularly patriotic, something which Charles and Louise had both noticed among Kazakhs. Werner was half European and had been educated in France. A weak attachment to his adopted country would make criminal activity easier for him.

Charles nodded, "We've seen them, even just outside Almaty. But what about the factories?"

Werner agreed. "Some plants do require oil. The smelters, for example."

"I know there's a big copper plant in Zhezkazgan. Is there anything else?" Their different projects seemed to be coming together in this interview. He sat attentively on the edge of his seat. Werner leaned back expansively.

"Yes, there are some other plants producing minerals, but the Samsung plant–Kazakhmys it is called–is the biggest in the country."

"That's the second time we've heard about Zhezkazgan." Louise said to Charles. She'd become very attentive after hearing the name of the town where the old prison camp was. She nudged Charles for a quick translation, which he did hastily.

Werner, thinking of getting rid of this inquisitive old couple, said, "It's an interesting town. You should visit there."

Charles nodded in agreement and took notes. They talked some more about the country, about the crumbling infrastructure and the slow pace of repair, but the two Americans had accomplished their mission and were just trying to maintain their cover. After everyone seemed to have had enough tea, cakes, and candies, and the exchange of more pleasantries, they excused themselves, said thank you again, put on their shoes, and left.

Outside the house, Charles looked quickly for a place to attach the transponder, a small oblong box about the size of a cigarette lighter, that would receive the weak signal from the Tatinan's apartment, boost it a little, and send it on to a receiver in Charles' and Louise's apartment. He found a place for it in a nearby telephone pole. The telephone poles in Almaty had two parts. The lower part, half buried in the ground, was a long thin block of concrete. The upper part was wood. The two parts were bound together by a dozen windings of heavy iron wire. Charles couldn't figure out why the poles had two parts. The concrete would resist insect damage underground, but why not make the whole pole of concrete, particularly when wood was so rare? His curiosity was at the moment not important; the juncture of the two overlapping sections provided a crevice where the transponder could be easily placed and held fast by adhesive. He made sure no one was watching, then reached up to attach the transponder in the crevice. Satisfied with the placement, they walked on down the street.

They hurried back to their apartment to begin listening, commenting as they walked on how poised the Tatinans were, and how innocent they seemed for people who were involved in a major drug operation. They didn't know, although they would soon learn, of Ainahan's involvement, or the extent of Werner's involvement. Nevertheless, the couple's graciousness and serenity was impressive as a cover. It made Werner's claim to be a legitimate businessman quite credible.

Chapter 25
The Gulag

Almaty's sidewalks were crowded with rush-hour pedestrians, and in the streets horns blared, the cars inching forward, their angry drivers yelling Russian and Kazakh insults. They both noticed, as before, how well dressed the women were.

"Sure," Louise answered, "they're dressed up but hardly fashionable, more like the '50s."

Charles had noticed several thongs, visible through tight white jeans, which were not at all out of the '50s, but he thought it the better part of spousal valor to keep that observation to himself.

When they got back to their room, they turned on their receiver and adjusted the frequency. What they heard confirmed their earliest suspicions, now grown well beyond suspicion, that Werner kept a set of books, legitimizing the vodka operation.

They'd already hacked into his electronic records and seen that he recorded the size and frequency of shipments of incoming alcohol and chemicals, and the flow of money. It looked completely legitimate, but knowing that the operation was actually the production of vodka with laudanum in it, the entries took on a more sinister meaning.

The finances were recorded using a simple conversion formula, so the amounts appeared normal for a vodka exporting business but were actually the much larger amounts of a drug operation. They cross-checked specific entries in Werner's books against Shen's bank accounts, and the dates and amounts made it obvious that Shen was being given money with which to pay off al-Riyadi. The evidence would, Louise thought, be convincing to a jury in the World Court. Louise was even able to derive the formula, by comparing the amounts of the deposits and withdrawals with the books Werner kept. When the time came for the operation to be fully exposed, she was ready with some powerful arguments.

At the moment, however, they were listening to conversations, mostly domestic matters and uninteresting but occasionally relevant. One conversation occurred a few days later. They spoke in Kazakh, but Charles, through his knowledge of Turkish and his continuing study of the Kazakh language, was able to get the gist of it. For the finer points, and to ensure the accuracy of his interpretation, he sent relevant parts of a transcription to Washington by diplomatic pouch, for analysis by experts in the language. But they didn't have to wait for the experts. What they heard was most interesting.

"This can't go on for very long," Ainahan was saying.

"I know. Only through the summer in any case." Werner tried to placate his nervous wife.

"But it may have to end sooner than that. You know how it goes when you bribe officials."

Werner's voice became a little impatient. "Yes, of course, sooner or later someone else offers them more, and elbows their way in."

Her voice rose, and they could hear her very clearly. "When that happens, your life will be in danger."

"I know. I have a contingency plan." He was still placating his wife.

"And what is it?" She wasn't convinced.

Werner now was feeling very sure of himself. "I've already introduced myself to the President of France, and told him who I am, reminding him of his friendship with my mother. When the time comes, if the operation begins to fall apart, I can ask for his help," he said with certainty.

There was scorn in Ainahan's voice. "Why would he want to help you? He doesn't even know you."

"Because," Werner's voice became that of the teacher explaining something elementary to a slow student, "it'll then be obvious that I'm involved in something illegal, and he'll want to keep that a secret. He is connected to me through my mother. Not closely of course but close enough so that my arrest would make harmful publicity for him. All I will want at that time is to be helped in leaving Kazakhstan, not be hindered at the borders. You know that if I try to buy airline tickets at that time, they'll stop us. He could buy them and send them to me. He'd do it out of friendship for my mother. He would appear innocent."

She was angry at being lectured to, but she had to concede, "Yes, it might work."

Charles and Louise would've jumped up and down if their aging joints had been up to it. It was just what they needed. For a while, they just sat there, realizing that for the most part they'd completed the mission they'd been sent to accomplish. Of course, there was now the "secondary" project, actually much more important, to pursue.

* * *

Logging on, they found encrypted email from Henderson, reporting the presence of laudanum on the streets not only of Marseilles, but also Paris, Moscow, and Rome. Go ahead and plant a homing device on the next outgoing truckload, Henderson urged. If the distribution route could be discovered, Interpol might be able to apprehend all those in the operation. Notices of cooperation from the relevant countries were already coming in.

The emails also suggested a plan for halting the drug ring's activities, a plan already endorsed by the DEA contacts. It would begin as soon as the truck, with homing device attached, left Almaty. If they were couldn't attach a homing device, a week would pass before another shipment would leave.

There were more congratulations too. Closing down the drug ring would save lives, probably many, very young lives and might prevent the re-establishment of the Korean heroin trade. But important work remained. The money from the first laudanum distribution had been added to al-Ryadi's accounts, now large enough to fund another suicide bomber, and everyone knew another attack would soon follow, but no one knew where. There were American targets all over the world. By monitoring al-Ryadi's accounts, they would recognize a withdrawal large enough to fund such an attack, and a transfer would pinpoint the location. They hoped it would be in time.

They had another worry. In the Arab world money was often transferred by the *hawala* system, an underground network of money dealers who'd learned to trust one another over many years of cooperation. If al-Ryadi began to distrust the privacy of his bank account, he could call a *halawadar* and would arrange for a counterpart anywhere in the Arab world to give a large amount of money to anyone designated, and it would be done. The Homeland Security people were surprised the terrorists hadn't used this system earlier. Maybe the amounts were too big for the *hawala* to handle comfortably. But if the terrorists suspected their bank accounts were being watched, they'd switch to the older way anyway, or use couriers, and it would be harder to trace them.

For Charles and Louise, monitoring al-Ryadi's accounts was boring beyond description, and they spent most of their time examining and discussing the records of the old prison camp in Zhezkazgan. It wasn't long before they found the real names of the three officials responsible for the camps. In Zhezkazgan and some of the other gulags, those who condemned prisoners to death often used aliases, worried that some day they would be hunted down by former prisoners seeking revenge. But researchers in Moscow had discovered their true names. The man in charge at the camp was Viktor Dmitrivich Gladin. He was in charge except that, in a certain way, he was subject to the authority of the second man.

This second man was Aleksander Aleksandrovich Briscov, a political operative who made sure those running the camp were loyal to the Communist Party. He also had to arrest and imprison anyone he was told to. Arresting innocent people, choosing them at random, was a policy Stalin used often to terrorize his own countrymen, and the web of political operatives, themselves susceptible to these acts of terror, were responsible for carrying out this policy of intimidation. He might be asked at any time to arrest anyone, including Gladin, so Gladin had to be wary of Briscov, and their mutual distrust and dislike kept the camp authorities in a perpetual state of anxiety, exactly as Stalin wanted.

The third man was Feodor Sergeivich Kerimov. His job was to carry out Gladin's decisions. For the easier jobs he used a group of toadies who'd worked their way into his confidence. For the majority of the work–the underground mining–he used regular prisoners if they were strong enough. For work that was particularly onerous or dangerous, he used the prisoners who were defiant, had misbehaved, tried to escape, etc. In charge of the daily operations of the camp and the mine it supported, Briscov ran the business. He too was subject to the threat of Briscov and had to be careful that what he said and didn't call his political tendencies into question. Kerimov wasn't a political person, and this made Briscov a little suspicious.

Charles and Louise, from the camp records and maps saw that the camp consisted of several rows of barracks and an administration building. The barracks housed new arrivals, who often didn't realize at first how hopeless their situation was and tried to escape by making false papers, stealing money and clothes, and then trying to get back to their home towns by train. There was no other way. Invariably they were caught at checkpoints and crossings and sent back to Zhezkazgan, where they found their situation changed for the worse. These men, those who had tried to escape, were put in the filthiest and flimsiest living quarters, and given jobs outdoors in bitter cold, or deep underground in the most dangerous parts of the mines.

Those who didn't attempt such foolishness were rewarded with better food and housing, better jobs, and eventually even the freedom of living in a small flat in the main part of town, sometimes with their wives and families if they were willing to come to such a remote and godforsaken place.

Charles and Louise, examining the camp records and the notes appended to them by modern Russian researchers, read that Briscov had been killed, bludgeoned to death in his bed, the killer never apprehended. Charles and Louise, fast becoming experts on the Russian gulag system, weren't surprised that Briscov's murder hadn't been solved. The murder of a political man in the Soviet era was common and often unsolved. Few who knew the victim would cooperate with the investigating authorities; these men were universally despised.

The chief, Gladin, was ten years older than the others, and when the camps were "shut down" in the 80s, he retired and returned to Russia to live on his pension. Unfortunately, all pensions were cancelled during an economic setback, and he lived in misery and squalor in Moscow, begging on the street. He wasn't young, and his sedentary life at the camp had left him too weak in his sixties to work, and he no money to start one of the small businesses that were now legal. His death was likely, but not recorded. He had disappeared into the vast grey ugliness of post-Soviet Russia.

Kerimov, however, was alive and well and still living in Zhezkazgan. His position as chief of operations had given him considerable expertise in managing personnel and running a large mining operation. He'd learned on the job, but his expertise was nonetheless thorough and deeply understood because of certain personal qualities. When the orders came to shut down the camps, he convinced the old authorities in Moscow and the new ones in Zhezkazgan to convert the camps into a legitimate mining operation. There was profit enough, he argued, to pay salaries for the managers and the miners and still produce plenty of copper for mother Russia at a handsome profit to the new Republic of Kazakhstan–provided, he emphasized, that the control of finances remained local.

Clearly an expert and was willing to work hard, he asked for a very handsome salary, which the newly created Board of Directors agreed to. In fact, they paid him more than he'd asked for, realizing that without Kerimov there would be no company. The local economy prospered from these changes, and the new Republic, now free from the Soviet system, had its own successful copper business in Zhezkazgan. Some of the former prisoners even stayed, willing to work for decent wages. Many went home, and local citizens snatched up their jobs. Jobs were hard to find, the pay was good, but the work was dangerous.

The continuing mines and smelter saved the town from extinction; there was no other economic basis for a town in the middle of the huge steppe–the summers were too hot to grow grass for grazing, and the winters were so cold that cattle had to be brought indoors until spring. The steppe was too dry to grow food crops, and the town was too remote to bring in raw materials or ship out the products of any manufacturing. There were only the mines. The quantity of ore seemed endless, and the quality was good enough to make copper mining an unending source of profitable industry.

Kerimov was the most important man in the post-Soviet company, but when it was sold in the early years of the new millennium to the Korean giant Samsung, he was let go. His association with the old camp was an embarrassment to the new owners, who were eager to put a more modern face on the company. He remained in Zhezkazgan, however, wealthy and independent, occasionally acting as a consultant for the new company.

Chapter 26
The Drunk

Charles and Louise took turns reading these reports while the other one kept an eye on the two buildings on Dyenuskova Street. Charles, looking through the telephoto lens, announced for the fourth time that day that a milk truck had pulled up at the garage doors. The previous three trucks had each connected their tanks to the pipe and discharged a load of milk bearing opium-laden condoms. Charles calculated that the four loads of opium would provide enough laudanum to fill a delivery-truck load with "vodka."

Sure enough, at three in the afternoon, a truck bearing the name and logo of Werner's vodka exporting business appeared at the house. Charles was ready. He put on a dirty, torn shirt and a pair of pants that looked like he'd slept in them. He wet the crotch as though he'd recently urinated in them. Then he laced up a pair of old work boots and went into the street, unsteady on his feet, looking half hung over and half still drunk. In his closed hand he clutched the little homing device, coated on one side with a soft material that would hold it in place long enough for the epoxy to set. The back of the truck was open, and a young Korean stood by it guarding the precious cargo, much of which had already been loaded while Charles was putting on his costume.

Muttering slurred Russian syllables, Charles walked toward the truck, his free hand outstretched, like a drunk who saw salvation through the open doors in front of him: many crates of vodka. As he got close, the Korean began to make warning sounds, which grew in intensity as Charles approached. At the last minute, with the truck's rear bumper within reach, the young man tried to push Charles away. Charles pretended to lose his balance and fell, adroitly evading the push and ending up with his hand holding the transponder under the truck's rear bumper.

"I'm awrigh', 'awrigh'. C'n get up by missel," he said in the Russian equivalent, steadying himself on the bumper while he pressed the homing device inside it, out of sight.

He rose, swaying a little, and blinking his eyes. The Korean gave him a hard push, which made him take one or two backward-leaning steps, then fall on his butt. He moaned and whined in drunken Russian about this treatment, then struggled to his feet and walked away feigning an inebriated attempt at dignity.

The Koreans finished loading the truck, banged the doors shut, and two of them drove the truck away. The rest watched it go and then went back into the house. Louise watched the whole episode from the window and was relieved when the truck pulled away. She waited until the last of the Koreans was out of sight, then called Charles by cell phone to make sure he'd succeeded in attaching the device securely to the bumper. Then she called the Embassy, who patched her through to a pilot in Florida, flying a drone invisibly high over Almaty. She told the pilot where the truck had just left Dyenuskova Street, heading west, and within seconds he had its position blinking on a map in front of him.

Over the next few days a series of drones would take off and rendezvous, handing off the tracking job one to the other, as the truck drove from Almaty, through Taraz, Shymkent, and Kyzel-Orda, and on to the western steppes of Kazakhstan, all the way to the northern shores of the Caspian Sea, skirting the shorter but more bribe-hungry route through the Caucasus, to the Russian border. At the border they stopped long enough to unload a portion of the cargo, which was reloaded onto another truck bound for Moscow.

The drones could, with their incredible imaging capabilities, see enough of this second truck to determine its general direction, and they gave a description of it to their command on the ground so that the Moscow police could pick it up and trail it once it got to the city. But they kept the first truck's signal blinking on their GPS display, as it continued to the port of Rostov-na-Donu, where the cargo of laudanum was unloaded into a ship.

The ship was easily identified and tracked through the Dardanelles, to the Mediterranean. It then stopped at Taranto, where the police watched the containers bearing the now infamous logo being unloaded and placed on a truck, which they followed to its destination in Rome. The same thing happened in Marseilles. The location of each local redistribution point was identified, and the people who took possession of the cargo were carefully described and noted, and, as soon as the authorities got the word, they would arrest all the people involved. But for the time being they held off.

An exception to this policy occurred in Marseilles. Not long after the truck's cargo had been unloaded in a small warehouse, staked-out plain-clothes police officers saw a young Korean leave the warehouse carrying a package which, by the size and shape and apparent heft, they took to be a pint of the contraband. They followed him to a nasty section of the city, and when they saw him sell his package to a couple of boys on the street, they moved in and arrested him, confiscated the bottle, took him to a holding center and locked him up, completely ignoring his shouted requests to see a lawyer, the Korean ambassador, and his "parents." By keeping him out of touch with his cohorts, they preserved the secrecy of the more general operation.

Chapter 27

The Moonbeam

In Almaty, Charles and Louise were running out of time. As soon as the police made arrests in Moscow and the other cities, the word would spread rapidly, and the culprits would disappear. Charles and Louise found an Embassy employee a tough-looking Marine fluent in Russian, who was often tapped for tasks like this. Lieutenant Thomas Hedley could pass for a Russian Mafioso. His blond crew cut was 6'5" above the floor and all 265 pounds was tightly packed into a well-toned muscular body. His father had been a Marine too and met a young Russian woman while stationed in St. Petersburg during the days of glasnost. He married her and brought her back to the States. She spoke only Russian, and young Thomas learned the language at his mother's knee.

Charles and Louise told him everything they'd learned about the Russian mafia. The Marines had stationed him in Almaty, but a Mafia presence there wasn't known. They also told him of their plans for Shen/Chung and Werner then made some phone calls to set it in motion.

Shen/Chung was the easiest. Charles, Louise, and the young marine went to Shen's hotel, and they were all sitting in different parts of the lobby, carefully dressed to look like respectable guests., when they saw him enter the hotel's restaurant for breakfast. Thomas followed him into the restaurant. Charles and Louise took a table to watch what transpired and be ready for anything that might go wrong. But nothing did. After Shen/Chung had picked up his food and found a table, Thomas went over and sat down across from him. Shen looked a little startled.

"Please, I'm sitting here," he said in Asian-accented but fluent Russian.

"Yes. I know. I'm sitting here too." Thomas played the cockiness of organized crime based on bullies he'd known in high school in New York City. They'd never stayed cocky for long.

"I don't understand."

"Exactly, I'm going to help you understand. I have a message for you from Nikita the Moonbeam."

Shen's face paled. Nikita was Nikolai Kalodna, no known patronym, leader of the "Moonwatchers' Society" in Moscow. No one knew exactly how they came to be called the Moonwatchers' Society, but from humble beginnings they'd risen to the top of Russian organized crime.

Nikita had been the leader from the beginning and maintained his position by rewarding loyal followers with riches unimaginable in post-Cold War Russia, and killing those whose loyalties were questionable, often killing their families at the same time. The bodies were marked with knife-cuts resembling a crescent moon. Some experts thought this symbol connected the Moonwatchers to Muslim fundamentalism, but it didn't. It was just the Society's way of letting people know what happened to those who interfered with the channeling of funds into the Society's bottomless pockets.

Nikita himself had been arrested, tried, and convicted in a German court and was currently being held in a maximum security German prison, but this did little to slow him down. He directed other members of the Society from his cell by telephone and email, and the German authorities seemed unable to pin anything on him that was clear and concrete enough to deny him his right to communicate with the outside world.

So, when Thomas told Shen he had a message from Nikita the Moonbeam, Shen listened closely, and his mouth went dry. He knew who Nikita was.

"Nikita's interested in your little operation. He thinks you have potential. It's clever. Make an initial payment of 1,000,000 rubles, and after that, we can talk again.

"But I don't..."

"Now, don't go using negatives. Nikita doesn't like that."

"I don't ..."

"Hmmm. Perhaps you didn't understand. Nikita hears negatives, and he thinks you disagree with him. You don't want to disagree with Nikita. Hardly anybody in the world left alive who disagrees with Nikita. Here's an account number at the Russian bank on Nekrasova street. Make a deposit." He smiled. "It'll be good for you."

And with these last ominous words, Thomas left the table. Shen trembled as he watched Thomas' broad back leave the restaurant. He got up and left hurriedly, looking first up and down the street, then walking quickly toward Werner's apartment. On the way, he had to stop and urinate behind a tree or he would've wet himself. As he rang the bell, he steadied his shaking finger with his other hand.

Werner came to the door in his bathrobe; it was only a little after seven. He was startled to see Shen. They limited their contact to the necessary times when money must be picked up, and this wasn't one of those times. Shen was babbling and was hard to understand. Werner looked down and saw an envelope under Shen's foot. Apparently slid under the door earlier, it hadn't been noticed. Werner picked it up, opened it, and read it with increasing alarm. It was from "Nikita."

"Go away!" he shouted to Shen. "Get out of here!"

Shen backed away, looking at the envelope as though it might explode. He turned and ran. He hailed a passing taxi went directly to the airport, where he bought a ticket for Seoul. He left his things in the hotel. Two Interpol agents waiting at the airport confirmed his destination then called Seoul and had him picked up as he got off the plane.

Shen called the five Koreans in the vodka plant from the cab on his way to the airport. The five left the building and fled on foot, disappearing into the streets of Almaty.

Werner, however, placed a call to MOLP, mentioning his mother's name. MOLP took the call, and Louise recorded it. MOLP called the airport authorities and bought an electronic ticket for Werner in the name of the President of France. That was enough for the airport authorities to let Werner and Ainahan go. They flew to Martinique, taking a large supply of cash but leaving much of their possessions behind. When the police broke into the house on Dyenuskova St. the next day, they found two shipments of opium packets in sour milk. They waited at the milk factory for a third shipment and arrested the driver.

That night, Charles and Louise had much to celebrate. They took out their instruments and played spirituals. Charles' strong baritone and thumping guitar accompaniment gave the songs power, and he held nothing back. Louise played harmonica riffs during the rests. They played "Do Lord," "Oh Mary Don't You Weep," "Joshua," and "Twelve Gates into the City," and then calmed down a little and sang "Swing Low," and "Deep River." For these, Louise's descant was glorious, soaring above the melody and lifting the songs to the spiritual heights they deserved. When they finally put their instruments away and went to bed, they slept well.

Chapter 28
The Train

Police in Rome, Paris, Marseilles, and Moscow identified the distribution cells and arrested the dealers. Shen was arrested as he stepped off the plane in Seoul. The workers at the house in Dyenuskova Street were never found. For a while, no one was sure what had happened to Werner and Ainahan Tatinan, but checking and cross-checking the records of flights leaving Almaty, the USDEA agents found a couple that seemed right, using a French name and bound for Martinique. A few days later the two Kazakhs were sunning themselves on a deserted beach in Martinique when they saw a group of four men walking up the beach. From the other direction another group was approaching. A sheer wall of rock behind them and the sea in front made escape unthinkable. By the time the men reached them, Werner was shaking. He was relieved and overjoyed to discover that he was only being arrested by French and Martinique police and not about to be executed by Mafiosi.

Charles and Louise closed up the apartment on Dyenuskova Street and prepared to move on. They still kept a close watch on the al-Ryadi bank account. They could monitor the account from any location, but they didn't want to leave Kazakhstan until they'd finished the last part of their job. Agents in Washington were also watching the account, so the elderly couple's monitoring was redundant. Charles and Louise decided to go to Zhezkazgan to investigate the old gulag. Maybe it would connect to their main mission. Maybe not. But they'd finished investigating MOLP, and their "secondary" project had shape-shifted from a drug ring to a terrorist plot. As so often in the past, they let their natural curiosity guide them. There was Raisa too. They wanted to meet her again, and she'd probably gone to Zhezkazgan.

They took the train. Zhezkazgan did have an airport, but they'd raised quite a hullabaloo in a small corner of the underworld, and the train seemed less conspicuous than flying. And maybe the train ride would be restful. This last judgment proved correct.

Their new friend Thomas, the burly Marine who'd done such a good job playing the part of mafia muscle suggested they buy extra tickets so they could have a compartment to themselves. The train pulled out in the evening, and just before leaving they bought bread, cheese, apples, sausage, and water for the two-day trip to Zhezkazgan, and lucky they did; the dining car that was supposed to be part of the train was unaccountably missing. Whenever the train stopped at a station, even in the middle of the night, people walked up and down the platform selling water, dried fish, and watermelons, but nothing appealed to them. The fish was particularly distasteful. Charles wrinkled his nose as he smelled it, smoked and rank, through their open window.

Their compartment contained four benches, covered with thin cushions for seating during the day, and a supply of sheets and blankets, and small, thin pillows for sleeping. It was meager but cozy, like a camping tent. At the end of the hallway outside the compartment was a large samovar, a small, open fire under it keeping it at the boil, so the passengers could make tea. Many stood in the corridor, sipping tea and looking out the windows as the lights of Almaty slid slowly by and the view changed to the empty blackness of the flat, endless steppes of Kazakhstan.

They put their luggage and the guitar on the upper bunks and their computer equipment in the compartments beneath one of the bottom benches, spread sheets on the lower bunks, and lay down in relative comfort. The movement of the train, and the rhythmic noises lulled them to sleep. But whenever the train stopped at a station they woke up, disturbed by the vendors hawking their wares and the sudden lack of motion. And when the train started up again, it was hard to fall back into a deep sleep. It was a long night. Morning finally came and found them still rolling steadily northward not too far from the city of Karaganda, where they would change trains.

A little before four o'clock in the afternoon, they arrived at Karaganda. Everyone gathered at the windows to watch the city appear. At the last minute they gathered their belongings, heaved down their bags, and lugged them through the narrow corridor and down the steep steps to the platform, each of them making two trips. The station was surprisingly small. Karaganda wasn't the metropolis they'd been led to believe, and they were too tired and grouchy to explore it.

They were both reminded of an earlier mission, when they'd had a layover in Stockholm after the cross-Atlantic flight. They'd wanted to explore the city, but as soon as they sat down on a park bench they sagged in unison to the left, and were soon sleeping. They woke up, sore and stiff, and decided to take a bus tour of the city, but again fell asleep and never did get to see much of Stockholm. This time, they didn't bother.

So they sat in the train station, reading what books they'd brought, looking at people, and taking little walks around the station, or napping. Charles went outside and sat on one of their suitcases and played chords on his guitar, even sang a few songs, which attracted a few curious listeners. Just as their boredom had sunk to such a low level that they'd have been grateful for any diversion, the train to Zhezkazgan pulled in. This train originated in Karaganda, so no one was aboard, and they quickly found a compartment and loaded their things. The train pulled out around 7:30. They watched the steppe roll by for several hours, with no relief from the flat emptiness, excepting only the occasional village. They began to appreciate the vastness of the country and the deadness of this part of it. The villages were no more than a small collection of farm buildings, and they were surprised the train even stopped. Small as they were, these villages all had electricity, bearing out Werner's statement about the nation's energy supply. Night fell and ended their gazing.

The little cabin felt cozy and separate, but it was hot, so they opened the door. Immediately, a woman appeared with a child. She was young, Asiatic, presumably Kazakh, and she wanted to sit in their cabin. It seemed that she had no ticket or had purchased a ticket that allowed her on the train but without a place to sleep. Small seats that folded up flat against the outside wall provided seating, but they had no backs and would be uncomfortable. Charles and Louise nodded, and the woman and child sat in their cabin. Charles found out that she was on her way to visit her mother. It was the grandmother's birthday.

In the cabin next door someone had broken out the vodka, and the voices were already getting loud. Since it was only around midday, Charles and Louise were a little worried that the party would be totally rowdy by bedtime.

Charles and Louise read, filled out crossword puzzles, and played cards. Occasionally, they would look out the window on the off chance that something to look at had appeared, but this hope was repeatedly stifled.

They visited the bathroom, which was eye-opening. There was no toilet paper. There never was in Kazakhstan, and they'd already learned to bring their own. There was a toilet seat, however, which wasn't always true in the country's bathrooms, but it was so dirty that sitting on it was unthinkable. Also, the rim of the toilet bowl had little antiskid patterns on it to steady the feet of the Kazakh people used to squat toilets. They couldn't imagine how anyone could balance themselves against the swaying of the train while perched, squatting, on the toilet rim.

Night came, and the woman with the little girl disappeared, apparently getting off in one of the little villages. This train traveled more slowly and stopped more often than the previous one. All through the night, it rumbled along, and each time it stopped at a little village, the grumbling, clicking train noises would die away with the motion of the train, to be instantly replaced by voices–selling food, greeting arrivals, saying goodbye to those departing–voices that seemed to carry in the night from one end of the train to the other, and disappearing, each one, into the emptiness of the steppes beyond. They lay awake on their cushioned benches, not talking, thinking about their work, the job now wrapped up in Almaty, their original mission, and the one to come in Zhezkazgan.

When dawn came, they roused themselves. They'd slept, but intermittently, and it left them feeling still tired in the morning, so getting up was a change from being a little more than half asleep to being a little more than half awake. Gradually, they became more alert as the new days' light streamed through the windows of the train, still rolling slowly through the steppes. They made tea in the samovar, using tea bags Louise carried in her purse and ate chunks of bread and cheese.

They arrived in Zhezkazgan at 9:00 in the morning. It was a chilly but warming rapidly in the sunlight, which seemed brighter than the light in Almaty, unfiltered by the pollutants and humidity of the bigger city. Here, in the middle of the steppe, there were no mountains to gather snow and send the water roaring down in the spring, only the emptiness stretching away for hundreds of miles in all directions. Their feeling of isolation grew when they realized that Zhezkazgan was the end of the railway, literally the end of the line. For many Russians during the Soviet era, it was also the end of the line in the figurative sense.

They lowered themselves slowly down the steep stairway onto the platform. A young man offered to help with their luggage, and they gratefully accepted. They made their way to the parking lot in several trips. Only one taxi waited, the others had already left with passengers who were faster at getting off the train. But there was this one, a little green Lada, and they stuffed their bags into it and dozed while they were driven to the "Business Center," one of several hotels in the town. The hotel was modern and clean, unlike the buildings they'd seen in town. They were shown to a pleasant, if simple, room overlooking a long, thin artificial lake. The locals, they later learned, often called it the "river," and a look at the map showed a river, but with no source, and it never emptied into any body of water. It just petered out in the middle of the desert. Once in ancient times, it had been a complete river, but now it came from nowhere and went nowhere. This seemed fitting, even ominously symbolic, to the Americans.

Some of the lakes in the region had dried up as a result of dams put in by the Russians upstream to capture electrical energy. Perhaps the locals still used the word "river" as a linguistic memory of former times when it did indeed flow from one place to another, but more likely it was just wishful thinking. A river would've been nice, connecting the city to something else.

Chapter 29
Zhezkazgan

They showered for the first time in several weeks–the Almaty apartment had had only a tub–then they took a long nap, enjoying the first comfortable beds their bodies had known for two days. After the nap they explored the hotel, which featured a nice restaurant with white tablecloths and a beautiful view of the lake, a sauna, a small but usable weight room, and conference rooms where businessmen could meet.

Then they ventured out. Zhezkazgan wasn't very large, 150,000 people they read, and cleaner than Almaty. A few modern glassy buildings dotted the commercial area, but mostly they saw old apartment buildings of the typical post-Soviet grey, with broken concrete steps, sagging windows, and no lights. Little buses scooted around the main streets, charging only 20 Kazakh tenge–about 15 cents–and many taxis for 100 tenge, or 75 cents, would take any number of passengers anywhere within the city limits.

The moment they stepped out of their hotel and headed toward the center of town their earlier notion of the pure air and unfiltered sunshine were dispelled by a long plume of smoke, high above the city, streaming westward in the steady wind. They could see the tall smokestack it came from, and saw another one, now quiet, not far away. Zhezkazgan, as they already knew from their reading, was a company town, sustained, maintained, and dominated by the Kazakhmys Corporation, a South Korean company that ran the copper mines and smelter.

The smelter itself, located right in the town, although away from the commercial center, was supplied with ore from mines in the smaller, nearby town of Satpaev. The two towns, about 15

181

miles apart, were mutually dependent on each other, like those celestial systems with one large and one small star orbit around each other in a wobbling, eccentric fashion, their mutual attraction rising and falling with each cycle. The two towns were economic systems, not at all celestial–often ugly, but just as predictable.

Charles and Louise had been warned that on weekends, particularly at the end of the month, busloads of miners from Satpaev would join the workers from the smelter in Zhezkazgan in the streets of the city, drinking vodka, fighting, and shouting and laughing through the night. The merchants, teachers, local politicians, and those who worked at keeping the city supplied with heat, water, and electricity stayed indoors during these times. It would all be over in a day or two, the broken heads patched, the drunks–a few dead each month from alcohol poisoning–collected from the gutters by small ambulances, leaving small puddles of vomit and broken vodka bottles behind for the street cleaners.

A bazaar centered the main shopping area, flanked by modern shops, some restaurants and shashlik houses, a few department stores, and many cafés, large and small. Oddly, the so-called "central" bazaar was older and farther away from the center of town.

For a town of modest size, Zhezkazgan boasted many schools, a gymnasium in the European manner where the university-bound high school students could prepare themselves, a large university with a curriculum focused on mining, and several smaller colleges and institutes, one of which trained teachers for the wider region, or oblast. The importance given to education, or at least the lip service paid to it, was typical of the whole country.

It was a pleasant place to be, self-contained, regulated, not too big and not too small. Money flowed out of the copper mining into the city. The streets were kept clean, and although there was only one main governmental building, the Akimat, or town hall, it was large and modern, set back from the street by an expansive stone courtyard. Public statues of heroic proportions honored the war dead, the more recent cosmonauts, many of whom had landed in the empty steppe not far from Zhezkazgan, and cultural heroes. Surely statues of Lenin had been removed.

Louise, characteristically, wanted to continue exploring and orienting herself to the new town. Charles, however, had walked enough, and returned to the hotel to set up the computer and link them to the wider world. He learned of Werner and Ainahan's arrest on the beach, of Shen's capture, and indeed that the whole ring, except al-Ryadi, had been shut down. Al-Ryadi was spared for a while to see if he might lead them to other connections. His role in the drug ring was tangential anyway, and soon enough he'd miss the man who periodically brought him briefcases full of money, and then he'd be arrested, too.

Charles took another look at al-Ryadi's bank account in Almaty and saw no major activity. Messages from Washington came in, mostly more praise for a job well done. One message told of intercepted traffic revealing that the Russian mafia didn't like having its reputation used to scare Werner and Shen.

Louise returned in a few hours. She'd bought a map and ridden the buses. She'd walked through the bazaar and been in a few stores. She knew the names of all the major streets, the main squares and parks, and the bus and train station.

She'd also spoken by cell phone to her library friend Raisa, and wasn't surprised to find that she was already in Zhezkazgan. They made an appointment to meet for tea that afternoon. Louise remembered her anger toward the men who'd run the camp, and knowing now that one of those men was still here in Zhezkazgan, was eager to prevent her from doing anything rash. Raisa knew Louise was researching the camps in Almaty and wanted to know if Louise had discovered anything new. Louise had discovered the identities of the men Raisa was interested in but wasn't sure how much information she wanted Raisa to have.

Louise went back to the hotel, and consulted Charles about the Raisa dilemma over a late lunch in the hotel restaurant. Charles ordered for them both. The restaurant was nice, but the menu was disappointingly familiar, mixing Russian and Kazakh dishes, except for the addition of Wiener schnitzel, doubtless to appease visiting German businessmen. The dining room had some elegance, which they were glad to see. Charles noted the menu had something for the German businessman but nothing for the more recent Korean or American counterparts.

"Do you think we should tell her about the men who ran the gulag?" Louise looked over her poised fork at Charles as she asked this question, eyebrows raised, before popping a forkful of cutlet into her mouth.

Charles thought about the question carefully, seeing it from several sides and considering possible outcomes in his often maddeningly academic way, while Louise chewed, swallowed, and speared another piece of cutlet. Her eyebrows went up again. "Well?"

"I'm thinking."

They were silent for a while.

"I think we should tell her that the man she is looking for–Gladin–is very old, probably dead, certainly missing, and was last seen in Moscow. And I think we should tell her about the death of Briscov."

"OK," Louise said. "I'd already figured that out, but what about Kerimov?"

"About Kerimov, I'm not so sure, Charles said. "Perhaps we should tell her about him, what he did and didn't do in the gulag, but not tell her who he is or that he's still here, until we've seen her reactions."

"OK," Louise said. "That sounds right. We don't really know where her anger is directed at this point."

"Or how much of it there is. Or its quality."

Louise asked, "What do you mean by quality?"

"Well, I think there are many kinds of anger. Or maybe there are levels instead of qualities. No, there are qualities, too. You know, there is simmering annoyance, like you seem to be feeling toward me at this moment. And on the other end, violent rage. In between are different levels and qualities."

Louise at this moment didn't think much of Charles' academic analysis, and dismissed it. "I see. Well, I think Raisa is an intelligent woman who has a good sense of herself and has found a balanced place within herself and her memories of the gulag. I feel that I can trust her to find the right answer. As for simmering annoyance, you are, as usual, up in your head when you should be looking at the whole picture."

Charles nodded his agreement with the last point. He was often too intellectual and knew it. Then he added another thought, confirming the conclusion they were reaching. "And from what we know of Kerimov, he's a complex man, who's participated in some evil acts, but who seems to have made a kind of amends for them, at least as far as the community is concerned."

Louise's mouth turned down a little, and she stirred her fork around in her plate. "When you say 'amends' do you mean he's apologized in some way?"

Charles shook his head emphatically while chewing and swallowing rapidly. "No, I mean he's taken the evil parts of his life and work and made them into something beneficial."

"Hmmm. That's different."

Louise thought some more about it.

They both started to talk at once, Charles to elaborate his idea, and Louise to express some admiration. Charles saw that she felt the same sense of admiration for Kerimov's behavior that he did and gestured for Louise to talk.

"There's creativity in what he did. It looks to me as though he took the very stuff the bad deeds were composed of–the mines and the smelter–and made them into good deeds, like making a beautiful ceramic pot out of a lump of clay," she said.

"Yes, that's what I mean," Charles said with enthusiasm. "Of course, it's kind of a theory."

"Sure. We need to talk to him," Louise said.

"Before we talk to Raisa," he added, to make sure she understood.

"Well, before we tell her about him," she clarified.

"Right," he said.

"The white tablecloths are nice, but the food is the same old stuff," Louise commented.

"Yeah," Charles sighed. He'd been hoping for a good meal. "Maybe there's a nice dessert." Charles' wistfulness wasn't lost on Louise, who grunted in agreement.

The ice cream wasn't half bad.

At the Reception Desk they asked for a phone book, and were surprised that there was none. They could call information for a telephone number.

"We're looking for Feodor Sergeivich Kerimov," Charles said to the man behind the desk.

"Oh yes, of course. He is here often."

"Do you have his number?"

"Yes, of course." The desk clerk, a young Kazakh man, tall, with high cheekbones, rifled with practiced fingers through an old-fashioned Rolodex and said, "77-23-23."

Charles and Louise both smiled at the simplicity and naiveté in the six digits and the ease with which they were given to strangers.

They returned to their room and called Kerimov. He answered and didn't hesitate to talk to an American journalist about the camp in Zhezkazgan. His forthrightness both impressed and puzzled them. He ought to be embarrassed, they thought. But then, they hadn't met the man. They made an appointment to see him at his house on the following day. Then they fell asleep for a couple of hours, curled in their beds, dreaming of America, and their home by the water in Virginia.

They woke to the sound of the telephone. It was Raisa, politely wondering where they should meet for tea. And it was time. Charles, eager not to be late, got dressed hastily. Louise was resigned to being late, not such a big deal for her anyway, and dressed more deliberately.

Raisa was waiting for them in a restaurant located on the main shopping street. They sat at wooden tables, set up in two long rows with an aisle between them leading back to the kitchen. The whole restaurant was down a few steps from the sidewalk and shaded by a large tent, the sides of which were open, letting whatever breeze there might be play over the customers. It was Kazakh air conditioning. They ordered tea and while the waitress was gone, Louise and Raisa caught up with each other. Charles, who'd never met Raisa, asked questions during breaks in Louise's conversation. By the time tea arrived, they were all on the same page.

"How is it for you, coming back here after so many years?" Louise asked.

"I'm not sure I can tell you what it feels like. But I'll try."

Raisa rested her head on her chin and blinked several times, then shook her head slightly. "First, I felt sad, thinking about Sergei. I still miss him. I think about him every day. He was my first and my only love. Right now I'd like to hold his face in my two hands and look at his kind eyes and kiss him."

Tears appeared in her eyes and overflowed down her cheeks, and her voice wavered a little. "But I can't do that." She paused for a moment, looking beyond them into the street. "So, then, I let that wish go out of my heart, and then, being here in Zhezkazgan, I feel closer to him." She gestured with her hand as if presenting the town to them. "This is where we lived together, and we were happy with each other. That was the only happiness we had—everything else in our lives was miserable, but with ourselves we were happy." She paused, and then went on.

"So now, it feels as though I'm a little closer to him, and that is good. But many things here have changed, and when I see something new, I first say, to myself, 'Look, Sergei, there's a new store on Mira St.' Then I see the new store a second time, just myself, and then it is just a new store."

"It's complicated, isn't it?" Louise said.

"Both sad and happy mixed together," Charles added.

She sighed. "Yes, it is complicated, and mixed as you say." She gave the same, very slight, shake of her head. It was a way she had, as if she were clearing her mind, as if raindrops had fallen on her head.

"And what about your anger?" Louise wanted to know. "Is it changed, being here? Is it more? Or less?"

"I think it is a little less. Before, when I was working in the library in Almaty, I'd think of Zhezkazgan, and I'd see the camp and the place where Sergei got on the bus to go to the mines, and each thought was like a piece of new coal that you throw on the fire. My anger burned very bright then." She looked away again, into the sunny street, where young girls in stiletto heels clicked by purposefully, and a policeman in a Soviet-style oversized hat walked along, bored, looking at the girls. Strapping middle-aged Russian ladies strode along, their inner arms interlocked in sisterly support, with shopping bags in their outer arms. Old Kazakh men wearing little blue skullcaps with embroidered gold designs walked slowly in the afternoon sun. Her shoulders relaxed, and she took her glasses off and wiped her eyes. "So much has changed here. It's not quite the same place. So, the fire isn't so hot now that I see all the changes."

"Have you been to the camp itself?" Louise was beginning to formulate a plan, a psychotherapeutic plan, for Raisa, a way for her to feel free of the past that she carried with her always like a heavy suitcase that couldn't be put down.

"No, I haven't. I'm a little nervous about it, but I feel as though it is something I should do."

"Would you like us to go with you?"

"Yes. That would be so nice."

Louise glanced at Charles. He knew what Louise was doing, bringing Raisa back into the present, letting her set down the burden she'd carried for so long, and he nodded.

"We'll go there with you," said Charles.

Raisa smiled, and her eyes glistened. "Thank you," she said, her voice a little hoarse.

She leaned forward. "Perhaps we could go later this afternoon."

"Yes. We have no plans." Charles statement was true enough. But they both knew that they might have to leave Zhezkazgan suddenly if al-Ryadi made a large withdrawal.

They drank their tea and nibbled at the small cookies that came with it. From time to time Charles or Louise would comment on the people passing by, an old form of entertainment they'd used in many cities around the world, or Raisa would mention something that was different now in the city. But there were long silences in their conversation too, times when each of them wondered what the scene would be like at the old gulag.

"Perhaps we should go now," said Raisa.

"If you feel that you'd like to," Louise said.

"Yes," said Raisa. "It is time."

Chapter 30
The Memory

The old camp site was on the other side of town, about a mile away, and it was hot, but they decided to walk anyway, realizing that a slow approach to the memory would be easier for Raisa than stepping out of a cab and looking up to see something that might be deeply disturbing.

But as they walked along slowly and gradually got nearer and nearer, Raisa's anxiety slowly increased, and in the last few hundred yards she was a little pale, and very quiet. The slow, steady approach had only allowed her anxiety to build up.

They were walking along Seifulina Street, divided down the middle by a broad greenway, and when they came to the last big intersection at Mira Street and stopped to wait for the traffic light, Raisa patted herself lightly on the chest and took a deep breath.

Then the light changed, and the three of them stepped off the curb toward something they were unsure of and crossed quickly. Raisa had a determined look in her eye and took bold steps. Charles and Louise quickened their pace to keep up with her. No one spoke.

Another short distance, half a block, and they were standing in an open area. Above their heads and to the left, a tall monument with heroically oversized figures of men and women loomed. A commemoration of the Great Patriotic War, as the Russians called World War II, it had a look of struggle and triumph over adversity that was appropriate for the present occasion.

Then they looked to the right. Raisa was looking intently, almost squinting, but not at the sunlight. She seemed to be looking for something. Charles and Louise saw only a school building, somewhat new, and a large lot, empty except for some crumbling, pink buildings, stretching back for several hundred yards, and beyond them houses that looked like private residences.

"It's gone," Raisa said finally. "It's just completely gone."

Charles and Louise, feeling stupid, looked in the direction of Raisa's gaze.

"Over there," she pointed, "those broken buildings are the remains of the barracks. There were many more rows of them then, low buildings made of red brick." She gestured again, pointing. "Our building was in that area, when we were living here before they let us move to the flat. But most of it has been torn down. Right here, where we're standing was a gate, the entrance to the barracks area, and there, where that school is, was the administration building. It was a place we dreaded, because we usually got bad news there."

Louise had been watching Raisa, assessing her reactions. Raisa shook her head again, making room in her thoughts for this new version of the place that she'd known so well. She stepped forward and walked down toward the front of the school. Charles and Louise watched without moving, to give her some privacy. She didn't seem to need any support. She walked around behind the school, out of sight. They waited. Perhaps they should've gone with her. In five minutes she returned, walking slowly with her head down. Then she stopped and looked again at the empty field, shook her head again with that small movement and came back to them. As she looked up at their faces, a half smile on her lips, "It's just gone. Not a trace of it. Nothing." She seemed relieved. Her walk was lighter. Her head came up. "Let's go look at the flat."

Charles and Louise looked at each other and smiled a little.

They walked to a bus stop and waited. Louise knew which bus to take after hearing the address and consulting the map she carried. Raisa didn't know how the buses worked; they'd been installed after she'd left the town. The bus was small, holding no more than 30 people. They climbed in and found seats. Curtains on the windows kept the sun out, but made it hard to see exactly where they were. A young girl came around and took their fares. In fifteen minutes they got off the bus and walked toward a group of very old buildings. The paint was peeling from the window frames, and the front door hung at an awkward angle. Raisa stopped and looked up. The flat was still there, the building discolored, even rusty in its metallic places, the concrete crumbling and broken, the rebar showing and springing up in places to catch the unwary trouser leg. They didn't try to visit the flat itself. Raisa seemed quite content just to look at the old building. Then she pointed. "Third window from the left, on the second floor. That was ours." She shook her head. "It was really a miserable little flat, old and dirty. The cabinet doors sagged, and often there was no water. But it was like paradise to us after barracks. We had privacy for the first time, and that was a wonderful luxury. The flat was awful, but it didn't matter."

She turned away. "I'm hungry."

Louise and Charles both smiled. Raisa had returned to the present. On some days she'd still think of the past, and she'd remember Sergei's beauty every day, but she had set down a heavy burden.

"Would you like to have dinner with us?"

She looked at Louise with gratitude, but in her new sense of strength, she declined the offer.

"No, I think I'd like to be alone for a while," she said as they turned and walked back to the bus stop. They waited there for a few minutes, not talking. Raisa's bus came first, and she got on, turning to smile and wave to them at the door. Charles and Louise waved back, happy for her triumph.

That night, in the hotel room, Charles and Louise unpacked their instruments and played and sang work songs, which seemed appropriate for the town they were in, with its long history of forced labor. They sang "John Henry," and "Follow the

Drinking Gourd," and two Odetta songs–"No More Auction Block" and "Oh Freedom"–remembering the power of her incredible voice.

Chapter 31
Kerimov

Feodor Sergeivich Kerimov met them at the front door of his house. He was a small, slightly paunchy, florid man with a round face, in his late sixties, balding, with a fringe of grey hear, wearing simple glasses and dressed in a tie and shirtsleeves. There was an air of intelligence and thoughtfulness about him, and Louise compared him to an ancient Greek philosopher. He might have been a retired university professor like Charles, except that he was also practical and forthright, traits Charles hadn't seen in the halls and on the quadrangles.

He didn't speak English, and Charles reverted to American-accented Russian and translated for Louise. Kerimov invited them to join him for tea. As they walked through the house on their way to a den, Louise noticed a number of small, copper sculptures. Charles smelled some unfamiliar chemical odors. Two small black dogs yipped a few times, but it was a formality, to show they knew strangers had come in, and soon they stopped protesting and followed the party into the den, their stumpy tails wagging.

The den was large, with books on one wall, a double window at the far end, and many framed photographs on the other–a good place for an interview. Before he sat down, Charles glanced at some of the books. He saw a collection of well used mining- engineering texts, some in English. Louise looked at the framed photographs of Zhezkazgan a few years earlier. Kerimov walked to the desk and sat down with ease and familiarity. He was comfortable in these surroundings and used to being interviewed. With his back to the window, it was difficult to see his face. Louise checked her camera, particularly the flash setting, which she would need.

"Thank you for having us in your house, Feodor Sergeivich." Charles used the formal first name and patronymic, equivalent to the English Mr. "We're interested in the old prison," Charles said as he sat in a large leather chair facing the desk. Louise remained standing, holding her camera at the ready, waiting for a good shot.

On a shelf to one side of the room stood a large, brass Russian samovar with a flame already burning under it. On a small table nearby, an assortment of little cakes and cookies on a plate sat next to a few lumps of sugar in a bowl that also contained hard candies. A box on the table contained an assortment of chocolates. Glasses in silver holders announced that tea would be served Russian style, not Kazakh.

"I haven't met many Americans, but I've been told they come directly to the point." He smiled warmly. "Have one of these little cookies or a piece of chocolate. They both came from St. Petersburg, as it is called now."

Charles noted the last phrase and took it to mean that the Cold War hadn't entirely ended for Kerimov. Charles leaned forward in the big leather chair, trying not to be swallowed in its folds.

"I apologize if my directness seems rude. It's a habit I acquired from interviewing busy people." Charles was careful to make some errors, using the wrong case ending, dropping in "yist" where it wasn't needed, and not trilling his r's.

Kerimov smiled. "That was nicely said. I will surely revise my opinion of Americans today."

Charles was quick to ask, "And what is your opinion?"

Kerimov sat back, smiled slightly, and made a little steeple of his hands. He tilted his head, and his smile became one-sided, "I was raised in Russia, first under Stalin, and then under a series of grey men with beliefs similar to Stalin's. We were bombarded with anti-American propaganda. If I believed a tenth of it, I wouldn't have let you in." Again, the smile spread, charmingly, to light up his face, and this time Louise captured it with her camera. Kerimov adjusted his tie, and his eyes twinkled. Charles realized he'd avoided answering the question in a most charming way.

Charles returned the smile and the compliment. "We've met some Russians since we've been in Kazakhstan, and they've helped us also overcome the propaganda we heard in previous years."

Kerimov's tone became avuncular. "That's the second very nice speech you've made. We were always told that Americans had no culture and were crude cowboys."

Charles nodded in agreement, remembering one or two politicians. "Some of us do fit that description."

Kerimov leaned forward in his chair, ready to get down to business. "What can I tell you about the old camp?"

Charles and Louise both noted that Kerimov had established control of the interview, which they hoped would make him more likely to speak freely. But they were also impressed by his adroit charm.

Charles became thoughtful. "I can imagine that it wasn't easy for you to run the camp." Charles thought that a statement of sympathy might lure Kerimov into admitting more than he wanted to, but he got more than he'd bargained for.

Kerimov nodded vigorously. "Of course, of course. And in many ways. First, Gladin was a difficult man to work for. He was without sympathy for those who were sent here, but I don't know if this attitude came out of genuine loyalty to the Party, or whether it was induced by the presence of Briscov, whom we all knew would denounce us in a minute if we appeared to waver." He gestured emphasis with a fist. "We never discussed anything remotely close to our political attitudes. It was terribly dangerous to say anything, even something supportive. Certainly not in front of Briscov, but the policy of denunciation also rewarded anyone who turned in a colleague, friend, or family member, so no one could ever speak the truth to anyone."

He paused thoughtfully for a moment, and then continued, "I had an advantage over Gladin in that my job was only to execute his policies, so the only way I could be disloyal was by failing to execute them. Gladin had to develop policies and rules, and he could never be sure if they would end up working to benefit the Party. If they'd ever turned out badly he could've been sacked, and in those days, very often, being sacked meant something more sinister than just losing your job.

I had only one way to be disloyal, which was a blessing in those days. Also, I could maneuver a little. Sometimes, if the policy was really awful I could drag my feet, and blame the slowness on the system, the lack of materials, or something else, but I could never refuse, or I'd find myself quickly in another one of the gulags. So I was always very quick to say 'yes, we'll do as you say,' but then, I made my feet drag."

Charles eyebrows went up. "Couldn't Briscov detect foot-dragging?"

"Certainly, he saw it immediately, but the whole system was in fact not very efficient. Materials and parts were delivered to us very slowly and sometimes not at all, and to build something took an age because the workers were very slow. Often, I could make arrangements or create small obstacles–filling a form out incorrectly for example–setting up the inefficiency in advance, and in this way I could prevent, or at least postpone, some real atrocity from being carried out. There was little Briscov could do about this kind of slowness; it had nothing in it that could be seen as political. Even he needed some kind of real evidence."

"Can you give me an example?"

Kerimov nodded easily. "Certainly. There was one section of the mine that was much more dangerous than the others. It had been dug hastily because the ore was of high quality, and Gladin wanted to get at it quickly. He was under pressure from Moscow to increase production–always–so the safety precautions in this section were inadequate and collapses were frequent. Gladin ordered me to take more ore from this section, but I knew that it would cause deaths, perhaps many, so I agreed readily to the policy, as I had to, but I set about improving the support structure.

"Eventually, Gladin would say, 'Why aren't we extracting from corridor B-4?' and I'd explain about the need for supports. He might agree to wait a little, but when the new support still didn't come, he'd tell me to send in the magpies. That's what we called the prisoners who continually got in trouble, for stealing, for laziness, etc. We called them magpies because they were always talking to each other as magpies do, probably hatching escape plans."

"And so the magpies were sent in?"

"Not right away. I could delay this too, for a while. I could first of all argue that it was simply inefficient to work a dangerous section because as soon as there was a collapse, we'd have to stop mining and make repairs. This was true, and undeniable, so it was an argument I used often. But eventually the pressure from Moscow, and the sly innuendoes from Briscov would override my arguments, and we'd end up working the corridor anyway, but by that time at least some repairs had been made. The prisoners, most of them anyway, were very good at slowing down when they needed to. Of course, they were political prisoners, and didn't want to help the Party, so if they could slow copper production they would. They would've stopped it altogether if they could have, but slowing production was the best they could do."

"How could they do that?" Charles, unable to visualize clearly the scene being described and genuinely interested in the answer to this question, looked up from his notepad.

Kerimov's face took on a wearied look, as if what he were about to say was too old a tale to bear repeating. "By breaking equipment, letting machines run out of oil, making 'innocent' mistakes, pretending to be sick, although that didn't work very well. I never told them to do these things—that would've cost me my life–but I came to believe, based on the timing of their activity, that the prisoners knew what I was trying to do, and did what they could to help. Of course, these tactics only worked part of the time. Many men died in the mines anyway."

"So, you fought the system as best you could." Charles worked hard to keep the skepticism out of his voice.

"Hmmm." Kerimov shook his head from side to side as if in some internal argument. "I'm not sure I'd put it that way. It is too generous to me." He raised two fingers. "I had two goals. The first was to survive, and I always did what I could to survive. If I could help some prisoners to survive also, and there was no risk to my survival, or at least not much," his hands moved together gesturing first to himself than to some imaginary prisoners, "then I'd do what I could to help them. But if it was a question of my survival versus theirs, I chose to survive." He sat back in his chair, with finality.

"And the second goal?" Charles, impressed by his honesty, was eager to hear the rest, and leaned forward. Louise, saw the tension, and took a picture of Kerimov over Charles' shoulder.

"It may surprise you," Kerimov smiled again and leaned forward with enthusiasm, "but I wanted the mines to work. I wanted to make them function well and produce copper, for mother Russia. Yes, I was patriotic in this old-fashioned way, but also for myself. It was my work, what I did, and if we produced more copper of higher quality, then I had produced more copper of higher quality. Gladin wasn't like that. He wanted only to please the supervisors in Moscow. He wanted to rise in the Party, if he could, and he wanted Briscov off his back. I wanted to produce copper."

"And when the Soviet Union collapsed, you were given a chance." Charles reached the obvious conclusion.

Kerimov almost bounced in his chair. "Yes. I was given that chance, and I worked hard to make the mines both safe and efficient–the two goals are not incompatible–but there was another thing that made me work hard after 1991."

"What was that?"

"I said before that my first goal was to survive."

"Yes?"

"So it was. And I did. But there were many who did not. Many died in the mines, usually from cold in the winter, or sickness, these were the worst killers. We had almost no medical care, and they laughed when I asked for it. 'It's a prison,' they said. 'People die in prison.' 'But we can make more copper if they live,' I'd answer. And they would brush off this idea, because it was both a prison and a mine. Often, the two things were incompatible, and when they were, the prison was more important to them. But for me the mine was more important."

"So you survived." Charles recognized that they were getting a little off track and sensed where they were going.

"Yes. I survived and many of them didn't. I kept trying to make the mine work well, and I tried to make the prison work not so well. I only succeeded a little in both."

"So..." Charles knew then where Kerimov was going and smiled a little.

"When the collapse came in '91, I didn't feel so happy with myself. I had what they call 'survivor guilt.' I read about this guilt, and I recognized it in myself. It is supposed to be about the guilt of prisoners who survive when others don't, but this guilt was also in my heart. My guilt may've been worse because I wasn't just a prisoner. I had been in a position where I could really help many of them, and, when my own survival was at risk, I didn't. This left a very bad smell in my nose, a smell that I myself made."

Charles nodded slowly, absorbing the idea. "In creating the company you were getting rid of the smell?"

"Exactly. When the new Ministry, the Kazakh Ministry, was established, it was easy to show them that we could make a lot of money by mining more efficiently and more safely. It was for me a wonderful time." He sighed, remembering the relief of having supervisors who wanted the mine to succeed.

"So your goals were the same."

"One of them was. Efficiency. And I had better cooperation, although resources–equipment, materials, even food–were very scarce in the beginning."

"And your new second goal..."

"Instead of my survival, I became able to do the things I couldn't do before for better safety. It was, to me anyway, a way of making a payment to those who had died. That's what it felt like. Each time I made a change for safety, I'd say, 'there, that is for the men who died in the collapse of corridor C-9.' Another improvement paid a debt to the ones who died of cold in the awful winter of '75. Of course, no one received any pay for these debts that I had in my heart, but I felt that I made such payments. It wasn't the same as actually paying the debts to the workers, but it was nonetheless helpful to me."

He drank from his tea, looking at Charles over the silver rim of the holder, but the tea had grown cold in the warmth of his descriptions and explanations. He made a little wrinkled face at the taste of it. Charles scribbled notes, and Louise took pictures. Their tea too was cold. They were both interested in, and impressed by, the complexity and intelligence of the man. Scientist, engineer, humanitarian, pragmatist, aware of his own inner contradictions and trying to reconcile them, accepting in the end the limits of that reconciliation. They wondered if Raisa would see him the same way. They thought that probably she would.

"Would you be able, and would you want, Charles asked carefully, "to meet a woman whose husband was here as a prisoner?" Then he added quickly "He died in the mines."

Kerimov looked up sharply. This was suddenly not just an interview, and he felt for a moment that he'd been trapped. He considered for a moment, not afraid but perhaps annoyed at being deceived, but then he answered quickly, "I'd be happy to talk with her."

After that, there were only pleasantries–kind words about the house and the town. Their tea was refreshed, and they drank it, all three thinking about a meeting between Raisa and Kerimov. Kerimov wondered how angry she'd be. So did Charles and Louise, but they at least had seen her reaction to the site of the former gulag that had been a source of such misery in her life. They had come to trust her reactions. Kerimov, as it would turn out, also knew Raisa, but dimly from the past.

Chapter 32
The Waiter

When Louise called Raisa that evening and explained what they could of their conversation with Kerimov, Raisa's reaction was immediate.

"I knew this man. I remember him, but with another name."

"And what was he like then?"

Raisa thought for so long that Louise thought the phone might've been disconnected.

"Raisa?"

"Yes, yes. I was thinking, remembering. I didn't see him very often. We called him Aleksei. Sergei would remember him better because Aleksei was often in mines, or at the main building. But Sergei wasn't sure about him. Some said he was a good man in difficult situation. Others saw little difference between him and Jozef–the one you call Gladin."

"We think it'll be good for you to meet him." Louise spoke softly, and Raisa heard the affection in her voice.

"When?" Raisa's heart beat faster as she said this word and committed herself to meeting a man who once held her husband's fate in his hands. She was afraid, but she'd begun to have more confidence in her ability to confront the past, and she saw the value in it, even if it meant talking to a man who had some hand, however indirect, in her husband's death. She also felt that she could rely Louise and maybe Charles.

"Tomorrow, if we can make the arrangements. At 3:00?"

"Yes."

They hung up and Charles called Kerimov. Three was fine, and they confirmed it with Raisa. Charles and Louise looked at each other. At least four eyebrows rose.

"It's going to happen."

"Yup."

Their dinner that night was quiet. There wasn't much more to say about the meeting tomorrow, but there was nothing else they wanted to talk about. So for much of the meal they were silent.

The waiter at their table spoke to them in English.

"You Englishmen, yes?"

"We're Americans."

"Ah, America." He said it as if it were a far off paradise. "I like Eminem."

"That's nice." Charles in particular disliked rap, considered it bad poetry on the wrong side of serious social issues, with no musical value.

"You meet Paul." It was a statement, not a question, so Charles and Louise both looked puzzled.

"Who is Paul?" Charles asked, using his American-accented Russian.

"Ah, you speak Russian. Great." He switched quickly. "My English not so good. Paul tried teach me. He Peace Corps Volunteer here in Zhezkazgan. He teach at university. You meet him."

"We'd like to. Do you have his phone number?

"Sure. The waiter looked in his wallet and produced a piece of paper, on which he wrote the requisite six numbers. Afterwards, however, Charles and Louise remembered that if they called Paul it would probably cost him his Peace Corps position, because the Volunteers were not permitted contact with any intelligence organization. Charles and Louise were a free-lance couple, but they figured what they did was close enough to intelligence to compromise the young Volunteer. They wouldn't be calling Paul.

The next morning, they saw the waiter again and explained that they were leaving Zhezkazgan soon and wouldn't be able to meet with Paul.

"Too bad." The waiter said, "Paul always want meet Americans."

"I'm sure." And then, to get the subject away from Paul, "What do you do when you're not waiting on tables?"

"I student."

Some things are universal, Charles thought, and waiting on tables to pay for a university education must be one of them.

He looked up at the young man, standing attentively at their table. "And what are you studying?"

"I want become mining engineer."

Charles nodded slowly. "The university here has some experts in that area, I understand."

A cloud passed over the waiter's face. "Yes, I must soon dropping out."

"Why?"

The waiter shrugged in a gesture that Charles and Louise were beginning to understand meant resignation, a deep resignation to the system, to life, to everything. "It costing much money. Must working to save for more school."

"Is the tuition so high?" Charles was genuinely surprised. He thought that in a country formerly in the Soviet Union, tuition would be reasonable.

"Not tuition! Must giving teacher moneys for good grades.."

"You have to pay the teachers for a good grade?" Charles was surprised. Of course, he knew there was corruption in most of the former Soviet Union, but it surprised him to find it in the university, and so common that this student would talk about it openly.

"Yes, 3,000 tenge for exam grade, 5,000 for final grade."

The amounts weren't large–about $40.00 for a final grade, but then there wasn't much money anywhere in Kazakhstan, and you could buy quite a lot for $40.00. For the teachers, of course, it would be multiplied by the number of students in the class. Nevertheless, Charles looked surprised.

The waiter explained. "When Soviet Union ended–I was just boy then but my father told me–teachers not paid and student gifts only way to live."

"I see." Charles could imagine how trained teachers, with no hope of receiving a salary, would accept money directly from students, and from this practice corruption could easily evolve.

"Are the teachers paid now?" Charles wanted to know.

"Yes, they're paid now, but poorly, and their salaries always month late, and they must give some back, for, for–how you call *baksheesh*," the waiter explained. "So, we still pay for good grades." The waiter shrugged. There was nothing to be done. The conversation ended, and the waiter returned to work. Charles and Louise left the table, feeling sorry for the many difficulties the country faced.

Chapter 33
The Meeting

Later that day, Kerimov, Raisa, Charles, and Louise met in a restaurant–a pleasant place, fittingly located on Mira (Peace) Street. They assembled outside under a pergola, covered against rain or sun but open to refreshing breezes. Plastic greenery flourished around the pergola, creating the illusion of a deeply shaded wood, a welcome relief from the sun, already quite hot, even though the worst of summer was yet to come.

Both Raisa and Kerimov were nervous. He wore a suit jacket and tie. Raisa had on her best dress and she'd had her hair done.

They were introduced and observed the formalities as the young waitress hung back, waiting for them to be seated. After they sat, an uncomfortable silence was broken only by their order for tea and a plate of cookies. Charles translated for Louise, as did Raisa from time to time, but sometimes the conversational pace increased and Louise missed entire exchanges. She then got up, camera in hand, and recorded the scene from various angles. The waitress, a college girl, came and went, trying not to overhear.

"I remember your husband," Kerimov announced this fact unexpectedly, and Raisa was surprised by it.

"Really?" she said. Her face reflected a mixture of gladness and suspicion.

"Yes. His name was Sergei." Kerimov went on a little nervously. "I remember seeing you with him. He was a gentle man, with soft hands, not at all suited to rough work like so many political prisoners. I believe he was an artist of some kind, a musician perhaps?"

Raisa swallowed the catch in her throat, "Thank you for remembering Sergei. He was a journalist by trade, but a poet at heart."

"Ah, journalism, a very dangerous field then. And poetry, too. I'm sorry he was sent to the camps and sorrier still that he died there." Kerimov looked at Raisa with a kindness that couldn't be anything but genuine, and she was deeply touched by it. Tears came to her eyes.

She filled in the details. "He died in February, of 1975, after being sick for a while with 'miners' cough.'"

Kerimov nodded, sadly but with certainty. "Yes, there were a number who died that year. The winter was harsher than usual, and we thought the cold lowered their resistance, but we didn't know what caused the cough in the first place. It began in summer as often as in winter."

Raisa made an offering of information. "Everyone said it was the dust in the mines."

Kerimov quickly agreed. "It was certainly the dust, but there was something deadly in it. Scientists are now trying to find out what in the dust is so dangerous. We still don't know. But I think we'll know soon."

"Couldn't the men have been protected from this dust?" Raisa's voice quivered.

Kerimov responded quickly. "Yes, certainly. I requested face coverings, like surgical masks, and eventually we got them, but I had to prove that using them would increase production. At first, Moscow thought it was ridiculous to protect the health of prisoners." He shrugged his shoulders and looked off into the distance. It wasn't hard to see the pain flicker across his face as though a cold wind from the past had blown momentarily through the open courtyard. "Mining is still dangerous, I'm afraid, but the successful companies protect the miners from the dust and from many of the other dangers."

Charles looked at Kerimov, his eyes narrowing, "Is it pragmatic, then, or is it humanitarian to protect workers?"

"It is both," Kerimov answered quickly. He seemed to warm to the subject. "And it is usually both. And it should always be both. If a job, any job," he said waving his hand in a broad gesture, "is dangerous, then the technology is lacking in some way and needs to be developed. Dangerous working conditions are always inefficient."

Charles was now sitting on the edge of his seat, shoulders thrown forward. "It seems to me that the desire of the bosses is always to make more money, and they use workers to do that. Surely, the workers and the bosses will always be in conflict."

Kerimov smiled. He was on very sure ground now. "That is the old way of thinking, and I'm a little surprised to hear such a Communistic idea from the mouth of an American."

Charles smiled, "Not Communist, but for the Unions."

"Ah, the Unions. They look at the mountain from only one side, the side opposite from the one the bosses see. But it is the same mountain. And today labor and management are beginning to see that they're both looking at the same mountain and that they need to work cooperatively."

"The Japanese model," Charles said quickly.

"No, no. The Japanese model was a kind of benevolent paternalism. The bosses tried to make the workers feel like part of the family, so that they would work harder for less money. It wasn't much different from Communism. These days in the forward-looking companies, labor relations is about communication, helping each side see the value of the other's point of view and helping both sides see the goals they have in common. If it works, the common goals override the tensions, and the two sides compromise, not because of strikes and pressure, but naturally, the way a tree grows."

Raisa sat quietly during this discussion, which was aside from her interest in Sergei's memory. Kerimov saw this and turned to her.

"Such ideas hadn't even begun to hatch when your husband worked in the mines. And even if they had, the supervisors in

Moscow would've killed them." He shook his head at the sorrow of it all.

She nodded sadly. "If only his death could've meant something. It seemed then, and it still seems, so useless. He was simply thrown away."

"No. I don't believe that." Kerimov was very sure on this point.

"Why not?" Raisa wanted more than anything to find the answer to this question.

"I think he, and all the prisoners, were in a kind of war. The supervisors in Moscow were the enemy. The prisoners, forced to work without compensation, were pure labor. Those who died were heroes in the war between labor and management. The Soviet bureaucrats were the purest form of management because for them profit wasn't the central issue, just production. As in most wars, the soldiers didn't know what the struggle was about, and Sergei, and many others, died so the truth could be known–that labor and management work for the same goal."

Charles interrupted him. "Now you're talking like a capitalist, for whom profit is the motive for both labor and management."

"No. It isn't profit that is the right motive. That is a step in the right direction, which is why the West won the Cold War, but it's not the final answer."

"So what is this final answer?" Charles was skeptical, and Kerimov saw it.

Kerimov pondered. "Perhaps 'final' is the wrong word. But the motive that unites labor and management isn't profit but quality."

"Quality?" Charles' voice rose to higher levels of skepticism. He'd seen poor quality in most things produced during the Soviet era.

"Yes. When labor and management communicate well with each other, and both realize they're working to produce a quality product, and then profits will also be better, but the community also benefits. When profit is the only motive, as in the USA, poor quality often results. In capitalism, quality has to be good enough only to result in a sale, and only with lots of advertising. Society suffers then, just as it did when production was the goal as in the old Soviet Union."

"I'm amazed," Charles said, "to hear someone from the old Soviet system talking about quality. It was missing from the products made in that system."

"You're right, of course. That's why it was so clear to me. When a company works only for production, there's no desire at all to improve quality, while when a company works only for profit, there's some desire to maintain quality, at least enough so that buyers will buy again. The profit motive drives companies to produce only just enough quality to avoid having the consumer choose another product, and that's not good enough. When the company works directly for quality, then everyone benefits–labor, management, and society."

"I can see that." Charles sat back, fascinated.

"So," Kerimov looked at Raisa. "It may seem too abstract or philosophical to be a consolation–doubtless it is no consolation–but I think Sergei died for a noble cause. He helped to advance the understanding between labor and management. All the prisoners were at the forefront of this battle. He was a brave solder. He went into the mines, which were not a good place for him, and died so that we could see these issues more clearly. But, as I said, I know this is no consolation for you. Perhaps it is a consolation for me. Sergei died working under the old system, and for you there can be little comfort in my philosophy. But know that I'm sorry for his death."

Charles admired Kerimov's interest in trying to help Raisa come to terms with Sergei's death. He'd shared some of his most profound thoughts, conclusions he'd reached from working in a particular crucible, in a way that might help Raisa see Sergei's death in a meaningful context. It didn't reduce her sadness; nothing could do that. But perhaps it gave her some perspective.

Louise hadn't been able to follow the discussion, but she heard the tone of Kerimov's voice and the changes in Raisa as she heard Kerimov talk. Although she knew no Russian, Louise knew what had happened that afternoon over tea on Mira Street in Zhezkazgan.

They left the restaurant together. Kerimov, waving goodbye, left in a taxi. Raisa took another cab to her hotel, embracing both of them before she climbed heavily into the taxi and left, waving through the window. Charles and Louise wanted to walk.

Chapter 34

The Rescue

At 5:30 a.m., hugging each other for warmth, covered only by prickly clumps of coarse grass, they heard the distinctive sound of helicopter blades to the east. Louise sat bolt upright, spilling grass clumps off her chest and fished her satphone out of her shirt pocket. She turned it on, saw the time, and quickly punched in a number. The sound of the rotors stopped, and a man's voice said "Hello?'"

"Red Dog?"

"Yes, ma'am. You guys OK?"

"We're fine. Where are you?"

"We have to wait for light. Advise you to shut down to save power."

"But we heard a helicopter."

"Yes, ma'am. We're not far off. Suggest you shut down now."

"OK."

Then there was silence. Puzzled, she looked toward the east but saw nothing. It was cold and still dark. The same steady wind that had cooled them in the afternoon now penetrated their clothes.

"What did he say?" Charles sat up.

"They want us to wait until there's light. He said they weren't far off, but how does he know?"

Charles piled grass clumps back over his legs. "Lie down again. We'll stay warmer."

They got back down low in the hole, piled some prickly grass over themselves, and curled their bodies together, trying to ignore the dead feeling of cold earth against one side of their bodies and the penetrating wind chilling the other.

215

Charles knew from her breathing that Louise was awake. She suddenly said, "They didn't want to show a light. I wonder why."

"Maybe the Russians are coming back for us."

"I doubt it. They thought we'd die out here in a few days. They wouldn't come back unless they had some use for us."

"Ransom?"

"It's a possibility. They think all Americans are rich."

"So they chill us down to show us who's boss, then come back and try to hold us for ransom."

"It's such a long shot for them."

"Because we're old?"

"Yes. There's less chance of anyone caring. That's a bad thought, isn't it?"

"Think they found out about us?"

"I don't think so. They're not that sophisticated. Just powerful and ruthless."

* * *

Dawn finally came. They were shivering and hated to give up the warmth of the other's body. But they sat up and looked around.

They walked off a few yards to pee, some atavistic instinct driving them away from their miserable bed.

As they walked back to their grave-like nest, they heard the cry of a steppe eagle, hunting high above them for his morning meal. With extraordinary vision, these birds could spot a rabbit or a desert vole thousands of feet away, then dive straight down in a silent stoop, flaring their wings at the last minute to brake the descent and sink their talons into the prey. The bird was the national symbol of Kazakhstan, but nothing could've been less representative of the blighted country. The eagle of the steppe was keen-eyed, strong, fast, and faultless in its methods, a predator that couldn't be avoided or stopped. The country was backward, slow, tainted with pervasive corruption, and weak-willed.

As the light increased, they saw a dark area on the eastern horizon, black against the brightening sky. They started walking toward it. It was probably several miles away, but distances were hard to judge against the emptiness. They wanted to run, but their knees were stiff and painful after a cold night, and they settled for a brisk walk. After half an hour of walking the dark spot had grown larger and three-dimensional. It was indeed a helicopter, but it didn't move. Its rotors drooped. Was it disabled or out of fuel? As they approached, a figure detached itself from the machine and came toward them.

"Howdy ma'am, sir."

The youthful Southern drawl was one of the best sounds they'd ever heard. "I'm Lieutenant Tolliver, 101st Airborne, out of Tajikistan. Y'all awright?"

"We're fine. A little chilly."

"We got heat in the chopper and a couple of friends of yours."

When they got closer, they heard the motor quietly idling, and were amazed it was so quiet.

The door on the side opened and hands reached down and helped them up. When the door closed behind them, it was nearly dark again, but it was warm. Voices, American voices, four or five of them, started talking at once, trying to introduce themselves. Tolliver interrupted. "No names just yet." Charles and Louise weren't about to reveal their true identities anyway and were thinking about how to introduce themselves when Charles suddenly stiffened, and said "They're here inside!" Louise knew exactly what he meant and gasped. Both of them wondered if they were being recaptured. Charles started for the door.

The man who'd called himself "Tolliver," next to Charles, took his shoulder and restrained him.

"It's OK," he said. "They're pretty well tied up."

Then he said, "Now how did you know who they were?"

Charles didn't answer, but he was trying to get a better look, in the growing light, at the men in the chopper, and at the same time reviewing the previous conversations, by phone and on the ground, with the helicopter crew, to see how they could've been played into a trap. It didn't add up.

"Your friends are back there." Tolliver pointed and oriented Charles. "Turn the light on Jim-Bob, show these folks our string of catfish."

An overhead light came on, and Charles saw the three Russians who'd kidnapped them. They were seated in a row, hidden behind the helicopter crewmen. The three Russians were leaning forward slightly with their hands behind them, and Charles and Louise knew then that they were handcuffed. The couple relaxed.

"Maybe before we take off and there's too much noise for conversation, I should explain to y'all what has transpired." The combination of Southern drawl and military words was delightful.

"Please."

"We followed that power line up from Kyzel-Orda like ya said 'til we were 135 mahls from Zhez-kaz-gan." He pronounced the name in three distinct syllables. "But it was dark and we knew we weren't goin' t' be able t'see y'all anyhow, and there was some danger of hittin' those wahrs." It took Charles a second to realize he was talking about the overhead wires.

"Just as we were settin' down to wait for light and talkin' to y'all on the phone, we saw a car comin' this way. So we set down and powered off for silence, armed and deployed ourselves and intercepted the car. Lieutenant … Hmmm, here (he hummed instead of saying the lieutenant's name) shot out one of their tahrs. Maybe you heard the shot." They both shook their heads. "And then we were all over them guys, like bees on a bayer."

Charles smiled. He hadn't heard that version of the idiom.

"They made a little show of resistance, but saw soon enough that there wasn't no point to it. And here they are."

"Well, excellent. That takes a big load off our minds. They must've gone home, partied a little, and then realized we might be worth some money."

"But how'd ya know they were in here, sittin' in the dark?"

Charles knew he couldn't tell them the truth; it was possible one of the prisoners spoke some English, and it would've led to a more general disclosure, which was something they never did unless absolutely necessary. Taking a cue from Tolliver's obviously rustic upbringing, Charles took a road away from concealment. "When ah was a boy in Arkansas," he began, suddenly sounding as Arkansan as could be, "Ah had a hay-ound that was the smartest dog you ever seen. He figgered out English purty quick when he was a pup, and could speak it purty well too, though he had a kind of accent you know, like he was from Tennessee or sump'n."

The men laughed, looking at one of them, punching him in the shoulder. Obviously, he was from Tennessee. "Anyhow, that dog loved me cuz ah was the only parent he ever had. We got him from a Star City man travelin' through, before he was even weaned, and ah bottle fed the little pup, so he loved me like ah was his own Momma, and he taught me everything he knew about bein' a dog, about scratchin' fleas, and tail position–that's important ya know–and pissin' on trees high up as you can, and a course, he taught me about smellin' out different things, grouse, rabbits, coons, you name it. And he taught me about smellin' out humans that mean ya harm too. It's not hard. Any of you fellas could do it with a little more trainin' during basic."

Tolliver laughed out loud, and the rest of the guys were smiling or chuckling. Those from deep in the country recognized the tall tale and appreciated it, Tolliver most of all.

"Well, if that ain't the best story I've heard since I've been a Marine, he said, laughing some more. "But now let's get off this desert. Lieutenant, let's take her up."

The men scrambled into flight stations. Someone helped Charles and Louise into seat belts, and the engine revved up and the rotors started to turn, increasing speed until they lurched off the ground. They made a sharp turn and headed south. In an hour, they were over Almaty. They circled down and landed on the roof of the embassy building. Thomas, the marine who'd helped them deal with Werner and Shen, came out to greet them. The Russians were unloaded and taken inside the building and out of sight. The crew waved, and the chopper took off.

Inside the building, they were shown to a small room with a telephone, which they used to call Henderson and give a report. He was relieved to hear that they were alive and well and that the Russians were in custody.

"The Russians will be treated as military prisoners for the time being," he said, "so they can't communicate with Nikita. And maybe they'll be discouraged from messing with Americans."

They also learned that al-Ryadi had made a large transfer to a bank in Aktau, a Kazakh town on the Caspian Sea. Aktau was filled with westerners negotiating the construction of a pipeline to transport oil from the Caspian Sea reserves to European and American markets. The westerners all stay in one hotel, which makes it an obvious target for a suicide bomb, although terrorist activity has been unknown in Kazakhstan. Maybe that was about to change.

Then, the aide who was squiring them around suggested politely that they might want to shower and clean up. Charles and Louise laughed as they realized they were still smudged and stained from spending the night in a hole, covered with coarse grass and roots. They looked like children who'd been playing in the dirt for several hours and encountered a fearful poison turning them prematurely into two old people.

They showered in a room containing several bathrooms with shower stalls. American who get into enough trouble to end up at the Embassy often get dirty at the same time. The showers were hot and the water plentiful, and they reveled in newfound cleanliness. There were thick, white towels available and new toothbrushes, shaving cream, razors, combs, and brushes, in little toiletry kits.

While they showered, their filthy clothes were washed by the Embassy staff, and after the shower they put on fluffy white bathrobes. For an hour, they sat in a small lounge, reading American magazines and newspapers. They were glad to see that the arrests of the Almaty drug ring had been kept out of the papers. The news would break soon enough, and they wanted to be far away when it did.

When their washed and dried clothes were returned, they changed and went to a cafeteria. Over a hearty breakfast they made plans for the next stage of their time in Central Asia.

Charles and Louise weren't sure what they could do to prevent the apparent attack, but Henderson suggested they go to Aktau.

An Embassy car took them to the Almaty airport, where they were waved through gates and checkpoints. From the car they made arrangements for someone to deal with their equipment and luggage.

Their driver took them directly to an Air Force jet. They climbed up a narrow ladder and were strapped into cramped passenger seating. Then the jet was pulled backwards out of the hangar and turned around. It taxied to the runway and was immediately cleared for takeoff. They sat back and enjoyed the luxury. Usually they tried to be anonymous and travel like ordinary citizens, but because of their rescue and arrival at the Embassy, they were treated like heroes.

With the money already in Aktau, every second counted, and they hoped that taking the time to eat breakfast wasn't foolish. Henderson reported, however, that no one had yet withdrawn the money from the bank. He'd informed the Marine Commander of the detail now being set up in Aktau that two American operatives would be on site, and he described but didn't identify them. The Commander was surprised to hear of two elderly American espionage operatives, at least that's how he thought of them, and he wasn't sure he liked the idea having such strange people under his wing.

Charles and Louise didn't consider themselves either strange or under the Commander's wing. For them, it was simple coordination to make their presence and descriptions known to the Marine Commander. But they were also unhappy with the arrangement. It was getting too public. But there was no choice, considering the gravity and urgency.

Chapter 35
The Target

During the flight to Aktau, they considered what they might be able to do. "There will be at least one other person, in addition to the bomber himself, who'll be part of the operation," Charles said.

"Someone to hold his hand, or at least pretend to be holding it, while in fact they make sure the attack actually takes place," offered Louise.

"Right," said Charles. "I'm sure that there's always some temptation for the bomber to take the money and run, or hand it over to his family and then hide from the terrorist network, hard as that might be. There must be some kind of handler, maybe more than one, who makes sure the bomber does his work."

"How does the money get to the bomber's family?" Louise asked.

"Maybe the handlers take care of that too," Charles offered.

"Mmm. Maybe," said Louise, "but I'll bet the bomber doesn't trust the handlers to deliver the funds any more than the handlers trust the bomber to blow himself up."

"Do you think they deliver the funds first, before the attack?" Charles asked.

"I can't think of any other way the bomber could be sure his family would actually benefit from his act."

"Of course," Charles noted, "some of the bombers do it for the glory of martyrdom and don't need any money, but in this case we know money is the incentive, and since the bomber dies in the operation, the money has to go to his family."

"The family must be right here in Aktau then," Louise said.

"Another possibility is that it's handled by a *hawaladar*," Charles said.

"Yes, maybe," Louise countered, "but we've already seen that they're either unwilling or unable to use that system. No, I'll bet the family is very near by, but don't know their son or daughter is about to blow himself up. They get the money, and before they get over the sudden windfall, they find they have to arrange a funeral."

Charles wasn't so sure. "How could they be sure of finding a willing bomber in the same town where they wanted to attack?"

"Maybe they choose the location because a willing bomber lives in the area," said Louise. "The family would be close by too."

"That makes sense," Charles concluded. "But I still think that they wouldn't want to deliver money to the family before the attack. And also, if the family knows about the attack beforehand, wouldn't they try to stop it?"

"So, what you're saying is that the bomber has to trust the handlers to deliver the money to the family after the attack," she said.

"I don't see how it could work any other way," he said.

"That's a lot of trust, Louise commented.

"Yes," said Charles, "but the bombers are usually young and idealistic."

"OK. So the family is in the same town but doesn't know what's going to happen."

"Right," said Charles. But that doesn't help us very much, unless we can identify the family before the bombing and tip them off, so they can try to change the bomber's mind. I can't see how we can identify the family until we identify the bomber."

"I know," said Louise, "but when we get there, we can start nosing around. Something may turn up."

"Yes," answered Charles. "Something may, but it's going to have to turn up very fast."

"Mmmm."

The target was obvious–the hotel where the Europeans and Americans stayed. The U.S. delegation was the largest group, occupying a whole floor. Charles and Louise would be staying there, too.

Both the bank and the hotel were already staked out so that no one could approach them without detection. The bank was equipped so that the moment account was accessed, the entire stakeout team would know. As the person making the withdrawal left the bank, an agent posing as a bank customer would leave just after him, alerting those watching from the outside. The idea was to identify the handler, or handlers, before the bomber could arm his bomb and carry out the attack.

That was the situation when they arrived in Aktau. More than thirty people were in the stakeout, although only six were on the scene at any one time. Charles and Louise made two more. There was always a danger that the bomber or the handler would look things over and discover the stakeout before making the withdrawal. Everyone took great care, usually in disguise, in approaching or leaving the scene. The Marine sharpshooters were hidden on the roofs of neighboring buildings.

The hotel was a different scene. There, the idea was to make sure the security was clearly visible. They hoped the bomber, seeing how well guarded the hotel was, would abandon the attempt or at least be identified, stopped, and disarmed. At the airport the Marines screened every new arrival. Everyone knew, however, that the handlers had probably already arrived. Or, the handlers might be a sleeper cell set up in the town long ago, waiting to be activated.

Looking over the scene, Charles and Louise thought no one could fail to see the extra protection, and they'd call off the whole operation, perhaps go somewhere else and transfer the money to a new target. That wouldn't be so bad, but capturing the bomber and any others before they did any harm would be even better. But probably the attackers had already arrived, reconnoitered, and were going forward. Catching the person taking the money out of the bank was the most likely way to stop the plot.

The terrorists would surely want to carry out the bombing as soon as the money was withdrawn. Or worse, the terrorists might persuade the bomber to go ahead with only the promise of payment, or with faked evidence that the money'd been transferred, so the bombing could take place without the money being withdrawn, and that was the only point at which a sure identification could be made.

Charles and Louise figured their best chance to be helpful was to hang out in the village and see if anyone was here from out of town. Almost everyone in Aktau was from out of town, but certain types–Arabs in particular–would be more suspicious than others.

Henderson had arranged for a Marine Communications Officer to keep them informed, so they knew what was going on at the bank and the hotel–nothing. The Communications Officer didn't know who they were, only a code name, like many in the operation. If anyone showed up at the bank, or if a known terrorist arrived at the airport, Charles and Louise would know immediately.

Posing as American journalists, they stayed at the targeted hotel. When they checked in, their luggage had already arrived from Zhezkazgan and was in a storage room. They were on the same floor as the rest of the Americans, which made Charles a little nervous, and he looked out the window at the scene on the street. Louise had a different reaction. All her senses were on high alert, a feeling that was familiar to her from previous missions. The upshot of this increased energy was a powerful sexual urgency, of which Charles was the chief beneficiary. This relieved Charles' anxieties about being in the target hotel. Both of them slept well, once they settled down.

Chapter 36
Aktau

The first night passed uneventfully. The next day, Charles decided to adopt a disguise. He spoke Turkish fluently, but only a little Arabic, although he understood it. With the application of some skin stain and other make-up, he could pass for Turkish. There was some risk in adopting any disguise. Discovery by a real Turk would arouse suspicion.

While he was getting ready, Louise set up the computer and let Henderson, and through him the Marine Communications Officer, know they were on the scene. There were some messages for them. Al-Ryadi was being closely watched in Almaty but wouldn't be picked up until the Aktau situation had been clarified. If al-Ryadi's contacts in Saudi Arabia heard that he'd been arrested, they might call off the Aktau operation, letting one or more terrorists get away. So, in spite of the danger to westerners in Aktau, it was thought best not to arrest al-Ryadi just now.

Henderson also told them that the President had asked when something might happen regarding MOLP. There was no pressure from Henderson. He knew how Charles and Louise worked to have everything aligned, set up, and organized, before pulling the trigger. But they felt pressured anyway. All they had to do was write a letter to a Paris newspaper to complete their mission. But they hesitated for two reasons. First, the embarrassment of MOLP would be greater if it were connected to a terrorist plot. His connection would be indirect and coincidental, but might still influence the election. The second reason was somewhat the opposite. They were having second thoughts. They didn't want to destroy the man, just put him on the defensive for a while so as to influence the election.

They thought this bucket of stones should be brought down on MOLP's head once the terrorist plot was exposed. They would then have a better idea of what was the right thing to do.

Charles went into the market, dressed and made up to look Turkish and acting like a Turkish emissary to the pipeline talks. The American government wanted the pipeline to go through Turkey, which had a long history of friendly relations with the U.S. But Charles, disguised as a Turk, had to steer clear of any genuine Turks, who would immediately know he was an imposter. He wanted to be able to approach Arabs, who wouldn't see through his Turkish disguise and wouldn't expect him to speak perfect Arabic. He thought Arabs would be most likely to have information about a plot to bomb the hotel.

He walked through the bazaar, fingering garments, asking prices, looking at displays, and listening to snatches of conversation. Whenever he heard Arabic, he'd surreptitiously get a good look at the speaker. He was looking for a certain type–young certainly, male or female, likely posing as Jordanian, because the Jordanians were accepted by everyone, but more likely to be Palestinian or Saudi, less likely Iraqi or Yemeni. The bomber would be a person, male or female, of Arabic descent living in Aktau but staying out of sight. But the handlers might come out into the public, and they were the ones Charles was looking for.

Aktau was a town that had grown too fast. Once a small port–the Caspian Sea afforded some trade routes but none very important–and before that a fishing village, now it swarmed with foreigners and was inundated with money. The markets often ran out of goods, their supply lines unable to ship fast enough to match demand, particularly items wanted by westerners–sunglasses, Coca-Cola, pens and pencils, electronics, and batteries. But everything was in short supply, even food. In the restaurants, patrons were given a menu, studied it while the waiter stood patiently by, then discovered that what they wanted wasn't available. Usually very little on the menu was available. It would've been better to post a sign that said "We have mutton today," but the owners knew that getting the customers in the restaurant and seated was the main thing. Then it was OK to tell them what the kitchen had.

Charles took care to stay downwind of anyone he thought looked the least bit suspicious. He was looking, or smelling, for any of the distinctive odors of explosives. If someone were carrying explosives, Charles would detect it immediately, but this would be most unlikely. What Charles expected was the more subtle scent of someone who'd handled explosives, building a bomb-vest for example. The scent would be strongest on the person's hands, although it could be reduced by washing. More likely it would linger on the fabric of any garments that had brushed against explosive material.

He spent the day in the market, spotted some men who might be Middle Eastern and got close to them, but detected nothing. He went back to the hotel discouraged. Louise was out, exploring the town, getting oriented.

He reviewed the way explosives could be brought into the town. Airport security wasn't very strict, but detection would result in confiscation of the explosive. Train or car, even by boat seemed more likely. There was no security on the overland entrances to the city, and the security measures for arrivals by sea were laughably lax.

Chapter 37

C4

Charles changed out of his Turkish disguise, which hadn't served his purpose well, into the more natural role of American journalist. Then he called Louise on her cell phone.

They met up for lunch in a small place with tables outside and air conditioning inside. It was the first air conditioning they'd seen in Kazakhstan, where the summer heat was brutal. Even now, in late May, midday was uncomfortably hot. They sat outside anyway, knowing that a few minutes of sitting still would let them feel comfortable, and that they could survey passersby.

The restaurant advertised western food, and they found hamburgers, French fries, fried chicken, and pizza on the menu. They decided that the fried chicken would be the most difficult to ruin, and luckily it was available. As in Zhezkazgan and Almaty, they felt conspicuous as Americans. There were others in town, but they seemed the only ones willing to show themselves. A group of men went by speaking Italian with characteristic vigor, and they heard Spanish with a South American accent from another group. The scene was cosmopolitan, like Almaty but with smaller numbers.

Their chicken came, and it was acceptable. Not like home, but good enough. After lunch, they walked past the bazaar to the water. A sea wall protected the town from the occasional storm, and they walked along it. The humid air that drifted in from the sea was unlike the Kazakhstan they knew, and it reminded them of their home on the Virginia shore. They saw no one suspicious and went back to the bazaar.

They were pushed and jostled by people, particularly around the vegetables where some sort of special offering was being made. As Charles peered over a number of heads, trying to see what was going on, a slight breeze blew over his back, and he caught a faint but unmistakable odor. It was the smell of C4, a powerful explosive used by the military. It was just what he had been on alert for, and his reaction was instantaneous. He whirled around, bumping hard against a very small, thick Kazakh lady trying to see the counter. The confusion and apologies took only a second, but when he looked up he saw nothing obvious. Three men, however, were walking away from him. The aisles among the various vendors took a 90° bend at this point, and it looked as though the three had approached in one aisle then turned down the other. Charles grabbed Louise's arm and tried to follow the three men, but the crowd got in their way, and the three men disappeared. Charles and Louise walked briskly along the aisle but didn't see them again.

But the implication was ominous: there was, here in Aktau, someone who'd recently been close to C4. When Charles explained what he'd smelled back by the vegetables, Louise asked him a few pointed questions. How sure was he, from one sniff, that it was C4 and not overripe bananas or something? The bazaar was filled with many smells. But he was sure he'd smelled C4. He'd tried before to explain the physiology of olfaction to her. Smell was the best sense for identification. Particular molecules floating in the air locked themselves physically to precisely matching cells in the nose. Once the person knew a particular odor, it was nearly impossible to mistake the identification.

She also wanted to know how he knew the scent had come from the three men whose backs he'd seen, as they walked away. Wasn't it hard to see them because of the people in his way? Charles' answers to these questions were less certain. He knew the direction the scent had come from, based on the waft of air that drifted across his back, but he hadn't been able to turn around quickly, and the scene had changed slightly.

But he knew there was C4 in Aktau. And the Marine Commander in charge of the stakeouts should know about it. They had to contact Henderson, who would then call the Commander. Henderson knew Charles' abilities, but even he might be skeptical about Charles' identification.

They found a quiet spot and called him on the satphone. He asked the same questions Louise had and got the same answers. He was convinced that Charles had detected the presence of explosives in Aktau. He called the Commander, but the Commander found it hard to believe the report and didn't pass the information on to the men watching the bank and hotel. Not that it mattered. Everyone was already on alert.

Charles found it frustrating when people undervalued his skill, as they often did, so he redoubled his efforts to identify the men, knowing there was little time left. Louise put the telephoto lens on her camera and got out her tiny digital camera, too. Either camera could take a picture without alerting the subject. Together they walked around the streets, coming back to the bazaar often.

Chapter 38
The Bomber

Louise was taking pictures for their scenic value, thinking of sending some to her grandchildren when they got their second look at the three terrorists.

She was capturing a long view of the streets with the Caspian in the background, trying to get a picture of the street with no people in it because the contrast of the white buildings in the sunlight with the sea in the background pleased her. She'd just snapped the shutter as three figures walked around the corner and spoiled the shot. She didn't even notice them at the time, but back in the hotel room she transferred the file and brought it up to the screen.

"Those damned three guys!" she cursed. Charles heard the curse first because Louise didn't often say "damned." She'd been brought up as the only child in a household of missionary women, and cursing wasn't part of her speech. His second reaction was to the number three.

"Wait! Don't delete it!"

He came and stood behind her, peering at the screen. The three men had just walked around the corner and were facing the camera, but they were too far away to see the camera and also too far for their faces to be seen. Louise, taking a picture of the wider scene, hadn't been using the telephoto lens. But these must be the same men Charles had seen the previous day, two of average height, one several inches shorter, all three wearing western clothes. She zoomed in and in spite of the distance they could see that their somewhat dark-skinned, and the two taller men had mustaches but not the shorter one. Maybe the short one was actually a woman, or a boy.

They called Henderson, who passed it on to the Marine Commander, but his skepticism remained, since the importance of this sighting depended on the earlier information. Surely these were the same three men Charles had seen in the bazaar, but the Marine was still not convinced they had anything to do with explosives.

Charles and Louise quickly went to the area where the three figures had been photographed. It was several blocks west of the bazaar and about the same distance from the bank. There were several banks in Aktau, but no branches, so it was obvious where a large withdrawal would be made. They walked toward the bank, hoping they wouldn't run into the trio.

Outside the bank, a taxi waited across the street with two men in the back seat. The back door on the side facing the bank was open. It wasn't obvious, looking through the windshield into the shaded interior, but Louise thought they were two of the three men from her picture. Charles had no doubts. The wind blew from the taxi toward him, and mingled with the smell of engine oil and exhaust fumes was the unmistakable odor of C4, and in quantity. They knew immediately that the third man was in the bank getting the money, and the bomber himself was sitting in the cab with the other handler. Worst of all, the bomber was armed and ready to detonate the device as soon as he knew the money was out of the bank and ready to be delivered to his family.

"It's them," Charles said quietly to Louise, "and he's wearing the bomb." He pushed Louise toward a storefront off to the side, hoping to get her where she'd be protected from a blast, but she resisted the shove and stayed next to him.

In the bank a withdrawal slip had been presented to a teller, who recognized the account number and was complying with the withdrawal request, as she'd been instructed in training, simultaneously pressing a button under the counter with a trembling hand. She pressed the button, but the terrorist saw her hand trembling and knew what it meant. He knew he'd been made. He didn't wait for the money. He took an ominous-looking machine pistol from beneath his jacket and turned around. The Marine posing as a customer in the bank heard the alarm in his earpiece, saw the man take out his gun, and hesitated. Should he still try to follow the man out of the bank? It seemed unproductive and risky. He did nothing.

A Marine guard, stationed in a small room where he couldn't be seen, heard the alarm sound in his earpiece and went into full alert, grabbed the automatic weapon lying in his lap, clicked off the safety, and opened the door. He saw the terrorist backing toward the front door with his automatic pistol displayed. The young Marine brought his automatic up into firing position, but the terrorist had begun to train his weapon as soon as the door started to open and squeezed off several rounds before the Marine's weapon had reached horizontal. The Marine crumpled in the doorway, his weapon clattering on the floor as his body wedged open the door. People screamed.

Outside, the men staking out the bank heard the alarm and were moving into position, clicking off weapon safeties when they heard the shots. To a man they swore under their breaths. Weapons fired inside the bank could mean only bad news.

For the second handler, sitting in the taxi, it was a moment of decision. In a few seconds, he realized from the gunfire that the suicide bombing couldn't happen, and he decided to save his own skin. He opened the taxi's other rear door and ran. The Marine Commander could tell by the speed of his movements that he wasn't carrying bulky explosives and ordered a marksman on the roof of the bank to fire. He fell like a running deer.

The cab driver was slower to realize what was happening. He'd looked toward the bank at the sound of shots but with more curiosity than fear. Nothing dangerous ever happened in his town. But when he saw the man he'd driven backing out of the bank, a machine pistol in his hand with wisps of smoke coming out of the muzzle, he knew he wanted no part of the scene. He opened his door and ran for a doorway only a few feet away. The Marine Commander barked an order not to fire.

The taxi driver got inside the store. Some people were dropping to the floor, while others foolishly looked out the window. This left the bomber sitting alone in the taxi, realizing that things had gone completely wrong.

Charles and Louise were only thirty feet away and started toward the waiting taxi. They saw the handler shot as he ran. From the roof a bullhorn sounded deafeningly with the English word "Freeze!" It wasn't directed at them, but they obeyed anyway, stopping in their tracks.

The man who'd backed out of the bank turned, saw his cohort fall and saw the cab driver run away. His zeal to carry out the attack, fueled by getting himself out of the bank, got the better of his judgment, and he started to aim his gun at the young man in the back of the cab to detonate the explosive. But several sharpshooters already had their weapons trained on him, and they quickly saw his intention. The Marine Commander ordered them to fire, and they did. The terrorist fell to the ground, and his weapon discharged as he fell, spraying rounds around the street, one of which whistled past Charles and Louise. They ducked, but by the time they ducked the bullets had sped past them.

There remained only the young man still sitting in the car. He made no threatening move. The Marine Commander knew he must be carrying explosives, but only Charles knew there was enough C4 in the taxi to level the surrounding buildings. Louise instinctively started to take pictures.

Charles walked toward the car, shouting "wait" in Arabic, then a phrase he hoped meant "take it easy, calm down." His voice steadied, and he began to say whatever came into his head. His Arabic wasn't that good, but he could say, "What's your name?" and "Where are you from?" These phrases barely penetrated the young man's bewildered mind. He was shaking violently and had peed in his pants. At first the wetness and warmth of the urine was puzzling. Maybe he'd been shot and was bleeding. The friendly voice asked him where he was from, which was confusing. But the thought that he might need medical help made him climb slowly out of the cab, looking back at the seat to see if there was blood, but finding none and looking down he realized from the smell that he'd wet himself. Suddenly he felt like a child, even younger than the 14 he was.

Charles continued to approach, now able to smile a little and continuing to talk. "It's OK. I can help you. Don't worry. It'll be OK." He said anything he could think of that would be soothing. As he got closer, he could see tears flowing down the boy's cheeks, as he slowly opened his jacket to reveal the vest, bulky with explosives. He was saying, "I'm sorry. I'm sorry." over and over again.

Charles made gestures with his hands intended to wave off anyone thinking of firing. The Commander saw him and saw the bomb vest and realized that firing would be both dangerous and unnecessary. He gave the order to put weapons on safety. The Marines complied. The boy stood still, arms at his side. Charles was saying, "Just stand still. It's going to be OK." Louise came up and looked at the boy with deep sympathy. She took one of his hands and touched his face, wiping away the tears. "Tell him what's going to happen," she said to Charles. "We don't want to surprise him. He's already terrified."

At the sound of English, the boy's eyes widened, but Louise's face reminded him of his grandmother. That, and Charles' repetition of "It's all right" kept him calm. Charles then told him in Arabic that men were going to come and help him get out of the vest. The boy nodded. He was eager to get out of it. "Don't take it off now," Charles said. "Wait. They'll help you."

They came, dressed in heavy garb and wearing helmets with transparent material over their faces. They looked like astronauts to the boy. He was still nervous but holding on.

"Who are these old people?" one bomb squad man said to another as they approached.

"I don't know, but they're keeping the guy calm."

Moving slowly, they slipped one of the boy's arms out of the jacket, making sure no triggering device connected the jacket to the bomb. Then they inspected the other arm.

"Keep talking to him," one of them said to Charles, who complied with more soothing words in Arabic. He couldn't think of anything new to say, so he kept repeating what he'd said before. Louise held the boy's hand, and he looked at her as if she were an angel. Having made sure that there was no trigger connecting the jacket to the vest, they slowly slipped the jacket off and dropped it on the ground. Now they'd have to remove the vest itself, but at least they could see it now.

The marksmen, too, wondered about the older couple, but they'd already been ordered not to fire, and their weapons were on safety. The Commander told the bomb squad men to continue. And they did, with the necessary care and patience, sometimes asking Charles to translate an instruction. He did his best. It wasn't perfect but it worked. The whole operation took about a half an hour. As they slowly slipped his arms out of the vest, his legs were shaking, and Charles and Louise had to hold his arms for support, carefully alternating as the vest was removed. When it was finally off and placed on the ground, the young man's legs were barely able to support his weight, and Charles and Louise helped him to the waiting custody of a couple of Marines. He was so glad to be out of the bomb vest he felt no fear of the Marines, although he should have.

Charles asked the Marines to go easy on him–he was young and desperate, but Charles knew he'd never know freedom again.

Both Charles and Louise felt close to the young man; proximity to enough C4 to blow a person into hamburger apparently was a bonding experience. They wanted to visit him during subsequent days, and he would've wanted it too, but they knew they'd be denied access. No crime was more serious than an attempted suicide bombing. But they continued to feel connected to the young man, and were sorry they had no way to express it.

After some time, the taxi driver crept back to his vehicle and was permitted, after some questioning, to drive away, disgusted at having to get the back seat cleaned. The people in nearby shops were evacuated because the live bomb still lay in the middle of the street.

Charles and Louise also left quickly in the confusion so they wouldn't have to give an account of what they'd seen. They seized an opportunity while the bomb vest was being covered with a heavy steel mesh. They went to their hotel room and quickly packed up their equipment, called Henderson to get transportation to Almaty, and were away from Aktau before anyone could figure out who they were. Their anonymity was one of their strongest weapons, and they protected it.

Chapter 39
The Trigger

"It's time to pull the trigger," Charles said.

"I know. But I'm reluctant," Louise answered, shaking her head.

They were back in Almaty, in a hotel room overlooking one of the main squares, now turned brown in the summer heat. They were waiting for a flight to Frankfurt, after which they would go on to Paris. Flights from Almaty left only twice a week, and they still had a day to go. They couldn't get on a military flight now that the situation was calm, and they knew it.

On the street Kazakhstanis were beginning to find out that a drama of international terrorism had occurred. They talked about it excitedly in the cafés and on the streets. Charles and Louise would've enjoyed sitting in a café and eavesdropping on these conversations, but they still had a few details to wrap up before they could "pull the trigger."

They'd made all the arrangements–hacked into bank accounts, changed figures in withdrawals and deposits, connected a lot of dots, and doctored up photographs. Charles was composing an anonymous letter to *Le Monde*, which would start the scandal.

They were hesitant, particularly Louise. "Maybe it could begin a new era of friendship between our two countries," she said.

"You mean not starting the scandal, but telling the French press that we could've if we'd wanted to?"

"Exactly."

"But France and the U.S. are already in an era of friendship. Revealing our plans could only derail it." He shared her opinion, but for different reasons.

"OK, but only for a while," she said.

He screwed up his face, wearing his indecision like a rubber mask. "It isn't that simple. Still, it wouldn't be out of line to ask Henderson to check with the big boss."

Louise was placated, but not happy. She muttered things about testosterone and schoolyard fights.

In the end they wrote a joint email to Henderson, arguing for restraint, noting that trying to alter the policies of other countries was profoundly undemocratic, and sent it off. Henderson reacted predictably. He called the President to ask for time and wasn't surprised to get it. The President had been briefed and knew how dangerous the situation had been for Charles and Louise and what an important part they'd played in preventing the bombing, which entitled them to some of his time.

Later that day, Henderson called them on the secure line.

"What did he say?" Louise asked.

"Nothing really. He can't just alter existing policy on a whim."

"It's no whim," Louise reacted strongly.

"No, of course not," Henderson said, backing down. "But he still has to talk to his people, Congressional leaders, etc., before moving on it."

"OK. So where does that leave us?"

"You'll have to wait, but he'll be in touch."

And they hung up.

"Well, that's not very satisfying," Louise said to Charles.

"No, but really, what else could you expect?"

Waiting in their hotel room, they felt a profound sense of accomplishment at their successes, mixed with relief at having survived a very close call. Louise, as usual after having been in danger, was feeling sexual urges. Charles saw the signs but decided to make her wait a little, which he knew increased her pleasure. He sang a song that showed the strength of his baritone voice–"City of New Orleans"–then switched to gentler songs he knew she liked: Woody Guthrie's "Hobo Lullaby" and "She's My Curly Headed Baby." She brought out her harmonica and played with him but was glad when they stopped and went to bed. Looking at her while they made love, smiling with joy and tenderness, Charles moved slowly, and Louise raised her voice at the end in a series of moans, throbbing with pleasure. Then the waves crested, her legs felt numb, and she had a profound need to sleep. Charles too was totally spent, and they both slept deeply and long.

The next day, they finished packing up, checked out, and went to the airport. Their flight to Frankfurt left in midmorning, and the small Almaty airport offered little. Charles found a book in his carry-on and settled down. Louise pulled out her journal and began writing, not about their mission—she never wrote about that—but about her feelings and thoughts. Self-reflection was a prominent trait.

Eventually their Lufthansa flight was called, and they boarded the plane, and immediately they left Central Asia and entered Europe. As the plane took off they saw out the window the flat steppes and the patchwork of windbreak trees receding, and the post-Soviet poverty and struggle fading into their past.

Charles was in one of his philosophical moods and dwelt on the suddenness of their departure.

"In the days of the Silk Road," he said, "leaving Kazakhstan would've been a slow process—a string of braying camels, their bells tinkling—stopping each night to set up tents and feed and water the animals. There were no national borders. The food, music, and clothing would change with imperceptible slowness. New kinds of people and variations in the landscape would loom, appear, pass. Even the language would change slowly, with more people speaking the language of an approaching country, and then, after you'd crossed the border, many would still speak the language of the country you'd just left."

They'd been able to sit together, and Charles was engrossed in his monologue, which Louise attended to from time to time, intermittently tuning him out without missing much. It reminded her of being a student–listening, taking notes, then daydreaming for a while and missing a little, then coming back to attention.

The loudspeaker blared, first in German, than in Russian, that those not going on to other destinations must fill out a German entry card.

"It still seems too slow," he said, nodding his head in the general direction of the loudspeaker. He was feeling grouchy, not having had lunch, and he slouched in his seat. Louise reached over and held his hand.

"It won't be long," she said.

He was always surprised, sometimes even grateful, when she read his mind, and he squeezed her hand affectionately. She smiled and tried to put her head on his shoulder, but the configuration of the airplane seats didn't allow it, and she gave up. International work was often exciting, even too exciting, followed by hours of boredom and discomfort.

Lunch was a combination of German and Kazakh influence, countering Charles' notion that modern cultural transitions take place at warp speed. They wolfed it down in silence. When she'd scraped the last morsel from her plate, and sipped at a cup of decent coffee, Louise said, "Do you think he'll change his mind?"

Charles knew she meant the President. "I don't know. We've seen him adopt lots of new policies."

"And the economy is happy about them."

"Absolutely. The whole country knows we're back on track, starting with the stock market." He pointed to a German headline in the paper he held–*The market has hit another new high*. He shook his head. "But about the other thing, I don't think so."

"Why not?" she asked.

"The policy is important to international relations. All countries have been working that way for a long time. No one's going to give it up," he answered.

"Humph." Louise's nonverbal response meant that she thought international relations would be better if left to women. She knew it was a dated view, and impractical besides, but she still felt that international antagonisms were largely caused by the belligerence and bellicosity of men.

Charles heard and understood. "That was the antitestosteronal 'harrumph' if I'm not mistaken."

"The countries of the world act like little boys in the playground," she said.

"Maybe," he said. "It's not an unfair comparison. But international relations aren't the same as personal relations. They're less civil."

"Why is that? Countries are made up of people," she argued.

"There are a lot of reasons, I think. When leaders make decisions, only their countrymen are present," Charles offered.

"They have summits," she threw in.

"But not always. Day-to-day decisions are made in state departments, with others who discuss the issues in the same language," he said. "They don't hear the other side."

"Well, why don't they have continuous summits?" she asked.

"Like the UN?" He felt a small sense of triumph.

"Oh." She realized the obvious with a corresponding letdown.

He shook his head. "But it's still the same problem. Even when representatives of other countries are there, they all caucus among themselves, reach a joint decision, and then have it translated."

"Do you think language is the main barrier?" Sometimes Charles saw language at the center of the universe.

"Language and culture. And the fear of strangers." He gestured toward the other passengers.

"There ought to be a United Nations of Women." Louise's eyes brightened and she turned toward him.

"There's a yearly International Women's Conference. "

"And so far they've looked only at women's issues, which is fine. Maybe they'll start looking at broader issues from a woman's perspective."

"It's an interesting idea," he agreed.

They lapsed into silence, wondering what a Women's U.N. would be like.

Charles wasn't ready to let the topic drop. "There are other reasons."

"For what?"

"For why international relations aren't as civil as personal ones."

"OK. Why?"

"There's much more at stake," he suggested.

"That's a reason to be more civil, not less," she argued.

"Maybe, but I don't think it works that way." He thought for a minute. "And there are politics to factor in, too."

"How so?"

"The decision-makers are always playing to an audience. Keeping their power depends on the audience. It changes everything."

"You can say that again," she commented.

He didn't, and they lapsed into silence.

The flight droned on, and they both fell asleep. A change in the plane's position woke them both up and the captain announced came that they were approaching Frankfurt Airport.

Once off the plane, they looked up their flight to Paris and ambled to the new departure gate, slumped in chairs there, and waited. Louise found a telephone line and logged on. Henderson had met with the President, who would write to them soon. She told Charles with considerable excitement. The President didn't usually correspond with them during an assignment.

This exciting information made the time pass even more slowly. Charles read newspapers. Louise wrote in her journal. After a while they watched people. Airport people looked different from street people–wealthier, more purposeful, but bored and frustrated, sometimes in very bad moods. They counted the people they thought were in a bad mood. They made up stories about why these people were in bad moods, and the stories got more and more outlandish.

With more than two hours to go before their flight, the gate area had been nearly empty. But now it was filling rapidly. No more seats were available, and people began to sit on the floor, arranging themselves along the outside walls, pillars, or anything that offered back support. Their projected stories about the people sitting around them helped pass the time, but soon Charles grew philosophical again.

"There isn't much incentive to make airports more comfortable, is there?" he asked rhetorically.

Louise glanced briefly in his direction, and went back to journaling. She took up self-reflection whenever circumstances permitted. It reduced emotional reactions and thoughts that might otherwise create noise in the complex system that she was. As a result, she was able to deal with straightforwardly with reality, orienting herself, not just geographically, but to immediate events with ease and speed.

Charles' response to her preoccupation was a monologue, usually silent, but occasionally vocal, as now. The monologues served him somewhat the same way her journals helped her, freeing his mind of the extraneous comments, conclusions, creations, and calculations, like so much pressurized steam, clearing the pipes and valves for any productive work that might come along. He'd given up on reading.

"No traveler decides to route his trip through Frankfurt instead of Mannheim or Bern, certainly not those paying for the flight. So why should the airport be comfortable?" He stopped, remembering Kerimov's argument about quality and trying to apply it to airport design, but failed to put the pieces together.

Charles saw Louise busily writing in her journal and realized he'd been rambling, and talking to himself, and he shut up.

He looked around at the people in the gate area, thinking they'd all be on the flight to Paris. He looked around the room, to see if there was anyone suspicious looking, an old habit. Everyone looked quite normal. He was glad; he'd had enough excitement for a while. The Aktau episode was still fresh in his mind, and in Louise's, he guessed, from the extent of her journaling. They'd been in danger many times, and it always left them thinking, almost obsessively, over the recent events.

Often they dreamed about these moments of danger, and in the dreams the recent events reoccurred but with dire consequences. If they'd escaped being shot, the bullets in the dream hit. If they'd been left to starve in the desert, as recently outside Zhezkazgan, in the dream the satphone battery died before they could contact rescuers, or the rescuers failed to find them, or the Russian mafia guys reached them before the Marines and held them prisoner for months. There was no limit to the number of alternative morbid possibilities. Within weeks or months, however, the morbid dreams stopped.

They both thought about the Marine who'd been shot inside the bank. He and the terrorist who fled from the taxi were flown to a medical facility in Germany. Though both had been seriously wounded, they were recovering. The other terrorist died on the ground outside the bank before he had a chance to detonate the explosives on the young man's body. The suicide bomber himself was taken into custody and not heard from again. They wondered what happened to the large sum of money in the Aktau account. The terrorist had presented a valid withdrawal slip, so legally the money had been withdrawn, even though the teller hadn't completed the transaction. They hoped it was put to good use.

They watched their plane being brought to the gate, watched fuel trucks and baggage trucks discharge their loads into it, and saw the pilot and flight crew get on board. All of these activities only accentuated their own inactivity and made the time pass more slowly.

Eventually their flight was announced, and they lined up at the gate and trundled onto the plane, stowing their carry-on bags, coats, cameras, and packages, and slid into their seats for the next round of waiting. There were no delays, and the flight pulled away from the gate on time, waved at by a collection of German well-wishers, and then taxied to the end of the runway. After a brief wait for clearance, they roared into the sky toward Paris.

In Paris, they retrieved their stowed luggage and took a taxi from the airport to a hotel, different from the one they'd stayed in a few weeks earlier. They checked in, two aging American journalists with a lot of camera and computer equipment. They didn't think of themselves as needing many amenities, but they were still grateful for those of Paris.

When Louise logged on, she found a note from the President himself, using a code name and a secure email connection. He was thoughtful and to the point.

I fully appreciate the sentiment expressed in your recent letter, and I have thought carefully about it. The possibility of beginning a new way of dealing with the world, possibly even ushering in an era of relationships with countries based on values more spiritual than physical is exciting to me. I would like the U.S. to take the lead in the beginning of such an era. I have balanced these possibilities against the possibility that other countries might see the U.S. as a paper tiger. I believe in your arguments as a matter of principle and have appointed a commission to study them and report back to me. But for now, I need you to go ahead with your plan.

They were both pleased and disappointed. Pleased certainly that the President had heard, understood, even agreed with their ideas, but disappointed that a different policy couldn't be immediately implemented. And a commission! It was a way to discard impractical suggestions, but the President might take it seriously and follow up. He'd always been a straight talker.

Of course he had to act in ways that reflected policy, and he couldn't change policy without study and reflection by himself and many other knowledgeable, thoughtful people. Otherwise, history would judge him as frivolous or whimsical. So, perhaps this was the best they could've hoped for. Somewhat heartened, but still with regret, they went forward as directed.

Chapter 40
The Press Release

Louise finished altering the records of Shen's bank account, making it look as though he'd made several transfers to an account in the name of MOLP's closest associate, the Minister of Agriculture. Her changes made it look as if they'd occurred some time ago. She altered the Minister's account to reflect the same incoming transfers. She also altered the records of a prominent Parisian travel agency and that of the Agricultural Minister so that they showed a transfer, reflecting airfare from Almaty to Martinique. The picture that they'd worked so hard to create when they were in Paris before was doctored so that the envelope showed, when electronically enlarged, the address of the same travel agency. Finally, Charles finished writing a press release, directed to *Le Monde*, Paris' most respected newspaper, as follows:

For immediate release: Anonymous sources have informed Le Monde that Monsieur Le President has ties, both sentimental and financial, to a recently discovered and apprehended drug trafficking group centered in Almaty, Kazakhstan, but with associates in Marseilles, Rome, Moscow, and other cities. A number of deaths by overdose have occurred as a result of the unique method by which the drugs were concealed and shipped. The connection with our President was originally established through a former girlfriend, Mme Tuttlies-Fourget of Marseilles, but communication has more recently occurred between MOLP and Mme Tuttlies-Fourget's son, Werner Tatinan. It is not certain at this time if the Almaty man is actually the natural son of our President. Shen Guo, a Korean citizen and apparent ringleader of the drug ring, was arrested last week in Kazakhstan while attempting to flee to Korea.

In addition, the profits from the drugs made in Almaty have been used to fund Muslim fundamentalist suicide attacks in a number of countries, one of which was recently thwarted in Aktau, a city on the Caspian Sea, where vast reserves of oil have recently been uncovered. The main financial backer, Azamat Ahmedovich al-Ryadi, was arrested on Saturday in Almaty, shortly after the attempted bombing in Aktau.

The accompanying photograph shows the Minister of Agriculture, M. Mijoux, the President's long-time friend and closest associate, giving an envelope containing confirmation of electronic airplane tickets to M. Costil, a confederate of M. Tatinan. The tickets were used by M. Tatinan to travel from Almaty to Martinique in order to evade capture. M. Tatinan was, however, captured anyway by American drug enforcement authorities several days later in Martinique, presumably at the request of the Kazakhstan government. Also shown are printed electronic records of bank accounts, showing the transfer of funds from al-Ryadi's account to banks in cities where suicide attacks have been attempted or carried out in recent years. The timing of these transfers makes them highly suspicious. The seized records of Mr. Shen reveal periodic transfers to M. Mijoux, the Minister of Agriculture, but there can be little doubt that they were made at the behest of the President.

The release was published the following day, although *Le Monde* appended a comment:

Le Monde notes that these accusations have been made by an anonymous source, and are consequently suspect. They were sent to us electronically from a computer in a library of the Cité Universitaire, which is available to the general public, and we have not been able to identify the source. Nevertheless, the charges are explicit, well documented, and correspond to current police accounts, which we have confirmed. Under these circumstances, we have no alternative but to ask for the resignation of our President and the formation of a new government.

By the next day all the newspapers of Paris, indeed the world, were carrying the story, and the President wasn't available for comment. A day later he made a public statement:

The accusations made against me and Minister Mijoux by unknown persons are false and without foundation. I did know Mme Tuttlies-Fourget 45 or 50 years ago in Marseilles when I was a student there, but I do not know her son Mr. Tatinan. I have no connections, financial or otherwise, with Mr. Shen or Mr. Al-Ryadi. The evidence presented from bank accounts has been manufactured and is false.

He failed to mention either the email request by Werner for tickets with which to leave Almaty or the fact that he supplied them. Within days, this deficiency was pointed out in the press, which made him look even guiltier.

The President's statement placated only his most ardent supporters, and his enemies continued to call vehemently for his resignation, as did foreign newspapers. Other heads of state–the Prime Minister of England, the Chancellor of Germany, and the President of the U.S.–were interviewed. Most commented that they had always found the French President to be amiable and forthright.

The American President was more reserved. In the reports written by journalists from major international papers and television stations, he refused to comment, but he noted to a reporter from his hometown paper that it was of interest to see the French President now eager for foreign support when he had often in the past argued against such support for the U.S. The French President read this and all other accounts of the scandal–in fact he had little time for anything else–and he correctly interpreted the comment in a paper associated with the American President as a signal to him that the current mess was an act of international retribution.

Charles and Louise took little pleasure in the destructive nature of their work and watched as the scandal unfolded. They were, however, pleased to see that MOLP didn't step down–although Minister Mijoux resigned.

They watched the story fade to journalistic obscurity from the comfort of their home on the Virginia shore.

Some months later they were pleased to receive a phone call from the White House. Louise answered the phone, and her eyes widened. She gestured to Charles to pick up an extension.

"I wanted to thank y'all for a job well done," said the President.

"You're entirely welcome, Mr. President," said Louise, "and I'm speaking for Charles as well," she added, seeing Charles nodding vigorously.

"That Commission I formed to consider your ideas..." he paused.

"Yes, Mr. President? Louise was eager to hear what he had to say.

"They've met twice during the past few months, and they've taken a close look at the policy that bears on acts of retribution. And they're writin' up a paper on it. I don't know exactly what they're gonna end up sayin' but they've taken their assignment seriously."

"We're very pleased to hear it," said Louise.

"It'll be ready in a few weeks, and I'd like you to see it before it goes public," he added.

"We'd be delighted."

"Of course, you know the right wing's gonna hate it," he added, "but I think the moderates might take to the idea. We'll see. So, thanks again. You'll be hearing from me. Bye for now."

Wow. They both looked at each other in quiet amazement. It was possible that things might change.

END

Reviews are more important to authors today than ever. If you enjoyed MOLP, please consider leaving a review at your favorite online retailer. Short reviews are just as valuable as long ones.

Thank you.

Want more Charles and Louise?

The *Charles and Louise* series continues with Book 2:
Kmedjzik (autumn, 2016)

The President gives Charles and Louise the job of capturing Zoltan Kmedjzik – a war criminal responsible for an ethnic cleansing campaign. He's holed up in a cave on a mountainside above a Serbian village. They capture him with the help of a remarkable eight-year-old girl and the U.S. Marines, but during transportation, he escapes and makes his way to Costa Rica, where the two agents resume the chase and finish their assignment in a tropical cloud forest.

Coming soon, Book 3:
The Woonboot (spring, 2017)

Sent to the Netherlands to harass a terrorist cell living in a houseboat, Charles and Louise use their unusual talents to sow seeds of doubt and confusion in the group.

Other stories from Woody Starkweather are making their way to publication. Keep an eye out for:

Cargo (autumn, 2017)
Jefferson, Connecticut: Stories of Insecure Youth (spring, 2018)
Talks With Man (autumn, 2018)

About The Author

Woody Starkweather has been a life-long lover of words: spoken, written, or sung. After a long career helping those who struggle with speech, he and his wife Janet Givens joined the Peace Corps and taught English in Central Asia. Now they write–she memoirs, he novels–amid the Vermont woods.

You may contact him at woody.starkweather@gmail.com

Acknowledgments
for the Second Edition

I continue to be grateful to the U.S. Peace Corps for my assignment in Kazakhstan and the time it gave me to work on this and other books. I am grateful too to John Heartson, of Dreamery Productions, whose enthusiasm on hearing me read for the audio version (coming soon) increased my own excitement. Thanks are also due to Reeve Lindbergh and her End of the Road writers' group for many helpful suggestions and expressions of support. I also appreciate the time and effort of George Mitchell, Bertie Koelewijn, and Winston Currier in developing the covers for the series, and the artistry and acumen of Maria Novillo Saravia, who designed the new cover. Finally, I am grateful to my wife Janet Givens for many kinds of inspiration and support and, oh yes, effort, in putting this edition together.

—Woody Starkweather,
still somewhere in the Vermont woods, September, 2016.